To Leah:

Love + a
your truest self.

[signature]

10.28.15

MW00675054

THE BLOOD ROCK PROPHECY

JASON N. SMITH

"No one can make you feel inferior without your consent."

- Eleanor Roosevelt

dedication

For my mom, dad, and husband. Thank you for always supporting and believing in me, even when I didn't believe in myself. I am so very lucky to have, and have always had, your love and guidance. To my mom, I miss you so much, but I know you are there with your hand on my shoulder watching over me forever and always.

thank you

A huge and eternal hug to Julie Hatcher, Carrie Deem, Kelley Mullins, and other great friends for everything you did to help me get my ideas together and down on paper. To Jenn, "my wife," thank you for using your keen eye with my writing, in my attempt to become an author. I couldn't have done this without your help. To my husband, Robert, thank you for not thinking I was completely crazy when I decided to write this book. You have supported me above and beyond in this new, exciting, and, at times scary, endeavor. All of your efforts and support will never be forgotten.

Thank you.

Copyright ©2015, Jason N. Smith

www.jasonnsmith.com

This is a work of fiction. Names, characters, businesses, places, events, and incidents are either the products of the author's imagination or used in a fictitious manner. Any resemblance to actual persons, living or dead, or actual events is purely coincidental.

All Rights Reserved. No part of this publication may be reproduced, stored in a retrieval system or transmitted in any form by any means electronic, mechanical, or photocopying, recording or otherwise without the permission in writing from the publisher.

Requests for permission to make copies of any part of the work should be submitted online at info@mascotbooks.com or mailed to Mascot Books, 560 Herndon Parkway #120, Herndon, VA 20170.

ISBN-13: 978-1-63177-120-0
Library of Congress Control Number: 2015902729
CPSIA Code: PRB0415A

Edited by Jennifer Bradford
Front Cover Design: Jason N. Smith
Printed in the United States

www.mascotbooks.com

Awakening

THE BLOOD ROCK PROPHECY

JASON N. SMITH

Prologue

We successfully made our escape from Paris on the 17 of September without commotion or delay. However, I must say neither of us breathed easily until we had left the medieval walls of Paris far behind us. I cannot say enough how much I appreciate the companionship of Madeleine in this endeavor. I do not think I would have been so resolute in leaving had she not been willing to risk her own life and future by coming with me. We have sat hand in hand since we left her home, and now, for the first time, we dared to smile slightly and utter a few words for the first time in hours, even though our fear persisted.

We both impatiently awaited the freedom we hoped to find in the New World, which lay on the other side of the Earth. We hoped that there we would be able to openly and freely practice our faith, unlike in the Catholic-

ruled lands of France. For centuries, people had relied on us for medicine, counsel and as conduits to the other side, but now the Church sought to destroy our peaceful and earthly religion: a religion that predated their Christian beliefs. We did not seek evil nor did we want to harm others. We only longed to continue our heritage as practitioners of white, natural magic. Unfortunately, those who had sought to practice and cast dark magic had ruined our peaceful and spiritual reputation and brought the Church's wrath upon us.

For hours, we watched the lush, French countryside as we made our way towards Orléans, the origin of my birth name, and the first stop on our journey to the coast. Throughout this first stage of our trip, Madeleine and I conjured images of what we thought might be waiting for us on the other side of the world and how we might be able to freely express ourselves as witches in a new coven. The majority of our fellow practitioners had either already taken refuge or had been violently burned for heresy in accordance with Church law. We deeply hoped and prayed religious freedom would soon find us.

Finally, we arrived in Orléans under the subterfuge of night, which was to be our plan of travel until we arrived at La Rochelle. Most privileged families had relatives living in the principal cities of France like Orléans, Bordeaux, and Tours; therefore, we had to be particularly careful while being in such places. Thankfully, La Rochelle was in a region of France where Protestantism had dominion over Catholicism. Perhaps there we would find a moment of solitude and peace before the next leg of our journey.

* * *

So far, the carriage driver has seen to our every need with grace and kindness. I will never be able to thank Guillaume enough for all he has done for his sister and me. We stop every couple of hours when the driver believes we are at our safest, so that we may stretch our legs and attend to other business as well as take a few moments to recite a protective incantation. I have continued to read the book while my sweet and dear companion naps off and on in the carriage. I have not yet told Madeleine about the book, and I'm not sure if I will. I feel conflicted about divulging its existence to anyone, even to her or to Guillaume. Allowing someone to discover its secrets would most certainly put my life and that of my true family in more danger than it already is.

We arrive in Orléans tonight, and I look forward to resting without being in constant motion.

Marie Françoise d'Orléans

Chapter 1

The death of innocents

THROUGHOUT THEIR LONG HISTORY, only the most malicious and vengeful members of the eastern nations of the Naukemag and Algonquian nations had conjured the Widjigo or "man-eater." It was a relentless demon that exacted revenge against their most hated enemies. The earliest uses of the Widjigo dated back to the first European settlers who had invaded and decimated the native tribes of New England and the eastern coast of the United States. Many shamans and chiefs ignored these blasphemous acts, justifying the action for the sake of saving their people. Nevertheless, in the present day, a member of the Sabbat du Cercle Noir had invoked this egregious spirit to hunt down, not an enemy, but innocent children.

* * *

Their hot breath clashed with the cold, damp air creating a mist-like trail behind them as they ran. Branches and limbs grabbed at and scratched their faces. The two boys ran haphazardly through the trees, their feet steadily becoming heavier from exhaustion with each step. Despite being athletically gifted, their conditioned bodies weren't responding to the adrenaline racing through their veins. *How could this be happening? Was it really happening?*

The entire situation created a surreal picture, and they both tried pinching themselves repeatedly, hoping it was nothing but a horrible nightmare. Neither of them was sure who or what hunted them, but it could move insanely fast and seemed to now be all around them in every direction.

"Stop! I ca...can't run any farther!" he tried to yell as he gasped for breath.

"We have to keep going! We can't stop, or it'll catch up with us!"

Unfortunately, the fate of the two young boys had dictated a different future than they had hoped. Without a moment of hesitation, it was upon them.

* * *

A conjuror, using the dark arts, had summoned and pulled me from my slumber in the nothingness between life and death. Although by whom, I do not know. Yet, for what reason is clear: my crossing over from the other side brought only cruelty, pain, and death to those unfortunate enough to be targeted.

Two weeks earlier, I had begun watching them. For them, they thought life would finally begin tomorrow with their first day of high school. They could hardly believe it. It felt like the day would never come when the twins would officially be freshmen. They had both already earned varsity spots on the lacrosse team as attackers, which was basically unheard of for freshmen. The school had an amazing lacrosse program, and they had garnered several state and national championships. Their futures were bright and full of amazing opportunities, but that did not concern me in the least because I hunted them for a singular need. Their lives would reveal the answers my secretive master needed.

I discovered them as they were walking home from a lacrosse summer camp at the high school. Their identical features offered me twice the pleasure in fulfilling the task. Their golden shaggy hair shimmered as it reflected the late summer sun, and I quivered at the manner in which their bright, green eyes revealed the pureness and innocence of their young, unassuming souls. For me, it would be a feast of horrific delights, and for them, a nightmarish end from which they would never wake.

They lived near the Achachak River, and the time it took them to walk home allowed for plenty of time for observation, learning all I could about them. My kind's ability to hunt and take life dispassionately had been perfected over the centuries to function seamlessly, swiftly, and effectively. Once summoned, we had no choice about returning to the chasm from which we were extracted until we had completed the task put upon us, lest we be expelled into oblivion.

One could not escape the impending inevitability of a gruesome and painful death. When evil pursues you, there is often no way of escaping it, except to give in to it or die.

After dinner, I watched as Alex and Mica headed upstairs to wind down for the evening. As I stalked them from outside their home, my cheek lightly brushed the window to the stairwell, an intricate pattern of ice crystals began to form, a tell-tale sign of my presence. I hovered in the night, shrouded by the treetops, to observe them, while succumbing to the dark euphoria concerning future delights. By 1 a.m., both had passed out, computers still glowing in the dim bedroom light. The anticipation and long summer of workouts and practices had culminated in an all-consuming fatigue for the twins, and their chests rose and fell in rhythm as they slowly drifted into a deeper sleep.

Oh, the joy I find in sleeping and unassuming prey, especially children. My decaying body, crooked appendages, and rotten innards smoldered with longing and pure ecstasy.

The churning seasonal wind did nothing in the way of waking or warning them of the danger approaching from outside their windows. Like the stealthy predator I am, I moved towards them, swirling through the treetops in a serpentine fashion, killing the already dying leaves on the branches my inhuman body touched. The air surrounding my carcass of a body crystallized and sucked the life from anything unfortunate enough to come in contact with my demonic aura.

No one had ever lived to describe my appearance. Only a single shaman of the Naukemag tribe had described the lore concerning my kind:

They exist as an opaque black mass with long out-reaching arms and glistening eyes, which shine an intense and hypnotizing gold, the eyes of a shrewd predator. Their gaping mouths are said to devour the souls of their victims after savagely torturing them. Rotting, sour-smelling cloth wraps their hollow bodies complete with an open chest cavity. Inside this cavity, they imprison their victims and torture them for eternity using their damnation as food. It is rumored the pain inflicted from this torture elicits the emotions sought to reveal the secrets or power the conjurer, who summoned the dark creature, desires.

As I drew closer to the window, it was easy for me to permeate the glass barrier meant to protect my prey from danger. Their breathing, once slow and steady, became more labored, a reaction to my presence. I could already perceive the stinging in their lungs brought about by the frigid air they inhaled through their noses. In unison, they began to wake. Their natural human defense mechanisms sent warning signals from their brains throughout their young bodies. The look of confusion splashed across their adolescent faces both thrilled and amused me.

He saw me first: the one called Alex. Fear gripped his throat so tightly, that he was unable to scream or even utter a single word of alarm to his brother. My eyes gazed upon them from above, my back rested against the ceiling, my hands pressed firmly as I readied myself to pounce; however, like a voracious feline hunter, I wanted to play with my kill first. Killing one's prey too quickly does nothing for the thrill. I swept down at them, and as humans are always predictable, they darted for the door, then the stairs. The smell of their sweat tantalized my putrefacient nostrils as the thumping of their small hearts gave me a great yearning for the climax of the coming hunt. Overcome with panic, they did not even attempt to wake their parents. They simply headed for the front door and fled into the woods. Let the game begin.

* * *

As they stood there, gasping aimlessly for air, drops of rancid fluid from my body dropped onto their heads, and as they looked upwards, I fell upon them, grabbing hold of their fragile necks. A surge of exhilaration raced through me as their pulses beat faster and faster toward certain death. I glided towards the clearing in the woods, which ran alongside the river where the Blood Rock stood, permeated with the blood of countless damned victims long since sacrificed. Their spirits would be trapped there forever. Clasped tightly in my grasp, their bare heels dragged the forest floor. The rocks, fallen branches, and other natural debris scraped them, drawing the first droplets of their life force, which began to litter the ground.

Concentric circles, five layers deep, erupted in flames in tandem with our presence at the sacred and cursed spot. The whispers of those long dead split the air as an unquenchable dread bore down on everything around us. I hung one of them on an adjacent tree bordering this macabre stage, so that he could get a glimpse of what was to come. Held there by forces he could not understand, I reveled at the sight of the tears that began to roll down his flushed, clammy cheeks. Using my left hand, I lifted the other out in front of my body and took the index finger of my right hand and pressed it against his lean abdomen. The exacting precision of my claw easily opened him up, warm blood seeping freely over my hand and onto the dead leaves below. He shut his eyes tightly as he winced in response to the excruciating pain, a warning sign that his young life would soon be over. The Rock reflected the glow of the surrounding flames, as I moved his limp and dying body over it. His blood splattered on the glittering rocky surface and vaporized as it fell, releasing a metallic smell and draping the ancient ritualistic stone in a garish red-brown shade of death.

Having drained these innocent victims, I placed their bodies across the circles of fire to eradicate any last flashes of life or hope. With what remained left of their blood, I scrawled the symbol needed to complete the casting of this sinister spell.

Having completed my part in this macabre act, I collected the confused souls of the two boys and vanished into a burst of fire shooting upwards from the Rock.

From between the trees and out of the inky darkness, a woman appeared, arms angled out from her body with her palms open and facing the rock, slowly moving towards the sadistic scene, which lay before her. The procurement of innocent blood, a favorite ingredient for the incantations of the Cercle Noir, had made the conjuring spell possible and now from the other side, she came forth, her only goal rooted in revealing the identity of her progeny, whose birth represented a break with and complete disregard of tradition. Now all magic and magical creatures found themselves in danger of being decimated. Simplistic superstitious nonsense had stated the blood of the Native Americans and that of the witches were never meant to combine, but she didn't give a damn about such naïve stories. The one, her child, must be reunited with her before their eighteenth year in order to seal the ultimate power contained within them. Only together could they destroy those responsible for her exile.

Chapter 2

The first day of the last year

AUTUMN IN NEW ENGLAND evokes sensations like no other place in the world, especially when the leaves begin to change and a slight nip in the air rolls over the land through the newly disrobed trees. The sun conspires with the heavy clouds as they cast a warm glow across the horizon and help to create a leisurely undulating mist from every corner of land as far as the eye can see. Many people don't like the overcast autumnal setting, but for me, it is so calming, as if everything in the natural world prepares for a long nap before its rebirth in the spring. It's exhausting spending so much of my time overanalyzing school and life and trying to always be the rational one. But for some reason, autumn is a time when I can let go and simply take a deep breath, inhaling in the essence of this season along with its placidity. From my window, the damp, cool air fills my lungs to capacity as I sit at my desk. Ah.

Many times while walking through the countryside, I got lost in my own thoughts and sometimes literally, while listening to the newly fallen leaves crackle beneath my feet. At times, it's as if I'm drawn to wander aimlessly through fields, which have seen the unwinding history of our country, scenes of both remarkable joy and unmerciful death. My family has lived on this farm since the first English settlers came to Massachusetts in the 1620s. Before the first of my ancestors touched the Atlantic coast centuries ago, the entire area surrounding our home formed part of the Naukemag and Algonquian Indians' land. Today their descendants, the Wampanoag tribe, continue to live here. I've always felt as if their deeply spiritual way of life permeated the land, leaving a lasting impression that must be felt to fully understand.

In our own history, the events of the Revolutionary War also made its mark on our town and people, creating a strong spirit of pride and determination of self through great sacrifice. The desire for independence spurred the early settlers of our town, then a village, to fight for freedom and help establish the foundations of our present government. I've learned, from the many stories I've read and been told by my parents and other relatives, about the heroic and many clandestine acts my ancestors accomplished during our fight for self-government.

Often times, I feel the spirits of the past when looking out on the land surrounding our home, a late seventeenth century Puritan-style house. The original home burned after a fire rampaged through our land in 1652 during an abnormally violent lightning storm; however, my unwavering ancestors were determined to remain despite unexplainable tragedies that plagued the area around our home and those who lived here. Edward Smythe, my four times great grandfather, rebuilt the house using remnants of the old house because he said it helped to give the home the same spirit and identity of the former. The house has always been and retained a deep burgundy color with black shutters that anchored the window casings (some of them a bit slanted due to centuries of support and combatting the elements), and a black door made of solid wood set back into the front façade. Being a tad bit sarcastic, one could say the Puritan-style promotes pureness in its simplicity, meaning most people did not appreciate the "bareness" of our ancestral home. I, on the other hand, admired the clean linear nature of the house and the way in which its stalwartness provided a visual representation of the Puritan commitment to living a simple, coherent, and unassuming life…if only the lives of my ancestors had followed the same simplistic model.

* * *

Life didn't get much better than being a senior in high school, in only eight short months the mundane existence that is high school would be over. I, Adeline Evie Smythe, had been busting my butt since freshman year to make sure I had the grades to get into my Harvard, my number one choice of universities. Both of my parents were alumni, and we'd been visiting the campus for as long as I could remember. My mother, Véronique (de la Fontaine) Smythe worked as a professor of French, and my father, Charles Edward Smythe, worked as a lecturer in the anthropology and history departments where he specialized in the early-English colonization of America. Needless to say, I'd grown up around the love of learning and being balanced and organized in all aspects of life. I was fairly well-versed in colonial New England history, and my French wasn't too bad either, despite my numerous attempts at dodging my weekly lessons and trying to always respond to my mother in English when she spoke to me in French. I should've been grateful for the opportunity to have a mother who was a native French speaker from La Rochelle, a city on the western coast and the capital of the Charente-Maritime department in France. Since I was a little girl, we had spent almost every summer in La Rochelle at the family home where the majority of my French ancestors fled religious persecution by the Catholics for being Protestants. They fled first to England then came to America along with some of the other first families who settled the area around Salem. Like I've said, we persevered and didn't change to blend in with the majority.

The family trips to La Rochelle inspired me to keep a journal. I am addicted to writing and recording everything I experience in life with great detail, from trips to France to my 5th grade field trip to the Salem Witch Museum.

On this particular morning, I was consumed in my own thoughts about new class schedules, assignments, and doodling in my tatty journal when I looked over and realized it was already 7:30. There was no way I was going to be late for my first day of senior year! Just being a minute late could throw the entire day into chaos, especially on the first day of school. Something, which I couldn't really describe, made my arriving on time this particular day really important. And besides, today began the first day of the last year of my high school career.

As I took two stairs at a time to reach the kitchen for breakfast, the same gut feeling told me that today was going to be an unforgettable one, the beginning of this next chapter of my life. I spun into the kitchen from the very narrow stairway and landing. Our kitchen maintained its historical charm and feel, despite the invasion of modern stainless steel appliances and technology. The ceiling hung very low, reaching maybe 6 feet as its peak. The walls of the kitchen were whitewashed. The knots in the planks looked out on the scene like hundreds of tiny eyes surveying the heart of the home. Copper and cast iron pots dangled from the ceiling where many different herbs had centuries ago. The original fireplace and hearth remained; however, many modern conveniences had of course been added, but in a way that didn't take away from the original architecture and character. Our farm-style kitchen table was made of oak and stained to match the amazingly preserved cabinets, which lined almost the entire kitchen except for where there were a few windows to let in natural light. The use of wood throughout our house created an organic environment. One could imagine that the house was a breathing living entity, a member of the family.

Per the normal daily routine, I saw my mom at the stove making coffee, in the French way of course, which if I were being honest, I absolutely loved. The typical American coffee tasted like water after drinking *le vrai café* throughout my teens.

"Bonjour, maman! Ça va?" I asked, racing into the kitchen at warp speed.

"Good morning, ma chérie…did you sleep well?" she responded in spit-fire French, competing with the growl of the coffee grinder. I nodded in the affirmative

"Are you just *so* excited to be starting the first day of the last year of high school?" she said in such a way that we both cracked up.

Keeping true to our sarcastic tone, "It's like so super fantastic, like really."

I laughed, but then I stopped as my mom's face became solemn and serious.

"Maman?"

Looking down at the stove, my mom took a deep breath, and I saw a tear fall, sizzling when it reached the heated stove. Both of her hands supported her as they pressed against the counter on either side of the stove. I immediately crossed over to her and put my hand on her back, fearing something terrible had happened.

When she looked up at me after a few moments, her eyes were red and puffy from crying, and I realized, without her saying a word, what was going on with her this morning. The realization had sunk in that it was the beginning of the "the end" of me being her little girl because I'd be leaving home in June and moving to Harvard. In that moment, I was completely caught off guard, a rarity for me. All I could do was start crying and I throw my arms around the most amazing woman and mother and hug her tightly. Despite our occasionally frequent mother-daughter disagreements, I could never have wished for a better parent.

I'm not sure how long we'd been standing their hugging each other and crying when my dad came into the kitchen from his tiny, yet overflowing, library-study.

"So it begins, the year of tears and fears. You guys are like big babies. We have her for another year before she leaves for college, and then she's only going less than an hour away from us."

We just ignored him as he continued.

"If this is going to be a morning ritual for the rest of year, could you both please not cry over the coffee? It's going to be watered down and damn well salty."

Well that was him, classic dad, always putting up the "tough love" front so he didn't have to show his feelings. I credit my ability to do the same to him. However, he generally fails miserably. He headed straight for us, and there we were all in the kitchen crying and having a group family hug. It was something we rarely did, which suited me just fine. My dad always smelled like the books that lined the walls of his very tiny library, the shelves constantly creaking under the weight. Maybe that was the reason I loved to read and write so much. It was one thing I'd never forget about him as long as I lived.

After the first of our many, rare, family moments bound to happen this year, I inhaled some toast and had filled my Harvard mug with a steaming serving of instant energy when I heard Ethan's car pulling up to the house. My cousin, and best friend, had picked me up for school ever since he had gotten his license and his new car. I still had yet to get my license, and I probably wouldn't get it anytime soon, especially, when I had my very own chauffeur. When it came to the relationship between my cousin and me, sometimes it was like we were one in the same. Sadly, being so close, we had had our fair share of falling victim to high school gossip. It was a sad day when a boy and a girl couldn't just be friends, especially in a small town like Salem. Thankfully, we had both learned to laugh off the close-minded whispers our friendship provoked. When you identified so much with another person, you tended not to care what others thought. The most important thing was having each other's backs, no matter what life threw your way, good or bad.

"Top of the morning to you, fine sir," I climbed into his new Jeep

Grand Cherokee, a present from his parents for senior year.

"I'm quite well, my lady."

For some crazy reason, we always spoke to each other in horrendous English accents. Maybe it was because we both had an appetite for anything and everything British when it came to TV and film. Thank you online streaming. It all had started as kids with "Are you being served?" on PBS.

As we exited out onto the road towards town from my circular gravel driveway, the sun began to poke through the dense autumn clouds covering the sky. Living outside of town, we were lucky to have a lot of privacy and quiet; however, it could sometimes be a pain to drive the fifteen to twenty minutes it took to get groceries, go to the movies, etc. Our families were the only ones who lived on the outskirts of town anymore. The two houses (ours and my cousin's) were about two miles apart and his, like mine, had stood for almost three centuries. The drive into town could be considered a historical one, taking into account the road was lined with the original stack-stoned fences that followed it until you reached the Olde Salem Village Bridge. It loomed there completely made of wood, nothing too remarkable to distinguish it from the multitude of trees on either side of the Achachak River, an Algonquian name meaning "spirit." I don't think the covered bridge had been updated or repaired since I was born.

The openings on each side gobbled up the cars as they entered and spit them out as they exited. Its wooden supports weakened with age, bended, creaked, and moaned as we passed through, as if it were enjoying a delicious snack. Going through the bridge scared the hell out of me. Every time I approached it, my body tensed, and I could feel every fiber of my being tingle as the proverbial hairs on my neck stood on end. The simple visualization of it in my mind brought with it an intense foreboding.

"Earth to Addie?" Ethan's question pulled me from my early morning daydream.

"Already focused on being out of here and at Harvard?"

"You don't even know me!" I laughed. "What's Harvard?"

"Yeah right! What's got you distracted this morning? Nervous about your insanely difficult schedule this year?"

Ethan was extremely smart but had never really applied himself at academics like he did sports. Some might have said I overextended myself, but school and getting into Harvard had always been my passion and goal in life. I wanted to get in on my own merit and not because both of my parents worked there.

"Oh, you know my mother. The year of tears has already started, and it really surprised me this morning how much I was affected by it. You know my mom and I haven't always seen eye-to-eye, but I guess with such a major change coming at the end of the year, I got a little emotional myself."

"You? Emotional? Headstrong and unaffected is more like it."

My cousin's words stung a little. He had a point. I had never really come across as an "emotional" person, but I did have them. I did realize I rarely gushed about them in public, but I did love my parents. It was just that I had always felt a "disconnect" between us, something I had never been able to fully define. At times I just found it easier to "turn off" my emotions like a certain famous pointy-eared alien. Focusing on school and college helped to give me an excuse, when needed, for my emotional distance. The only person with whom I had ever truly revealed my feelings was my cousin. I wanted to be more open, emotionally, with my parents and hoped the distance between us, after I began college, might help.

"What the hell?"

The jeep slowed as we turned into the student parking lot. I looked up to see several police cars parked with their lights flashing. A mob of students and teachers were standing around, more or less surrounding the cruisers, worried expressions showed their concern.

I don't think I'd ever seen the police at our school, except for antidrug and alcohol assemblies or for show and tell in the elementary school. To say our town is sleepy and crime free was an understatement. The only time anyone heard police sirens was during parades, which we had for everything from founder's day to pumpkins. Like I said, it was a slow-moving little town, but I loved it.

Ethan and I grabbed our bags and hopped out of the car to the sight of our shocked and confused classmates and teachers filling the parking lot. There was a noticeable icy tension in the air, and I wrapped my scarf around my neck and slipped on my jacket as I began to shiver. The sight of the police scrambling around not knowing exactly what to do looked comical and strange. For many of the police, they were placed in a difficult situation, which was not something they were used to doing. As I looked around, everyone had lost their individuality and had become one large indistinguishable blur of faces. I noticed several students were crying and others vomited, not caring they were in plain view of everyone else. I placed my hand on my stomach and took longer, steadier breaths as I absorbed everything I was witnessing.

"I asked around, and I couldn't get a clear answer from anyone," Ethan said.

I had leaned forward to keep from passing out and I jumped suddenly when I felt him place his hand on my shoulder as he spoke. I hadn't even realized he'd walked away from my side.

"Whatever it is, it can't be good. Not the way everyone is reacting."

All of sudden the school's rusted PA system crackled and electrified the air before screeching to life, "All students are to report to the gym immediately."

* * *

By 9 a.m., all students and faculty were seated or standing against the walls in the gym. Principal McIntyre didn't even have to ask for silence. He presented himself as a confident, stern, and incorruptible person; however, he always had a caring demeanor with both students and faculty. I imagined he must be in his forties, but he looked to be in his early thirties. He stood over six feet tall and had a knack for getting the truth out of anyone he encountered, whether it were a student or parent. His muscular frame and serious continence demanded attention, and, no doubt, was an overwhelming reason why we had very few discipline issues. All in all, he was not the type of person or principal who was disrespected.

The only thing to be heard throughout the gym was the sniffling of students who were or had been crying. The ceiling of our gym still reflected the architectural innovations of the 1970s. The insulation was coming down and pieces of it wafted down every now and then along with the green-grey paint peeling off of the cinderblock walls. The paper from the insulation, looking like a rat's nest, dangled down creating an ominous and oppressing feel, which didn't help the current mood in the gym. Making matters worse, the bleachers, made of hardwood, seemed to be made to torture students, always causing us severe discomfort and the constant need to shift back and forth to try and get comfortable.

There was no wonder why no one could pay attention during regular assemblies. However, this time, boredom wasn't the cause of everyone's discomfort and anxiety. Numbness permeated the room, and for the first time in my life, I didn't notice the discomfort. We all knew something serious had happened, and with our imaginations running wild, we yearned to know the truth behind why we had all been summoned here, and why police had infiltrated the school.

As Principal McIntyre stood and moved towards the podium, there was a collective sound of people adjusting on the bleachers while those standing against the gym walls straightened. What in the world had happened to warrant all of this?

"Ladies and gentlemen, thank you for getting here so quickly. I have the very sad duty of telling you that two of your classmates have been found in the woods just outside of town near the Achachak River, dead."

His words faded away as flashes of red and blood-chilling screams filled my mind, causing an intense and shooting pain. My hands began to shake uncontrollably, and I had a hard time sitting upright. My body felt heavy as if it were sinking downward through the bleachers. The sounds from Principal McIntyre and others seated near me sounded foreign, and I couldn't focus my mind on what was going on around me.

Was it possible to be in two places at once? My mind and emotions twisted and turned in multiple directions.

The silence was deafening.

Chapter 3

Resisting the truth

IT WAS ONLY TWO in the morning, the clock mocking me with its neon blue numbers. I lay there wide-awake. Why did I incessantly run away from every opportunity to be honest? That's just who I was and had always been. I'd struggled so long and hard with life, with being honest with myself, with being . . . Ethan. How could I truly be myself after putting up a front my entire life? Do I continue to lead others to believe in a persona, which only bared the slightest resemblance of the truth or, am I honest and forthcoming despite feeling nauseous at the very thought of doing so?

I always took the route of plausible deniability. I lay there on my bed being quite the successful insomniac, hands behind my head pondering how to proceed, sometimes *if* to proceed. I saw myself as part of that magic act where people were sawed, not only in half, but also in multiple pieces. Here, everyone, here's a little bit for you, and you, and you too. It was mentally and emotionally exhausting to feel I had no choice but to deny myself the freedom to be open with others. I was quickly approaching my breaking point and didn't know what would happen when I finally broke. I was eighteen, athletic, smart (albeit a little lazy on the academic side of things), popular, and good-looking, but it wasn't enough. Most guys, and girls, my age and in my position, the star athlete and all, would be reveling in life and moving forward with a much clearer vision of their future than I was.

I lived more or less alone in the barn out behind our house. I was at least one hundred yards out of earshot of my parents. I had the entire place to myself and never had to worry about my parents butting into my personal business. I could have had some damn good parties, but I didn't, even with the constant protests from friends and teammates. I couldn't. I needed the alone time to filter through my own issues, most of which alcohol couldn't help. I'd tried that when I was fourteen with disastrous consequences.

The barn, in typical barn fashion, was painted red with a relatively new tin roof, which perfected sleeping when it rained. The beams, massive supports of hardwood made from the surrounding trees, in the ceiling were original and, more often than not, the focus of my far off stares as I pondered my life. When my parents allowed me to move out to the barn, they installed a brand new bathroom at the far end of my room. My room spanned almost the entire length of the barn, and was decorated with trophies for various sports, none of which I particularly cared for, except the ones for lacrosse. Simply put, it gave me the chance to escape my own thoughts. I was constantly running on an open field filled with teammates and opponents. Stopping was not an option, being defensive and offensive were the keys to survival. Games were an endless series of movements and the continual struggle to be the one standing victorious in the end. The rest of my room exhibited the fruits of my hobby, photography. I never knew I had a passion for it, until I went with my cousin, Addy, to visit her mom's family in France a couple of summers ago. I became obsessed with capturing the history of La Rochelle and the surrounding area with my lens, and then later realized, after uploading my photos, I wasn't half bad. After that, I started taking pictures of everything around me: people, nature, and landmarks. I loved discovering how a camera could capture images and emotions not seen by the naked eye.

Despite the fact my father and Addy's father were brothers, when it came to my family, the difference in the sense of family unity were evident. My father, Franklin Xavier Smythe, worked as an Associate Professor of Anthropology at Boston University and traveled constantly because of his work. I rarely saw him for more than a few days at a time. On the other hand my mom, Kelley Friedman Smythe, worked the night shift as a nurse at the local hospital. Deep down, I knew they loved me and I loved them, but I had always had this nagging feeling something didn't "fit" between the three of us. I wondered if they somehow knew my secret.

Addy's parents were easier to be around, and I probably spent most of my time with them instead of in my own home. Addy and I were one and the same. She and I even shared the same birthday, October 31. We told each other almost everything. Yet there was one thing I just couldn't say out loud without potentially ruining everything, or could I?

"Ethan, stop it!" I said to myself, lost in my thoughts, all of which were too profound for this time of night.

Dwelling over things started to wear me down, so I decided to go for a long run. The solitude I found in running helped me to organize my thoughts and deal with them without the usual over analyzing of every detail.

I mean after all, I was too young to be having an existential crisis, right?

Looking out the window of my room, even in the darkness, nature looked so inviting and the nighttime was perfect for running. The moon glistened high in the sky and the blue-purple clouds dispersed the moonlight, casting a gothic glow over everything in sight. Our back yard extended for several hundred yards before losing itself in the dense woods, which stretched for miles on end around Salem. I appreciated the historical allure of the woods and land around my house. It fascinated me to wonder what it would have been like to be one of the first settlers here, arriving in a completely unknown world to establish a new society, braving the inherent dangers all around. I thrived on seeking out the unknown.

When I was about six years old, I got lost for several hours in the woods behind our house. I remembered walking through the incredibly tall and menacing trees and thinking how small I was in comparison. They swallowed me whole as I entered. The strangest part was that I did not remember walking into the woods. I was found hours later, all the way past my cousin's house along the banks of the Achachak River. The policeman who found me said I was just talking to myself and playing near a rock. I did not remember feeling scared at all while I was lost, which, in retrospect, is odd for a six year old. The entire time I was in the forest, I didn't feel alone. Even today, I swore I had heard someone's voice, intriguing and oddly familiar, guiding and reassuring me throughout the whole experience until that officer, who is now my principal, found me. Ever since having that very strange experience as a child, I had felt drawn to the woods, and often went there, unbeknownst to anyone, to run, relax, and sometimes camp. I felt more in touch with the trees of the forest protecting me than I sometimes did with my own family.

I pulled myself out of bed and headed over to my dresser to grab some running shorts, socks, and my shoes. Dressing in front my mirror, I noticed the discrepancies in my physical features and those of my parents. My strong cheekbones sat high on my face, my almond eyes ice blue, a prominent nose, and full, deep red lips. My hair was dark brown, but looked black if I wasn't out in the sun. My lean, toned, and naturally tanned body was the result a life filled with athletic endeavors and there was no doubt I had become more mature, considering I began high school as a scrawnier more uncoordinated version of my current self. I took great pride in taking care of myself physically and perfecting my skills on the field alongside my teammates. But, feeling physically mature and agile was one thing. On the flipside, I lacked emotional confidence and had quite a long way to go before I felt the same about my inner self as I did my physical prowess.

Descending the creaking pine stairs, I began to feel invigorated about my run through the woods, completely bathed in the tranquil liquid darkness. Looking out at the trees, I headed out, starting with a balanced jog before picking up my speed and striding into a full run. It didn't take long to escape the meager light of the two floodlights on the back of the barn before plunging into the blackness of the trees.

Despite my love for the solitude and quietness of the dark of nighttime, I had to wear a headlamp, so I didn't break an ankle or worse. After all, my life centered on the hope of winning a scholarship to a university far away from here.

There was nothing like feeling the cool damp air swish past your face as it did when I ran. Every muscle in my body, beginning in my legs and moving upwards, absorbed the oxygen in the air. Every fiber tingled and came alive as I built speed and continued my forward momentum. I generally followed one of two paths, both leading towards the river. I'd thoroughly carved them out over the years and usually ended up running their entire six to eight mile length. The all-consuming silence was so meditative, and I had always been able to clear my mind and refocus during my jogs. The runner's high consumed both the body and soul.

Tonight, something pulled me in a direction I hadn't travelled in a long time. The same direction I had gone when I got lost all those years ago. I was shocked to see a path emerging before me as I ventured into a part of the woods I didn't know that well. The now pale yellow moon held itself at its apex, the silky black sky devoid of even a single star.

Without warning, I heard a peculiar sound coming from between the trees, and I ground to an unsettling halt, coming close to tripping over my own feet. Several unfamiliar words reached my ears, carried through the trees on the whistling wind. I recognized a few words here and there as the wind swirled past my ears. They sounded like they were in Latin, but I couldn't be sure. All I knew was they weren't English, and I shouldn't have been hearing anything in the woods at this time of night, except for the occasional sounds of animals.

My hands became clammy and a cold sweat claimed hold of my body. I sniffed back the mucous beginning to flow freely from my nose. For the first time during my run, my breath appeared before me as I took deeper breaths to calm my pounding heart. Free from any conscious decision, my body leaned into a full sprint without worrying about where I might end up. Guided solely by instinct, I attempted to turn back and retrace my steps, but all of my senses had gone haywire. It felt as if I were running in circles as the sensation of being watched and chased from all sides assaulted me. Tree limbs scratched my face, as I fled through the thick brush, finding it abnormally difficult to control my breathing. Then a new sound touched my ears . . . water. I must have been close to the river. I extended my sprint to get to the water before whatever was hunting me attacked first.

The "fight or flight" instinct overpowered me. I misjudged the opening to the river, forgetting the drop off leading down to the water, and sailed over the rocky edge. My forward momentum propelled me helplessly through the air towards the menacing shoreline. As I fell, I scrambled to grab something, anything, without success. I slammed into the earth with my shoulder striking the rocky sandy bank of the river. An overwhelming jolt of pain shot from the point of impact and throughout my entire body as I rolled helplessly towards the water. When my roller coaster of a tumble finally came to an end, at the edge of the river, I lay face up, eyes towards the now blurry sky. I must have cut my forehead because a warm liquid trickled down my hairline and alongside my nose and cheek. I shivered uncontrollably against the elements. Both of my legs were submerged in the frigid water of the Achachak River as warm blood bathed my head.

My senses regained their grasp over me, and I listened intently for any other types of abnormal sounds around me. I struggled to move, frozen by fear and confusion.

A guttural groan marred the still night air before fading again into complete silence. Once more, the forest offered new sounds, a steady murmuring similar to singing. I didn't understand what the hell it could have been. There were no animals capable of making such sounds. Using the reminder of my energy, I strained to listen out for other clues as the frigid air poured over my body bringing back the convulsions. I prepared myself for what I thought was certain death.

* * *

When I regained consciousness, I was completely disoriented and not sure what had exactly happened. I remembered running and then everything else escaped my memory. I sat up and realized I was up on the shore above the river in a place that struck me as familiar. I believed it was the same place where Office McIntyre found me twelve years ago. I shook my head hoping to clear the fog from my thoughts. Nothing. I had no idea how I'd ended up here.

This was too weird. I had gotten lost on September 22, the same date as today. The first day of school.

"Dammit!" I said out loud as I looked down at my watch. It was 6:30, and I had to go get ready for school before I picked up Addy.

As I stood in the shower, lost in my thoughts, I worried over the fact I'd lost over four hours of time. How the hell was that possible? Standing under the jets of hot steamy water, I had a flashback to my run. I wasn't me, but rather I was watching myself running, fear streaked across my face moments before falling, blood over my face, chest, and legs. In reaction to my vision, I put my hand to my head, searching for the wound, but there was nothing. No part of my body showed signs of scrapes, scratches, or any other type of injury like those I had seen in my mind.

"Screw it," I told myself.

I decided to push those thoughts out of my mind, and busy myself with getting ready for school and a new year. I was definitely no slave to fashion and decided to throw on a long-sleeve t-shirt and some jeans before I grabbed my black leather jacket and headed out the door.

There she sat. My beautiful jeep. She, which I loved almost more than anything else in the world, was a much unexpected gift from my parents for my senior year. Thanks to her, I could escape from the act that was my day-to-day life. My jeep was a solid onyx that shimmered in direct sunlight and the deep brown leather seats conformed perfectly to my body when I sat down.

I cranked her up and headed out of the driveway for the short, maybe one-mile drive towards Addy's house. The sun hadn't heated the ground long enough to burn off the lingering mist created by the cool night air, much like my in ability to shake the nagging feeling I had about what had happened hours earlier.

Within seconds of my arrival, Addy shot out of her front door and climbed in the car. As per our usual morning routine, we exchanged our good mornings in stereotypical British accents. Every time I saw her, which was often, I became more aware of the bizarre physical similarities between Addy and myself. Like me, she had incredibly dark brown hair accompanied by strong angular features, the only difference being our eyes. Where my eyes were ice blue, hers were a very attention-grabbing emerald green, which forced you to look her in the eye when she spoke. She wasn't athletic like me, but she had always maintained a slender body. She was the type who really pissed people off when they learned she didn't exercise. When we were younger, lots of people assumed we were siblings and were always surprised to find out we were only cousins.

Leaving her driveway, I accelerated down the only road into town from our houses. After a lot of thought, I decided to ever so vaguely tell her about my night.

"I think I may have slept walked last night. I woke up this morning down by the river, in the exact same spot where they found me when I got lost that time. Pretty damn crazy, huh?"

Nothing.

"Earth to Addy?"

She didn't have the slightest idea what I had just told her, so I made the decision to let it go for the moment. I knew she was focused, more like obsessed, on Harvard and not much else mattered. I couldn't blame her. If I had had a full-ride to an Ivy League school, I wouldn't be worried about much else either. Lucky for me, I guess, I didn't really have to worry about all of that.

When we made it to school, there was no mistaking that something serious had happened and whatever it was had warranted the police. Their cars filled the parking lots and officers filtered in between students and teachers in an aimless and quasi-lost manner. After I'd finally found a parking space, I ran over to ask some other classmates about the situation, but they were all as clueless as Addy and I. I had always found it surprising how high school students, in particular, always reacted so dramatically to events before they discovered the cause of something.

When I walked back to the car, I found Addy hunched over with her head between her legs and unintentionally scared her when I touched her arm.

"My bad, I didn't mean to make you jump."

"All students please report immediately to the gym," Principal McIntyre said, his voice echoing and far-reaching over the intercom.

* * *

As we all sat in the gym on the ass-numbing bleachers, the principal, other administrators, and town council members filled out the gym floor in front of us, worry betraying their cool demeanors. The gym echoed with an eerie silence, not often felt during assemblies.

"Dude, what the hell is going on?" a classmate asked me. I could barely hear him.

"No clue, but it sure as hell can't be good."

Principal McIntyre stood and approached the podium.

"Ladies and gentlemen, thank you for getting here so quickly. I have the very sad duty of telling you two of your classmates have been found in the woods outside of town near the Achachak River, dead."

A slew of gasps and stifled screams rippled through the crowd of students and teachers. How was that possible? Nothing ever happened here, especially not murder.

"We have no specific information at this time, but we do want you to know school will proceed as scheduled today as it is the first day of the year. Counselors and myself will be available throughout the day should you feel you need to talk. At times like these, please lean on your classmates and friends for support."

Suddenly, an animalistic shrill filled everyone's ears, followed by a loud thud. As I looked over to my left, I realized Addy lay unconscious and seizing in between the bleachers.

"Somebody help!"

Chapter 4

Guardian

I WAS BORN DEVON Archibald McIntyre in1619 to a wealthy and noble Irish family, who had moved to London at the beginning of the seventeenth century to extend their mercantile business. I grew up with the many advantages and opportunities my situation presented to people of my social status. However, I, along with others, became increasingly malcontented with the changes in England and the Civil War, which ravaged our country. As a consequence, my wife and I had come to the colonies in 1648 in the hopes of raising our family in a new environment removed from the rule of Charles I and the English Civil War. Our journey was a difficult one. We mourned the death of our infant daughter during the trip across the stormy, unpredictable Atlantic. Standing on the rancid-smelling, mold-laden deck of the ship, we let our precious baby girl slip away into the foamy dark depths of the cold ocean, never to hold her sweet little body in our arms again. In addition to the death of our daughter, we buried a total of four of our six children before they reached five years of age. After landing in the Americas, the only two to survive were a beautiful boy and girl. Unfortunately, we were forever hardened and affected by the voyage and each of these unendingly painful deaths. In those incredibly difficult years, I learned the value of life and family, a passion that continues to burn deep within my soul.

After our arrival, we set up our home on a plot of land outside of Olde Salem Village and near the site that would become the village proper of Salem. With the help from our new community and Wampanoag tribe, I built my family a modest home while I cultivated our new land and brought crops to the daily markets. I could not afford to hire extra hands, so my son and daughter helped me as best they could, but the work was arduous. Thankfully, we were lucky enough to have several tribesmen willing to help us several days a week. After their arrival in New England, the colonists had established a treaty with the local tribe. I felt guilty that we had come from across the sea and taken their land from them, sometimes using violent and bloody methods to do so. I had lived a life filled with entitlement and had seen how such arrogance ruined the lives of those directly and indirectly affected. Who were we to dominate a people we had not even cared to fully understand?

Because of the strife we suffered during our voyage and in this new home, we had had to depend on the knowledge of our new Native friends when the others refused to help us. Despite the pre-established treaty, my family and I were glad to have actually worked to create deeper friendships with several of the Natives living near us. All of us enjoyed learning about farming, traditions, and history from them. For all of our Christian kindness, many of our fellow god-fearing colonists thought poorly of our close relationships with the Wampanoag people. To their chagrin, we did not let their refusal to understand others different from themselves deter our desire to learn more about their ways and further nurture our new friendships.

Regrettably, we quickly learned to what extent the demeanor of the other colonist could be one of judgment and discrimination, which left us very isolated at times. The only colonists in the vicinity of Old Salem Village who extended the hand of friendship were William Smythe and his French wife, Agathe de la Marchande. They lived just outside the town center on the other side of the river and had made us feel welcome ever since our arrival, unlike the other citizens of the village.

However, their friendship brought suffering. I became aware of a supernatural war between the forces of good and evil fought amongst the Native tribes and two feuding covens of witches in and around Salem Village. This war would eventually bring about the death of my wife at the young age of twenty-four. It would also give me an unwanted immortal life, a life that would force me to never forget the soul-eating pain brought by the murder of my wife and disappearance of my family.

Now, almost three hundred years later, I stood in the shower repeatedly scrubbing my entire body. The dark gritty water ran down the drain as I rubbed my mud-caked body. After decades of peace, the recent murders had awakened me to prepare to perform my duty and save what I had been sworn to guard so many centuries ago. My destiny forged in a time when the magical entanglements between good and evil brought lightning to the starry, dark-blue sky and blood to the lush green village fields.

My body throbbed and burned from the intense scrubbing, as I got out of the shower and began to dry off. Since I was a young boy, I had had no choice in staying fit, both mentally and physically. When I wasn't working, a rare occurrence since my promotion to principal, I trained by practicing various disciplines of martial arts in addition to running and lifting weights alongside my lacrosse players. As I dried my body, my hands grazed the reminders that told of the long and, at times, difficult story of my life. My psyche also showed the scars from a life filled with love and loss. In the back of my mind, I hoped to never again be the one creating such a loss for others, knowing all too well its everlasting effects.

As I stood staring into the steamy mirror, I began to come to the realization that, unfortunately, there was no doubting *it* had been set in motion. For years, I had wondered when the signs would appear in Salem, which had already suffered from a long, turbulent past. So many years of peace and quiet had now been shattered by the first murders in over a hundred years. I had hoped this day would never come to be, but today I had been awoken by a sickening vision of mutilation and the savage murder of two boys, identical twins, who were only thirteen years old. Now, I knew all tranquility had ended. My destiny lay before me, and as I watched the streaks of the blood orange morning horizon from the bathroom window, I wondered who would survive the relentless evil coming.

"Hey babe, have you seen my badge?" Ayden asked from the closet in the bedroom. "Babe?"

Snapped from my own thoughts, I replied that I thought it was in the bathroom. I've got to pull it together.

"Here it is," he said. He wore his golden blond hair so that it looked messy even though he took time fixing it every day. He had the broadest shoulders of any man I had ever known giving him a commanding presence. His ever-present five o'clock shadow pushed his image beyond his thirty-three years.

Letting on that something was wrong could put both of us in danger, and I would not let that happen. Since the moment we first met, I had been in love with him, one of the greatest loves of my life, after the first, my wife Elizabeth.

"Can you believe it's already nearing the end of September and time for you to welcome back your students?"

"It's crazy," I said.

He was right. Today was September 22, and the beginning of what I was sure could be a trying and more than likely, a deadly year.

"Are you okay? You seem like you're way off somewhere else this morning?"

"I'm sorry, babe. I just have a million and one things on my mind with the kids returning today and making sure we start the year off without any hiccups."

Coming around behind me, he put his strong hands on my shoulders and began to massage the tension out of them.

"You always stress about things you know are going to turn out fine. And besides, you know I'll always be here for you if you need me. I mean, I have gun if it's needed," he said with a wry smile, causing me to laugh.

"I know. I'm sorry for being so distracted lately. It's the fault of too many restless nights the past several weeks."

"No worries. I more than understand the effects of too little sleep," he said.

"Well, it's not the way I wanted to start the morning. How about I make it up to you tonight by cooking us dinner? I can go by Frank's and get some fresh fish to grill."

"It's a date. Love you and see you later tonight."

"Bye."

As I was getting ready, I struggled to get the images from last night out of my mind. I had acclimated to living in relative peace for the past several decades after what happened to my family all those years ago. Finally enjoying a decent night's sleep, I had shot upright in bed last night and raced towards the woods without a moment's hesitation. Since Ethan's brief disappearance twelve years ago, the murders marked the beginning of something the world wasn't ready to know existed. I feared she had returned.

* * *

The first sign of the awakening came twelve years ago today, September 22, and I would never forget it, no matter how long I lived. The panic on their faces was overwhelming even for the officers who were supposed to be immune to such emotions, especially when one considers their jobs. We were there to serve and protect the people of

Salem making them believe everything would turn out okay in the end, but this time it was different. Something about their reactions to their missing son, rippled through all of those involved in the search and rescue. Nothing like this had ever happened in this town, at least in recent recorded history. For many, this was the first missing person's case they had ever worked, and, also, the first ever recorded in the history of the SPD.

Early that morning around nine, the department had received a frantic call from Kelley Smythe, Ethan's mom. According to the initial report, she had walked into Ethan's room only to discover he wasn't in his bed. She told the operator she had searched all over the house and couldn't find any trace of him or any clue about where he might have gone, except for the fact his red down jacket wasn't hung beside the back door like it had been the night before when she had let the dog out.

I got the call over the radio while I was making my mundane patrol and although the dispatcher's voice sounded as banal as usual, a reverberating chill slashed through my body, a feeling I had not felt in a long time. Flipping my lights on, I turned around in the middle of the road and headed straight towards the Smythe house, which sat on acres of land with plenty of space for a small child to get lost or, worse. After crossing the unchanged Olde Salem Bridge, I used the loud speaker on my cruiser to call out for Ethan, hoping he might hear me and walk towards the sound.

Nothing.

As I turned onto the gravel driveway, the deep blue family home came into view. It had not changed since it had been rebuilt in 1652. His house and that of his cousin had been built again from the ground up after a fire ravaged their property. Being back in this place, I had a flood of memories of the life I had had centuries ago. In my approach, I noticed Frank and Kelley methodically moving around the perimeter of the house, yelling Ethan's name. Their voices had become hoarse and cracked from exhaustion.

"Oh my god, Devon! We don't know what to do. He's alone, cold, and he's probably scared to death. It got below freezing last night," she said, choking on her words.

"Kelley, just try and calm down. I know it's tough, but we're going to find him."

As I tried to calm her down, other cruisers arrived. Frank went to talk with them to give them as much information about their son as possible.

"I know you've already told the 911 operator this Kelley, but when was the last time you saw Ethan and what was he wearing?"

"Around 8:30 last night when I put him to bed...he was wearing...I can't, I can't remember," she said, tears cascading down her face.

The tears turned to sobs as her knees betrayed her trembling body. She slithered through my arms and melted to the ground. I called Frank over to help me to get her into the house.

Kissing her on the forehead, the two of them embraced one another for what seemed like forever, doing their best to comfort one another, hoping he would be found soon.

The one thing we had going for us was that it was daylight and would hopefully be easier to find him, especially if he were wearing the missing red down jacket. After a brief review of the facts we had, we quickly organized a search party composed of officers and asked another officer to stay with the parents at the house just in case he returned home or, in the horrible event, we found his body. I dreaded the thought of relaying such news to them and knew having someone there to keep them occupied would be best for them as we searched.

An early and untimely artic chill had descended upon Salem as we began our search into the woods surrounding the property. The once green grass, now a dirty brown, was littered with scattering leaves as the thinner trees of the woods swayed back and forth in the wind in unison with the treetops of the older, stronger trees. The environment around us reminded me of how this place used to look in the past: serene and safe before the trouble began. Now I steadied my labored breathing as the beginning of the search for Ethan, who may or may not be alive, lay before me. Upon my arrival here, I had always worked near or in the woods. At one time, I had played endless games with my children about the aging trees. They were a way for us to get away from the backbreaking work of the farm.

We entered the forest in three different areas in an effort to more effectively search the densely wooded area. I and another officer took the area farthest to the left of the house where the trees created a natural barrier between the two family homes. The section of forest between them was not as dense as those behind the house, and, therefore, we were able to cover the area more quickly. As we made our way through the trees, clouds formed, molding together like marshmallows, and the sky darkened despite the fact that no rain had been forecasted for New England for the entire week. I pulled out my flashlight as I inched forward, deeper into the woods. After only a few moments, I lost sight of my partner and stood still to see if I could hear his foot falls in the blanket of brittle lifeless leaves.

There was nothing, not even the sound of birds from above or other animals scurrying around the forest floor. I couldn't even hear the bellowing wind that continued to irritate the trees. A dead silence had engulfed the entire area around me.

"Simmons?"

The sound of my voice only reached a few feet before disappearing into the silent void.

Focusing on finding both my partner and Ethan, I continued my search and weaved my way in and out of the forest along the property line of Edward's, Frank's brother's, house on the other side of the natural barrier of trees and undergrowth. Due to the increasing darkness and the dense natural veil of trunks and branches, I could no longer see Frank and Kelley's house to my right. Perspiration dripped from my hairline and down my back as I wriggled my way through the thick brush, only to discover that I had become lost. How was that possible? I knew the woods better than anyone in town. In order to reorient myself, I looked upward, but the clouds blocked the entire sky and swirled about in a spiral-like formation, conspiring against my attempts to find my position. I called out to whoever might be listening without hearing anything in response to my shouts.

Physically, I knew I was moving forward, but the scenery around me did not change, and I began to feel more disorientated. In the eerie silence, I thought I heard something rustling through the trees, all around me. Instinctively, I spun around to look in every direction as quickly as possible, but failed to see anything physical in the vicinity of my position. An uneasy feeling came over me and I started moving more quickly through the thick undergrowth desperately pursuing my, as yet futile, search. The whole time, the otherworldly movement crept closer towards me no matter how speedily I maneuvered the forest. I stopped almost falling forward as breathing grew difficult, the air around me turning colder and heavier. Suddenly, whispers bombarded my ears from every possible direction, adding to the tension already consuming my body. Their sound subtly penetrated my soul and I deciphered what sounded like Latin-sounding words, but I couldn't understand them clearly enough to translate them. Any last doubt about this possibly being natural vanished. I knew I was in danger, but from what I had no idea. History had taught me not to question my acute senses, and I quickened my pace.

The temperature had dropped to such a degree that I could see my breath before me as I rushed forward into unknown woods. A bone chilling sweat covered my entire face and body as I looked and listened for any clue as to where I might be in relation to either house.

For the first time, I heard a sound other than the rustling and whispers that had been plaguing me. In the distance, I picked up on the sound of tricking water from the river.

With my heart pulsing in my ears, my body jerked towards the sound of the river even though I couldn't tell how close or far I was from it. As I approached the growing sounds of the Achachak, I slowed, feeling whatever had been chasing me had moved away from me, back between the trees.

In the distance, in the same direction as the river, I heard someone talking.

"I dunno," a child's voice said.

Ethan.

Creeping as stealthily as humanly possible, I made my way forward using his voice as a point of reference. I came to the shocking realization, the closer I got to him, that he was having a conversation with someone. The other voice sounded deep and hollow, like nothing I had ever heard before. The voice directed the conversation without allowing Ethan to ask it questions. Hearing the gravelly voice sent chills down my back, and I couldn't understand how Ethan wasn't afraid. Finally, I reached the tree line and as I leaned forward to get a better view of him and his interviewer, something moved in the trees above me and emitted a piercing shriek that brought me to my knees.

After the ringing in my ears stopped, I got to my feet and rushed towards where I heard Ethan's voice. I broke through the edge of the forest and saw him there, sitting on a large boulder near the edge of the water. He looked at me and we locked eyes for a moment, his expression very perturbed yet innocent, his small, round and red face aging to that of an adult for a split second.

I ran to him, and, while checking to make sure he was unharmed, I asked him about his conversation. He looked at me with his ice blue eyes, confused, and then shrugged his shoulders. It was as if he didn't even remember the conversation, and, after questioning him a little further, I gathered he didn't even understand how long he had been gone from his house. At first, he didn't want to get down off of the rock, and I had to coax him with the promise of a ride in my car with the sirens and lights blaring before he would budge.

We made it back to the house in less than thirty minutes after following the creek to the bridge and then going along the road. I was relieved to be free of the woods and whatever creatures they held. Frank and Kelley were overjoyed to see their baby boy placed in their arms. The both of them cried happy tears, while Ethan remained unaffected by the entire ordeal. His amnesia surrounding the ordeal has never gone away. After additional questions, most of which were tailored for a six year old, no one could figure out what had happened or how or why he had ended up at the river several miles from his home.

Unlike the majority of the town's people, I understood much more and knew of the centuries old secrets buried deep in the past, which now, appeared to be affecting the present and possible future of our small village in Massachusetts. I found it difficult to fathom what the residents of this town would think or if they could even comprehend what was at work so close to them and their children.

Did *I* even fully understand them myself? I prayed I did, for the sake of the lives of the ones I had been charged to watch and protect. I had "survived" the same perils, natural and supernatural, many years ago in the winter of 1652. Internally, I struggled with the questions I had and their possible answers. Was I doing the right thing? Should a person with such power be allowed to exist and possibly threaten the wellbeing of innocents? I was just thirty-five years old on the night I received this "gift," some might say curse, including myself. During the winter of 1652, I had no clue how my life and world was transforming or what would be expected of me. Hundreds of years later, I still wasn't sure I did.

* * *

Horns honking snapped me back into the present. I had stopped and was just sitting at a green light. As I drove to work, I couldn't help but be proud of how far the town had come over the centuries, but the nostalgia was short lived. The maliciousness headed this way would wreak havoc on everything the town held dear. I tried to stay positive by remembering everything that had happened to me throughout my existence had empowered me. In the weeks to come, I knew I would need every ounce of my strength and experience. Giving into my fear was pointless.

All of a sudden my phone bounced and blared to life over the car's Bluetooth.

"Hello?"

"Principal McIntyre, something terrible has happened. You need to get to school ASAP." It was my secretary Karen.

"What do you mean? What's going on?" I asked, knowing exactly what she was going to tell me.

"The police are here. There has been a horrible accident. The Bower twins have been found murdered down by the river."

There was no doubt the prophecy had begun.

"I'll be there in a few minutes. I'm already on my way."

When I got to school, I forwent my usual task of walking throughout the building, greeting the students and, instead, headed straight for my office. Officers roamed the halls of the school like ants, in circles with no real idea of what they were supposed to be doing. Ayden and Detective Williams were waiting for me when I entered the office. Ayden and I exchanged looks as Williams began explaining what a local fisherman had found earlier this morning. I had known Williams and everyone in my office, in fact, for their entire lives. I was always amazed at how human beings could be so unaware of the world around them. They had perfected the art of misperception, and, because of that, I had been able to live my entire life in the same town without being discovered.

Henry Williams was a very capable and competent cop, but this was the first homicide in Salem in decades, and it would be trying for all of those involved in the investigation. I was told the twins were found brutally attacked and carved open near a large boulder alongside the river. Now, I had faces and names to go with the vision I had had the night before. I had held back from believing what Karen had told me until I had the facts for the SPD. The reality hit me harder than I had initially thought it might. Each of the boys was found with symbols burned into their flesh. They had been placed around the rock, the entire combined blood supply of the young twins poured about the area to create various images and words. Small wooden figures and shapes similar those used by the Algonquian people had also been found in the vicinity of the murders. They were calling it a ritual killing and they were right. Williams had spoken to the F.B.I. and hoped a team would be arriving by the end of the day.

"However, there is one thing, which is stranger than everything else. There were no footprints in the area. The only tracks we could find look to be from their heels being dragged through the soil. We have no idea how the hell someone could do to them what was done without leaving any evidence behind," he said.

"That is strange," I said.

I had my own ideas about what happened, but I hesitated to make any sort of judgment until I could do some research.

"We're going to need access to both of the boys' lockers as part of the investigation."

I understood and told them we would be more than happy to cooperate with them.

"Karen, please do not answer the phones this morning or talk to any parents who may arrive. I have to let the kids know before gossip runs rampant. Then I'll send a message to everyone's parents."

*　*　*

Silence abounded in the gym as I sat there looking at the weary student body seated before me. Every face showed varying degrees of fear and worry. They understood something grave had happened. As I scanned the crowd, I saw that he was safe and seated next to his cousin. Thank god he was safe. I decided to stand and get this duty, the worst thing to do for anyone in my position, done.

"Ladies and gentlemen, thank you for getting here so quickly. I have the very sad duty of telling you that two of your classmates have been found in the woods outside of town near the Achachak River, dead."

Gasps and tiny screams echoed around the gym.

"I know this a shock for all of you. We, the faculty, are here for each of you if and when you need to talk. Please respect the Bower family's wishes to be alone and together at this time. We will begin the school year today as scheduled, but will follow a modified schedule."

Above the growing sea of voices, a cry for help suddenly reverberated throughout the entire space and everyone turned to see what had happened. Addy Smythe was convulsing violently in the bleachers as her cousin Ethan tried in vain to help her. My fears were coming true. The prophecy, recounted to me centuries ago, had begun and I was being called to protect the one I had been bound to that bleak winter night in 1652.

Chapter 5

An unexpected reunion

I HUNG UP THE phone in disbelief over what I had just heard from my friend, who taught at the high school where Addy was a student. I had had no premonitions about their deaths, as I had been able to do in the past since my awakening. Most naturally gifted witches experienced their awakening when they turned eighteen, but some had been known to fully realize their gifts earlier. I had been blessed with the powers of telekinesis and foresight. I had also studied my family's book of spells, our grimoire, to master the art of spell casting. Years ago, when I left France, I had smuggled the secret book from my parents' stronghold. I couldn't risk the chance of it being stolen by anyone from the Sabbat du Cercle Noir. Thanks to the magic contained within its pages, I had succeeded in fortifying my own gifts, all of which I had used to protect Addy against those who sought her.

After hanging up the phone, I called Kelley, Ethan's mom, and my closest confidant in both mortal and supernatural circles. The phone rang until the answering machine greeted me on the other end. Without leaving a message, I hung up the phone and sat deep in thought, my cold hands coddling a warm cup of coffee. How in the world can this be happening now after all of these years of peace and quiet? I had learned about the prophecy when I was younger. It had been whispered about among covens throughout Europe and as part of Native American tribal traditions for generations. Throughout the years of peace, we had become complacent, not even noticing the emerging signs of its fulfillment on the horizon. With the realization of the prophecy, the entire future of Wiccan and Native American magic would hang in the balance and sway one of two ways: towards evil or good. It was the classic battle between the two forever warring sides of being, but this battle involved allies and foes who were not known to everyone. Therefore, we had no way to know who we could trust.

The clock struck 10 a.m. and the family heirloom grandfather clock shook me from my trance. I needed to figure just exactly what had happened to those twins. I walked into Ed's library that was strewn with papers, books, and other artifacts from his work on the history of the area where his ancestors had lived. His ancestral line wove together the heritages of the first English colonist as well as the Naukemag and Algonquian tribes, who had lived here centuries before the arrival of the English. He found such pride in being a representation of the native peoples of New England and the first European presence here. I have always admired his passion and desire to learn more about the magical history of New England. I was so proud of the work he had done, and that he was considered one of the foremost scholars in the area. He was an amazing man and father who knew much more about the supernatural history and events of New England and Salem, which most didn't even realize existed. The myths and legends most inhabitants discounted as folklore, actually portrayed the true history and experiences of the early settlers in the northeastern United States.

I approached the bookcase in the far left corner of my husband's cluttered study, I grasped the antique brass knob and opened the glass cabinet. Behind a book containing the treatise on the traditions and beliefs of the Algonquian tribes was a false back, which when pressed in the upper right-hand corner clicked and opened. The interior of this sacred, secret cavity contained my family's grimoire as well as series of scrolls containing ancient incantations and rituals passed down from my husband's father: all fruits of his research in the same area of history. A white witch's magical gifts were derived from nature, just like that of the Algonquian medicine men and shamans. When I was younger, I had studied and learned the traditions of the local tribe, but I was unable to use their spells and rituals just as they were unable to use mine. It was nature's way of controlling the amount of power one supernatural being could have so as not to create a torrent of destructive chaos. The most important aspect was to keep all of this hidden from Addy because we could not risk her discovering our secrets.

I pulled the book out of hiding and cleared a space on Ed's desk to find the location spell needed for such a situation. I had no doubt the murderer of the twins was an inhuman entity conjured by someone with considerable power, enough to direct it in killing two innocents. The blood of innocents was incredibly powerful and only ever used in spells when absolutely necessary. My grimoire contained hundreds of spells handed down over the centuries. Creating spells was extremely difficult and no new ones had been created in almost twenty years. The last was created and cast by my mother, and as a consequence, she sacrificed herself in order to save others.

The pages of the book were crisp, brittle, and brown after so many years. I turned them carefully as I looked for a divination, or location spell. In order to better preserve our heritage, I had actually started working on rewriting the book in both a rewritten and a new electronic form. The one caveat to scrying, or a location spell, was having something that was touched by the person or another object, which had belonged to them. In this case, unfortunately, I had neither, so I decided to cast a detection spell instead to see if anything supernaturally dark had appeared around the village within the last couple of days. A detection spell wouldn't be as accurate as locator spell, but at least I'd have some idea of the magical happenings taking place recently.

To use the spell, I needed to use the blood of a supernatural being, and having no other candidates waiting around to have their finger pricked, I used my own. I really did hate that part. I reached back into the hidden compartment and retrieved an old, tarnished brass goblet used to create small potions or cast certain spells. I also grabbed black pepper corns, cloves, and dandelion root. With a pestle, I ground the herbs together before adding the last of the ingredients. I hovered my hand over the goblet with my index finger extended, and with a small sewing needle, I punctured the tip of my finger and allowed three small droplets of blood to fall, forming the three points of a triangle on top of the dried herbs.

I closed my eyes, and as soon as I threw a lit match into the goblet, I began to meditate. The smoke inching out from the spicy mixture entered my nose, tingling with magical energy. The air became charged and the temperature dropped several degrees as the spell began to scour the surrounding area for whatever supernatural being was responsible for this atrocity. I sat in dead silence until a loud, body-shaking scream leapt out from the silence and pummeled my ears. Images materialized within my mind's eye as the events of last night started to come into view. Red flashed multiple times in my thoughts accompanied by slashing claws and flowing tears. I found it difficult to calm my mind and focus because of the abhorrent violence of the moment I was witnessing. What on this Earth or beyond could have done these unnatural things?

The smell of rotting flesh dominated. It couldn't be that. But it was. The one responsible for the death of two innocent boys was the Widjigo, one of the most demonic and violent spirits to ever have existed. Once summoned, it was relentless in its desire to complete its task. Only the most depraved and sadistic witch or shaman would summon such an inhuman entity. But who in Salem would do such a thing? All the magical beings, witches, and Native Americans, knew one another, and I believed none of them would be crazy enough to bring forth a creature as malicious as this one. Widjigos hadn't been used in centuries because of their unending hunger for human flesh and blood and their unpredictable nature. Those poor children. They never had a chance against such a monster.

In my vision, there was something about the place where the Widjigo had sacrificed the twins that I recognized. It was in the woods, near water. The river. The energy, like their blood, flowed along the river in both directions, but where exactly were they? I pushed myself to concentrate further despite the risk it might pose. The images slowed as they passed through my mind, and I focused on the area surrounding the brutal attack, next to the river close to the thick line of trees marking the entrance to the forest. The image of a boulder crept into my thoughts, the Blood Rock.

The Blood Rock was one of very few magical vortexes found within the United States, and the only one in New England. It had long been revered and protected by both Wiccans and Native Americans because of its unimaginable power and its ability to amplify the magic of supernatural creatures. There was only one reason why this ritual sacrifice would have been performed here: someone had broken the ancient commandment and put the prophecy in motion, which would forever change the world, when their awakening occurred on their eighteenth birthday, if not sooner.

* * *

Casting the spell had zapped me of my energy, and I sat down at Ed's desk in his worn red leather chair. There was no need in attempting another detection spell for further information, considering Widjigos ceased to exist on this plane after their mission was completed. Trying to find the one who had cast the summoning spell would be futile. If they were powerful enough to summon such a beast, they would most likely be able to deflect any type of other spell written within the pages of my grimoire. However, one question remained. Did they already know the identity of the one described in the prophecy?

My thoughts were scattered, and I wasn't sure how I should proceed with this new information. One thing was certain, I had to let my coven and the local Wampanoag community, who were descendants of the Algonquians, know what I had divined. The head of our coven and the tribal shaman would know what to do next, I hoped. We all had to work together to protect the world from what had been mentioned in the prophecy centuries ago. The One, as foretold in the prophecy, would not even know they possessed such power and abilities. That was why finding them and mentoring them was key, so that they used their gifts for good.

I grabbed the phone on Ed's desk to call Kelley again, but before I could press the talk button, it rang, making me jump.

"Hello?"

"Véronique, it's Devon, Principal McIntyre."

"Hey Devon, I heard about the boys. It's so horrible."

"I see. Yes, it is, but that's not why I'm calling."

"What do you mean?"

"I'm afraid something has happened."

"Yes, like I said, I already know about what happened to the boys."

"It's not about the boys Véronique, it's Addy. She's had a seizure, and she's in an ambulance on her way to the hospital."

"Oh dear god."

"Do you need someone to take you to the hospital?"

Disbelief and all-consuming fear overtook me. Surely, this had nothing to do with her impending awakening?

"Véronique?"

"Yes, yes I'm here. I'll be fine to drive myself. Thank you for offering to send someone."

"Okay. I'll see you in a few minutes at the hospital."

"Bye," I said just as a reaction without really hearing the end of our conversation.

Addy had never been in the hospital, but I knew she would be strong. That's the way she was and had always been: like mother, like daughter whether it be good or bad.

As I gathered my thoughts, I took a few things from the hidden compartment, put the rest back, and covered the evidence of its seams. There may have been something I could do for her once I reached the hospital. She couldn't find out the truth about who she was no matter the cost of keeping the secret. Before walking out the door, I called my husband and gave him a very quick rundown of what the morning had revealed.

"Are you sure?"

"I don't see any other reason for all of these things happening. Do you?"

"I just don't want to believe she has made her way back to this plane. Whoever the child is as described in the prophecy can't fathom the things that are to come."

"I know, but we're going to have to tell her, and eventually him, the truth. If we don't, these incidents are going to grow in number and bloody violence. We will need their help if we're to stop this."

"You're right."

"I'm headed to the hospital now, and I'm taking a few things from the cupboard in case there is something I can do."

"Okay. I'll call the tribal council, and the coven to let them know what you've learned this morning. Maybe they've also learned something new or created something that can help all of us."

"I hope so."

"Be careful. I'll head that way, while I'm on the phone with them."

"I love you, Edward."

"Toi aussi (You too)."

* * *

The unnaturally arctic autumnal wind chilled my body as I locked the door and walked to my car. The polar blast only added to my already shaken feeling. I have never much cared for this season. There was the death of nature in every direction you looked. My powers of premonition pulsated in my head, calling on my other senses trying to clearly see who from the Sabbat du Cercle Noir had made the prophecy a reality. I couldn't wrap my brain around how it was possible, and I hoped to god it wasn't a sign of the return of my sister. How could she have broken through the veil between the two planes? I jumped as a gaggle of geese, flying south before the impending New England winter, passed overhead. Their flight overhead was followed by the sound of forest animals scattering sporadically through the woods, in the opposite direction of town and our house. It was an eerie sound that ruined the resounding tranquil silence of the countryside.

A feeling I hadn't felt in years came to life in the center of my being. Someone was stalking me from the edge of the woods. I didn't waste any time getting in the car and pulling out of the driveway, throwing a little gravel here and there as my emotions got the best of me. En route, the foggy mist, which was commonplace this time of year, laid heavy over the ground and the road ahead of me. The sea of white cast an ominous glow over everything not covered by it, and I hoped I could see the covered bridge clearly when I reached it. Only one car could safely enter at a time. I turned the knob and let music fill the car. My heart began to beat less furiously and my white knuckles saw their natural pink color return. Breathing was easier than it had been before reaching the relative safety of the car. I was one of those people who focused better when there was background noise. The dip in adrenaline brought clearer images to my mind, but I still wasn't sure what I was seeing. There were just splashes of red and faces blurring back and forth in my head. Then, all I heard was static. No stations were coming through clearly enough for me to make out a single word. I scanned through all the channels without success, so I looked for a CD in the center console. There had to be something, anything better than the crackling coming from the speakers.

With one eye on the road and one eye searching the endless depths of the console, my phone fell onto the floorboard by the accelerator. As the unending static screeched throughout the car, increasing my stress, I noticed something out of the corner of my eye running towards me. I slammed on brakes just in time to avoid crashing into a deer streaking across the road.

"Jesus!"

After it crossed to the other side, it stopped dead in its tracks and turned its head towards me, its eyes challenging my own with focused concentration and what struck me as conscious intent. Was a wild animal staring me down? The large buck, with a full, dagger-like set of antlers, moved forward a little and manipulated his stance so that he could face me directly. I pushed down hard on the horn multiple times, but nothing changed in his demeanor. We were transfixed in an unwinnable game of staring each other down.

Lowering the window, I yelled, "What the hell are you looking at? Move! Get out of here, you stupid animal!"

Nothing.

His cold, black eyes bore into my soul, and my body rejected the signals from my brain that told my limbs to function. Then, all of sudden, his irises flashed a bright, translucent gold. His sturdy body tensed and he kicked his front legs up into the air. Instead of falling back to the wet ground, they remained suspended in the air as he began to stand upright, like a person. His legs, now like arms, stretched towards the sky, his antlers wilted and slid down the back of the creature, becoming radiant, flowing locks of flaxen, human hair. The fur, running the length of its body, began thinning, absorbing into its torso, revealing flawless, tan human skin. His hooves split and became ten fingers and toes as his stance straightened to better reflect a human posture.

His body was tight and compact, revealing the body of someone with more than a passing athletic inclination. During this transformation, the creature, he, never broke eye contact with me. In fact, his stare intensified as he went from his animal to human form. I had never seen or read anything about this, and I had been studying and learning about all aspects of magic throughout my entire life. Surely my family, my mentors and teachers would have mentioned something like this to me, considering they had seen and experienced much more than I. I was flabbergasted at what I was seeing, and I couldn't convince my body to react. Who was this person and why in the world would they allow me to be witness to such an intimate display of magic?

In reaction to something I couldn't see, the fully transformed man broke eye contact and whipped his head to look at the land across the road, beyond my car. He furrowed his brow and snarled, baring his unchanged animalistic teeth, as he hunched down closer to the ground taking on the form of a sprinter. Despite his human form, he readied himself to attack his prey. With a loud bang, something landed on the roof of the car accompanied by the sound of claws scraping and twisting metal. Instinctively, I slumped down in the driver seat and eyed the roof, watching for anything breaking through, but there was nothing. I looked back to my left, over my shoulder, but the "man-buck" had disappeared, causing the knot in my stomach to intensify.

Even though I wasn't sure what was attacking my car, I knew I had to get to the hospital, to Addy. I took several deep breaths and coached myself into action. I grabbed the steering wheel and sat up enough to see the road, put the car in drive and slammed my foot on the accelerator. The car faltered a bit and struggled to pick up speed, which I assumed was due to the excess weight of whatever the hell was holding on to the roof. The mist had yet to burn off thanks to the almost nonexistent sun, and I struggled to see the road, which meant crossing the bridge without stopping before entering carried more danger than usual. Should I swerve? Maybe I should force the car back and forth. It always worked in the movies, right? Slowly at first and then more franticly, I turned the steering wheel and drove the car back and forth across the dirt road, hoping this might dislodge the creature from the top of the car. Unfortunately, the only thing my stunt did was kick up wet dirt and mud from the road that coated the windshield in a murky mix of sludge. The situation was going from bad to worse, and I wasn't really sure what I could do to ameliorate it.

Thinking it might help my visibility, I turned on the windshield wipers and pushed the button to spray the cleaner but it only made everything in view blurrier. Now, I couldn't even see the road directly in front of me, which didn't help to quell my fears of crashing. More of the same racket of grinding metal broke into the cab of the car, and I had no doubt something would be breaking through the roof at any minute, poised to rip me from the diminishing safety of my vehicle. Hoping to finally throw whatever it was off the roof, I drove both feet down on the brakes, sending the car fishtailing on the muddy road. As the erratic movement turned into a violent spinning, I was thrust back and forth in the driver seat. I desperately groped to regain control, but the car struck a ditch and flipped into the air. The heavy metal automobile rolled numerous times through the vacant pasture. The world spun wildly around me, and I couldn't resist the urge of vomiting from the disorientation. The only sounds I heard were twisting metal and thuds as the car impacted with the ground over and over again. Even when my carnival ride had ended, I maintained my white-knuckled grasp on the steering wheel, unwilling and unable to relax.

The car had finally come to rest on the driver-side with the left side of my face firmly planted in mud. I prayed I would be safer and more protected inside the totaled heap of metal than from the thing that had come for me. I tuned in my ears to the surroundings, listening for any clue concerning the creature's whereabouts. Nothing.

By some miracle, I was still alive. However, my body was reeling from the somersaulting crash. Slowly and painfully, I attempted to unfasten my seatbelt, but it wouldn't budge no matter how hard I pulled or cursed. Desperate times call for desperate measures, and despite the rule against it, I decided to use my gifts to free myself from the car. I concentrated my thoughts on the seatbelt lock and placed my hand over it. After a few moments, I heard a welcomed clicking-sound and the buckle released. I twisted my body so I was facing upward, out through the passenger-side window and began crawling out of the totaled car. I took advantage of the center console and hoisted myself up, and, being careful, peeked my head out of the shattered window to see if I could spot what had attacked the car and me. I wiped some blood away from my face and eyes to scan the surrounding countryside, and thankfully, I did not see anything strange or otherworldly. A part of me honestly hoped to see the deer spirit, but he was nowhere to be seen. There was absolutely nothing to be seen. I was alone, or at least I thought I was.

Standing there with both feet trying to balance on the console, I caught the sound of something moving in the trees, but I failed to see a damn thing. I craned my head and body to get a 360-degree view of my surroundings, which exacerbated the already intense throbbing and stiffness I was experiencing, causing involuntary tears to accumulate and drop from my burning eyes. Wind rippled across the ground scattering leaves as far as I could see. My hair covered my face, and I tried desperately to sweep it away when something grabbed me by it and yanked me out of the car and into the air. Calling upon my powers of telekinesis, I tried to release the hold it had on me. I had to see what had assaulted me. Unfortunately, my powers had no effect on the creature, and I was trapped, struggling as a mortal would. Regardless of the impending pain, I thrashed violently trying to break the grip of whatever had me by my hair. I realized that if I were able to break free, I would most likely break a leg. I dangled at least 10 feet above the broken remains of my car, and the ground below looked just as uninviting, but I had no choice. I had to escape.

"Who are you? What do you want with me?" I yelled.

"Aren't you self-important! What makes you think it's you I want?" a raspy voice bellowed in response.

"No! Why?"

Something sharp pierced my back, and looking down, I saw the end of a staff with a sharpened silver tip immerge covered in blood from my abdomen. My blood revealed a symbol carved into the metallic tip. It was one I had observed before in books on dark and demonic magic, the Sabbat du Cercle Noir. My worst fears surged though my body as blood flowed more freely with my rapidly palpitating heart. They employed this mark to summon only the darkest of magic. Normally, the caster used blood, just like I had done, to seek out magical creatures, but using the blood of the innocents refined the search. It searched for malicious and diabolical creatures. In that moment, I realized who had invoked the Widjigo and who had me now. But how was it possible?

I managed, just barely, to let out a visceral scream as my insides writhed in torment. My blood splashed onto the ground below us.

My last thoughts were of Addy before there existed only nothingness.

Chapter 6

Secrets between sisters

I AM SÉVERINE ARABELLA de la Fontaine. My sister, Véronique, and I were born a mere eight seconds apart, fraternal twins, on January 1, 1973 in La Rochelle, France, to naturally-gifted Wiccan parents. Our father descended from a long line of witches from England while our mother came from one of French heritage. We spent much of our time between our family homes in France and England, and for all intents and purposes, our childhood passed by as normally as those of ordinary mortal children. Despite their now combined households, our parents took overwhelming pride in each of their lineages, and we were expected to do the same. My sister and I only ever spoke French with my mother as required, whereas we would only speak English with our father as well as when visiting the United Kingdom. Each of our lives would be sculpted by a very strong magical hand with only moments of love and caring from our parents and other family members.

Our home in France dated back to the thirteenth century and had always been occupied by our mother's family, all of whom had been magically inclined. Intricate, ornate, and pristinely manicured gardens designed by a famous eighteenth century landscape artist greeted visitors as they approached the house via the long gravel drive. Flanking the entrance sprawled two stone and mortar turrets, the only remnants of a long deceased medieval stronghold, which encapsulated a set of ancient grand oak doors. The vertical distance of the towers climbing into the sky plus the immensity of the wooden doors framed a commanding façade to everyone who visited our fortified home. The home was built of white stone from the surrounding region and shone luminously in the daylight. The three story square structure was built around and contained a large patio and interior garden, which could be seen from any one of the hundreds of windows looking inward from the main house. Our parents used this garden to grow many different types of herbs needed for castings and potions. In some ways, our home continued to resemble the citadel it had once been and from which one could not easily escape.

Our home was rarely empty . . . of people. More often than not, the halls saw lots of traffic as family or coven members occupied its rooms, especially during important Wiccan festivals and holidays. I always hated these incessant visits from people with whom I had nothing in common except for being magical. Even as a child, I saw them as weak and too happy to lead a more mortal life. I had power, and I deserved to use it whenever and wherever I pleased. Unfortunately, as a universal rule, witches did not use their magic for personal needs in fear that such acts would incur dangerous and costly consequences. The cosmos demanded a delicate balance of all things and certain spells could evoke deadly and unforeseen consequences. Never being one easily dissuaded by silly ancient commandments, I looked at things very differently, as did my sister for a while, and rebelled against their moral restraints of using magic. Soon I was to learn, the design of our home hid an impressive network of secret passages and hidden rooms, in which I would discover our family's most sinister buried secrets. Ones I would embrace wholeheartedly and the same ones my sister would realize she was too scared to embrace the true power available to us.

Throughout our childhood, our parents remained distanced from us, unwilling to show either of us much emotion or actual parental care. In creating and propagating this type of behavior, they had also denied us from knowing about the house's secret inner sanctums and passageways, which guarded the marred secrets and history of our family. But as if guided by another's desire for unearthing the truth, the house gave life to long dead memories. When I was 13 years old, I accidently discovered the entrance to one such long-hidden and forgotten parts of our house's innards while playing hide and seek with my sister. As I crouched in the back corner of my closet, a light sour-smelling breeze tickled the back of my neck as it circulated through the wooden planks and cracked plaster. I pressed my ear against the corner of my closet and heard a sound, like a voice, seeping from the other side. Leaning against the back wall of the closet, I listened intently, trying to prove to myself I wasn't just imagining things. Snap. The back of my closet creaked and popped as a hidden door slowly opened, revealing a stone tunnel populated by cobwebs, spiders and the rampant sounds of scurrying rodents. My heart thumped in my chest while my stomach churned with supernatural hunger. My body licked up the energy oozing from the once concealed hallway causing my limbs to become limp with longing, my lungs swelled in my chest and a charged breath exploded from my mouth, lighting the ancient torches still holding to the rocky walls. I moved forward along the glowing stone passage, guided by some invisible being. I did nothing to deter its control of my body. I am not sure how far I had penetrated the fortified shaft when I reached a wooden door marked with a pentagram carved into it. However, this pentagram did not reflect the usual symbol used as protection by white witches, instead horns branched off of every one of the five-pointed star, breaking the Guardian circle surrounding it.

The unseen force crawled into my body and levitated me until my toes barely brushed the slimy, wet floor. My head pitched upwards. My eyes opened, my pupils fully dilating as I glared at the corrupt star. The door opened graciously without causing the slightest groan despite their apparent age and I drifted across the threshold. Dozens of black candles ignited with black flames and cast their supernatural glow around the dome shaped room, unveiling stacks upon stacks of ancient tomes lining the curved walls and a single table occupying the center of the room. An enormous red leather bound book sat closed on the medium-sized table. Again, I floated out of control of my own body towards the table. In front of the book, my body stopped and I hung there suspended. The book violently opened and its pages tussled back and forth by some non-existent wind. My mouth opened savagely farther than humanly possible. Suddenly the pages stopped and released a dense storm cloud of energy, which forced itself into my gaping mouth and down into my soul.

"Arabella, wake up!" my sister screamed.

She shook me ferociously until finally I opened my eyes and peered up at her tear stained face looking down at me. We were in my closet.

"Are you okay? Say something!" she persisted.

"I'm okay, I think."

"What happened? I've been looking for you for hours!"

"I, I'm not sure. I think maybe I fell asleep."

She looked at me quizzically and I didn't blame her, but I couldn't remember anything after I had entered the closet.

"I need some water. I have a really strange taste in my mouth." I said.

"Okay, let's go down to the kitchen. You scared the crap out of me!"

I gave a weak smile in response.

"You've never been that good at hiding before. You'd better not have used your gifts, that's cheating you know."

"I didn't use them, I swear." I said. *Or did I?*

Several weeks passed without any idea of what may have happened to me during those lost hours. Then, one night my life and destiny changed forever. Familiar earthy scents of decay filled my room. I slept soundly in my wrought iron bed dreaming of childish things when, suddenly, I awoke. I was not alone in my room. The floorboards creaked and moaned supporting whatever watched me in my bed. Breathing in the air created an acidic taste in my mouth and I swallowed multiple times to try and cleanse my pallet. In the corner, in the impenetrable blackness, something darker than the deepest depths of the night ogled me, but I wasn't scared. It felt familiar and we simply looked at each other. We understood each other without using words. In that moment, I recalled what had happen during the game of hide and seek and the sullied past of my family and their predilections for black magic. The wraith inched forward and enveloped me in his shroud. Inside me, the power and knowledge of the Sabbat du Cercle Noir brewed and transferred to me when the magically charged cloud consumed me. In the nights and weeks that followed, I devoured the secrets told to me by the wraith, a remnant of a long dead ancestor, but one who would not reveal their name. I learned I couldn't trust anyone, not even my sister, without risking them stealing my newfound gifts and knowledge. And I couldn't get enough of the power given to me by the evil coven, so I would die before it was taken from me. Finally, in the deepest depths of my soul and being, I knew I had found my purpose of being born into this world.

Recent revelations helped me to see that the majority of the people in my entire life were talking about me and had never truly loved or cared for me, most of all, my sister. We had always been best friends or so I thought. For the next four years, I secretly plotted a way to remove her from my life and an upcoming trip to our family's home in England provided the perfect moment to do so.

We arrived at the sixteenth century Tudor manor house in Yorkshire on a typically stormy and rainy English day, which charged me with exhilaration. We had come to England to celebrate the birthday of a great aunt who we had only ever met once, years before when we were much younger. Another waste of time celebrating the mortality facing those who relegated themselves to living a human existence rather than access the truer, darker magic already flowing through our pulsing red veins. Now that my sister and I were seventeen we were expected to act like the other adults and help with the festivity's preparations; however, we managed, as always, to slip away and brush off our newly assigned duties.

As commanded by the wraith and as a promise to myself, I had never discussed anything about the past four years to anyone, especially my sister. The passage of time had taught me to see through her lies about half-hearted attempts at showing her sisterly love for me. Today would be the day. I would rid myself of her false witness of love.

Like we had done numerous times in the past as children, we entered the wood surrounding the home through one of the ornate side gardens and slipped out of the view of everyone infesting the manor. Both of us had always loved the rain and storms and venturing out into them when they approached. The brisk wind swept through the treetops and down onto the forest floor, blowing leaves and small branches into tiny cyclonic vortices, which we ran through, just as we had done as kids. Nature always became irreverently charged during such storms and as a consequence, our powers were also increased. The gods above must have been smiling down on me, embracing my plans for my sister.

"Come on, slow poke!" my sister said as she darted back and forth from behind the trees.

As we had grown up, my sister had stopped using her gifts for everyday activities, a sign of fear and weakness. A sudden clap of thunder came with a bolt of lightning which stuck a large English oak, causing the middle of the enormous tree to explode into a cloud of splinters and charred wood. My sister screamed and ran, but she was too slow and the larger upper part of the massive oak pinned her to the ground with a crushing thud.

Her frantic shrills shattered through the claps of thunder and I walked over to where she lay trapped between the trunk and the steadily increasing muddy ground. Her eyes called out to me as her mouth filled with a mixture of water and mud, choking as she desperately gasped for air. I stared into her eyes, my own sister's eyes, without saying anything. I felt no connection, no loyalty, and no love for her. There was nothing, not even a smidgen of anything resembling compassion or desire to help her as she helplessly struggled against encroaching death. Blood trickled from her nose and misted the cooling night air a scarlet hue as she coughed, the weight of the wooden behemoth slowly crushing her insides.

"Please, Arabella, help me! Go get help!" she pleaded.

Perhaps I could have used my gifts, been strong enough to save her in that moment, but I did not. I didn't care what happened to her.

"You impudent little brat!" a voice said inside my head. "You are not the one who decides the death of your sister. Do not think you are above reproach."

The voice inside my head stopped and the next thing I remembered was lying beside my sister on the muddy forest floor. She was alive, her injuries healed.

"Arabella, what happened?"

I was reminded of the booming vexed voice in my head a few moments earlier.

"I'm not sure. What do you remember?" I asked.

"Nothing. Absolutely nothing."

After the incident in the English forest, I never attempted to take the life of my sister, partly because of a sickening hint of sisterly love, but more so due to the commanding words of the wraith that rainy night. I pretended as if nothing happened, and after a few months, Véronique pushed that night out of her mind as we left the life with our parents in France. One chapter in our lives verged on ending with a new one lying before us. The overbearing, yet unloving influence of our parents had culminated in our overwhelming desires to escape our home and our country.

Chapter 7

A new beginning

FOR MONTHS ON END, we had both counted down the days until we finished our studies, always with private tutors. For as long as I could remember, Arabella and I had ignored and, at times, mocked our tutors. We had always preferred to spend our time practicing the craft, not studying languages, literature and history. When we were younger, we never understood why we were forced to study such unimportant mortal things, which had nothing to do with perfecting our gifts. Unlike Arabella, however, now that I was older, I realized the importance of developing and using my non-magical gifts to the same high standards as my magical ones. Secretly, I had applied to Harvard and been accepted. Not even Arabella knew and I worried what her reaction might be when she found out why I had been so determined to move to Massachusetts.

Then, when we were eighteen, my sister and I fled to the United

States from France and found a new home in Salem, the place where the English-side of our family, the Harwoods, had gone nearly three hundred years before us and close enough for me to attend university. Our English ancestors had been cunning and lucky enough to stay hidden and safe during the chaotic and murderous times of the Salem witch trials. All in all, their safety was thanks to their relationships with the Native peoples who had helped them to remain unnoticed, while at the same time, allowing them to continue practicing their craft alongside the Algonquian shamans and tribe members.

We stepped off the train in Salem on a gray snowy day in early November having nothing but a few clothes and tomes we managed to sneak out of our home. A cold Arctic front had invaded the New England coast. Snow, like rolling hills of sparkling sugar, had conquered the entire landscape as far as one could see, while the bitterly frigid deep blue inlet from the Atlantic Ocean popped and cracked as enormous growing sheets of ice encroached upon the rocky coast with an unnatural speed. The low-hanging ashen clouds resisted the winter sun, painting a shadowy canopy over the tranquil seventeenth century village turned town. People, bundled in warm billowing layers, walked along the streets reluctantly easing into their day, the warm steam from their cups of coffee, tea or cocoa swirling elegantly into the glacial air.

Suddenly, I was overcome by the oddest sensation, I felt at home here even though I had only arrived moments earlier. The town reminded me of a postcard I had seen in a shop in France about the seasons in New England. I think that was the first time I dreamed of moving to America, specifically New England.

We made our way into town fighting against the bristling polar wind when, in the distance, I caught a glimpse of a deep green sign swinging violently on cast iron hinges, which said "Harwood Realty est. 1800" in gold lettering. A bell jingled as the door opened and we stepped into the warm cozy entry of the realty office. In a hearth that probably dated back centuries, a fire bustled, emitting very welcome heat. The interior of the office greatly resembled the library in our father's family home in England, only adding to the welcoming feeling I had already been experiencing. At a deep-stained oak desk, an older woman with high cheekbones, beautiful shoulder-length heather grey hair and rimless reading glasses that aided deep set, yet caring olive green eyes behind them, greeted us with a smile as I shut the weighty wooden and glass pane door behind us.

"Good morning. How can I help you young ladies this fine chilly day?" she said.

Although her question was completely expected and normal, neither of us had actually thought beyond making it to Salem and what we might say when we went in search of our ancestral family. We must have looked idiotic standing there, ours mouths gaping open as we looked at each other dumfounded as to how to proceed.

After a few seconds of awkward silence, the elegantly mature receptionist asked, "You're here to see Mr. Harwood, correct? We've been expecting you for a couple of days."

"But how could you know?" I asked. She couldn't have been a witch because there was no magical aura surrounding her.

"Witches aren't the only supernatural beings who know how to use nature to their advantage. Of course no spell is ever one hundred percent accurate, hence the mystery about the exact date of your arrival in Salem." she explained.

"I think I'm really going to like this place." Arabella said in a hushed tone.

"I'm sure you both will. I'll let Mr. Harwood know you're here. Please have a seat and help yourself to something warm to drink." she said as she motioned over to two comfortable looking worn-in leather chairs on either side of the stone fireplace.

Neither of us said a word to the other. I think both of us were suffering a bit from jetlag and also surprised at the knowledge about our arrival even before we knew the date. Suddenly, the bell above the door jingled to life and a very attractive sun-kissed boy around our age barreled in from the cold outside.

"Daniel, you're fifteen minutes late. Mr. Harwood has been waiting on those for his 12:30 closing," the receptionist said showing a slight crack in her pleasant demeanor.

"I know. I know. Sorry mom, but it's the freaking North Pole out there and traffic is insane."

"Please watch your language. We have guests."

He looked over at us, but he saw right through me and focused on Arabella, the connection supernaturally visible for those with gifts. Seeing the electricity flow between the two of them, I wondered if the intuitive receptionist perceived the light show too.

*   *   *

It felt hard to breathe and I unconsciously gripped the leather bound armrest tightly, digging my nails into their soft surface. Never had I experienced such a connection with another person, not even my own family. The only other connection of such intensity occurred when I met the wraith for the first time in my room as a child. Come hell or high water, I would find out why we were linked in such a supernatural and human manner. Sweat formed on my forehead and droplets of cooling perspiration dripped down my temples and rolled down my back. Luminous and intoxicating heat swallowed up the room with radiating force and I stood up.

"Could I have some water please?" I asked.

Before the old woman could answer my question, he, Daniel, butted in and offered to show me where the water machine was kept. I followed him out of the intense heat of the reception area and into a small kitchen off to the side.

*   *   *

"Is your sister quite all right?" she asked me after Arabella and Daniel had left the room.

"Ugh, yes I believe so. I think she just might be a little dehydrated after our journey." I started to ask how she knew she was my sister, but then remembered her ability to know things before they happened.

Arabella had never acted or reacted in such a way with anyone else she had ever met. It was true we'd spent the majority of our lives separated from boys, but we were never forbidden to be near them. She rarely showed much emotion towards a person, even with me. Something was at work and I wasn't all that sure what it was. Recently, her aura fluctuated almost constantly and even I couldn't get a solid reading on what she was feeling or thinking for that matter. Unfortunately, we didn't share things as we once did as children and I saw the future as one full of less camaraderie and more solitude.

"Miss? Miss?"

"Yes?"

"Mr. Harwood can see you now."

"I'm sorry. I was lost in my thoughts. I'll go and get my sister if I may."

She nodded and I followed the path taken by Daniel and my sister a few moments earlier. As I turned the tiny corner, which led into the kitchen, flabbergasted was the only way I could describe my reaction.

"Arabella, what are you doing!"

I scared both of them. Arabella jumped off the counter and Daniel stepped too far back and crashed into the refrigerator. They both looked at me with faces full of shock, but also with hints of humor glimmering in their eyes and trembling in the corners of their mouths.

"Let's go. He's ready to see us."

I grabbed the back of her arm as she passed me and asked her what in the world did she think she was doing.

"You don't even know him!"

"I thought we left our parents back in France," she said cutting her eyes at me.

We passed through the cozy sitting area and then followed the kind receptionist into Mr. Harwood's very welcoming office. The two sidewalls were filled with bookshelves stuffed with all types of books, new and old. The walls behind his desk were replete with photos, most of which depicted people in various stages of life instead of the usual banal decorations found in offices. One felt immediately at home in this large combination library and family room. We both sat in chairs facing his desk and sunk into comfort.

A few minutes passed before Mr. Harwood entered from a hidden door behind one of his bookshelves.

"We all need our little sanctuaries," he said with a large and heartening smile.

"Thank you so much for seeing us, especially without an appointment," I said.

"Oh, think nothing of it. Genevieve predicted you would be arriving around this time."

Before I could comment, Arabella asked him the question I had been pondering since we arrived but didn't want to ask and be rude.

"How's that possible? She's not a witch."

I shot her a look, livid with the way she was acting.

"It's quite all right, my dear. I've always admired people who are direct."

"Then you'll love her," I said, knowing I was being childish and petty.

"You are correct, she is not a witch. She's a member of the Algonquian tribe near Salem. Certain members of the tribe possess gifts very similar to ours, but unlike us, they do not radiate aural rings."

Of course we knew Native Americans were very spiritual people with traditions purporting to be based in magic and the supernatural, but neither of us had ever heard of the rumors actually being true. It actually made sense because most witches were simply practitioners who mixed herbs and communed with nature, but unlike us, possessed no supernatural gifts or power.

"Just like us as I'm sure you know. Most witches have nothing in the way of powers. They merely appreciate the study and love of a more naturally based life."

Was he telepathic or was this just some sort of coincidence? Being taken off guard by the declaration about Genevieve had shaken me a bit.

An uneasy silence ticked by the three of us looking back and forth at one another, not sure of how to continue. In some ways, I waited for him to continue with information he'd already heard about us from his receptionist, but he did not.

The embarrassed pause didn't last too long before, of course, Arabella rectified the exchange of blank looks.

"So, we are here to learn more about our magical gifts. Our parents were, let's just say, a little too strict for our liking and we needed freedom from them. We hoped coming to where our ancestors came centuries ago might be an imaginative way to explore and discover our gifts."

Mr. Harwood just smiled.

"I told you you'd love her," I repeated.

"I think both of you will benefit from and enjoy life here in Salem."

A knock at the door brought a stop to our conversation and Daniel poked his head inside the office with files in his hand, which had been further delayed after his helping Arabella find some water.

"Ah Daniel, please do come in. Ladies, I'd like to introduce Genevieve's son. He helps out a lot around here and is heading to Harvard in the next year."

"We met earlier," Arabella said and I instantly turned bright red.

Mr. Harwood's expression shifted abruptly and he asked Daniel to leave us after taking the files from him.

"You are both very welcome to stay here and practice with our coven and even participate in rituals with the Wampanoag tribe. Having said that, it is strictly forbidden for witches and Native Americans to carry on romantic relationships. If anyone is discovered to be involved in something of the sort, they face expulsion, binding or possibly even death."

"And just why is that?" Arabella retorted, her directness having lost its appreciative element.

"It is true you probably do not know about our reasoning, but you must follow our rules here."

"That's not a good enough reason. I want to know why."

I sat there silent, embarrassed, yet, all the while curious myself about the rationale for such a rule.

Mr. Harwood clinched his fists and supported his weight on the desk as he gazed outside for a moment before responding. He brought his stare from the window and directed it straight at Arabella.

"Centuries ago when our ancestors arrived here, we quickly established a friendship and understanding with the native peoples in the Massachusetts area. Thanks to that relationship, an exchange of ideas, beliefs and magic occurred and as a result we learned of a particular prophecy, which had been orally handed down through the generations."

"And?"

"It states that if a naturally gifted witch and Native American produce a child, it will bring about a cataclysmic event that would reshape the world and exterminate all supernatural and mortal creatures. Basically, the end of the world as we know it."

"Change is always a good thing in my opinion."

"This is no joking matter young lady. This is something we can never allow to happen. Do you understand?"

"Yes," we said in unison.

"I apologize for my sister being disrespectful Mr. Harwood."

Just as quickly as his tone had turned serious earlier, his jovial demeanor returned and he invited us to have lunch at his house so we could meet his wife and children, and some other members of the coven.

* * *

The family had established itself, using its history as a founding family to its advantage. Driving through the snowy town, the name Harwood appeared on several signs offering an array of services from butchers to healthcare. The Harwoods lived in a house just outside the town limits of Salem. It was a colonial style brick clad house with deep green accents, just like the color of the sign outside the realty office. The same welcoming feeling found in the office could be used to describe the interior of the home. Much of the interior architecture did not look like it had changed since it was built centuries earlier. Exposed wooden beams wrapped the dining room, which held a dark stained table for six, set for a full lunch of delectable looking food.

Mr. Harwood's family was so gracious to have us for lunch and we spent hours afterwards talking about our lives in France as well as our family's magical heritage in Europe and in the States. It was so nice to find people with whom we could share our magical gifts. The Harwood family made it clear that we were never to use magic in public or in front of mortals who did not know of our existence. I understood the rule and the reasoning, but I worried about Arabella's fervor for using her powers when and where she desired. The consequences of breaking these "directives" concerned me. Already, I liked Salem and the options we would have here, as long as we, more specifically Arabella, stayed within the lines of what was expected and asked of us.

Only a short time after arriving at the Harwood home, I knew Arabella had already tired of the functioning family dynamic and the laws of being a witch here. As soon as the food had been cleared, she asked to be excused and said she was going to go for a walk in the woods surrounding the house and property. She was out of the door before anyone could give his or her consent or even acknowledge she had said anything, more than likely surprised by the fact she had actually muttered more than a one-syllable response since we had arrived. I, on the other hand, longed to know more about our ancestors and the Harwood family, so I stayed to talk with the family and research our lineage in their incredible collection of ancestral books.

* * *

My lungs contracted as soon as the outside air reached them. A fresh aroma of ice, snow and decay dominated the land around the

Harwood house. What an incredibly weak and sheepish family. How they had managed to maintain any sort of control here for so many centuries escaped me. Daniel, on the other hand, was someone I looked forward to getting to know despite the nonsense spouted repeatedly by Mr. Harwood. The bleak winter landscape invited me into the fold of the now barren trees of the wood bordering the Harwood property. The forest floor lay bare without even the slightest sign of anything living or dead for that matter. I meandered down a path, not knowing where I was going until I reached a river. I did not remember passing over water when we left the real estate office for the Harwood residence. Of course nothing looked familiar and I crawled onto a large rock to sit and simply gaze out into the winter nothingness.

Steady footfalls disturbed the frozen silence and I turned back towards the trail I had followed earlier expecting to see Véronique, but it wasn't her. I watched him quizzically in the distance. He said nothing as he headed towards me, determination focused in his eyes as they met mine. He emerged from the tree line revealing his sinewy nude silhouette, seemingly unaffected by the polar landscape. Instinctually, I retreated farther back on the giant stone as he stepped towards me, reaching the top of the rocky surface in one predatory stride. I raised a hand, every hair at attention when he grabbed my head, my hair, twisting and pulling my hair, the tension causing my scalp to stretch to its limits. His mouth met mine as he jerked my head towards him, our deep kiss emitting a cloud of condensed heavy, balmy breath. Within moments, my outer layer no longer existed and my back arched when it contacted the bone-chilling surface of the crystalline boulder. My legs quivered as he lay between them, the sweat evaporating into steam off of his back. My nails gripped it ardently and dug deep into his flesh. The mix of warm blood and bitterly cold air a paradox as it oozed down my fingers and dripped from my knuckles onto the sparkling surface of rock. An otherworldly desire overwhelmed both of us and we sunk into the moment, in writhing exaltation.

Afterwards, Daniel and I continued to see each other, not caring what the consequences might be if we were discovered. For the first and only time in my life, I fell in love, the son of an Algonquian shaman, and the type of person I least expected to ever meet in my life. However, after several months of studying with the Harwood's coven and members of the Wampanoag tribe, I realized they could and would never help me tap into the more powerful and darker side of nature. I grew impatient and angry at their lack of willingness to answer my questions regarding what I had learned in those dark and damp passages as a teenager. My anger grew to hatred as the members of the coven discovered my darker predilections and, along with the consent of my sister, banned me from further interactions with them.

"How can you do to this to me Véronique?"

"Do you not understand what you're doing is dangerous and could cause rippling consequences for not only you but all of us? You know better than to practice the black arts. Did you learn nothing?"

"It's not my fault you're scared of greater power. What happened to my sister who wanted more, who wanted to use her magic all the time?"

"She grew up and realized there are more important things in life, like having a life outside of magic, a mortal life."

"You are not the sister I knew before coming here. This was a mistake and I am leaving to pursue what I truly want to practice, real power and magic, not these petty tricks and potions."

"Arabella, wait! Please don't go."

"Goodbye, Véronique. Enjoy Salem and good luck with your new family."

* * *

Despite multiple attempts to contact Daniel, I never spoke to him again. After he heard of my expulsion and the reasons behind it, he had refused to see me. The only contact being a letter to me saying he would never see me the same way and suggested I leave forever because in his eyes, I was dead. My anguish and confusion devoured me and I pushed all thoughts of my sister, Daniel, and Salem from my mind. I packed my few belongings and left for a place where I would be able to pursue my deepest desires, New Orleans.

Chapter 8

New Orleans

BEING IN NEW ORLEANS was so invigorating for me. The use of magic, voodoo and hoodoo presented itself at every corner of the French Quarter. An infusion of French and African traditions, beliefs and rituals ignited the air with a flurry of magical currents, creating an atmosphere of pure energy, both good and evil. My skin tingled and vibrated with excitement and energy as I walked down Bourbon Street, every part of me bathing in the fluid mystical energy running rampant as far as the eye could see. Here was a place I could call home and realize my iniquitous destiny.

To fully tap into dark magic, one must prove one's self worthy by the act of sacrificing an innocent, whether it is an animal or a human. When choosing a sacrificial victim, the greater the innocence of the creature, the more plentiful the rewards when conjuring the dark arts. I, myself, had no compunctions about killing another human if it allowed me to claim what was rightfully mine.

The hunt for the catalyst, the blood of an innocent, was exhilarating. My new family accompanied me: a dark coven rooted in the supernatural history and energy of New Orleans. We had met in a voodoo shop in the Quarter. It's not difficult to recognize the serious followers of magic, both black and white, from the incessant whine and silly giggles of the tourists. Germaine St. Claire stood strong and almost arrogant in the voodoo herb shop. The mocha skin of her long, lean body glistened in the humidity that constantly bombarded every inch of the swamp that was now New Orleans. Her raven hair was held back tightly from her face and a long ponytail dipped down her back. Her full lips anchored her angular face and gave full prominence to her naturally bright blue eyes hidden below long, full eyelashes. Instantly, I knew we would be great friends and companions in releasing the torrent of black magic buried within me.

Germaine's group gathered in the basement of an antebellum home located in the historic Garden District. The white nineteenth century home belonged to one of her followers who was not naturally gifted, but did possess the ability to cast basic spells. Overall, Germaine seemed to attract more people, who fancied themselves witches, than naturally gifted ones. I saw that as a weakness within her coven, but for the time being I kept this disappointment to myself. Thankfully, these want-to-be witches could do something right because they had succeeded in discovering several axis of power located in the eastern half of the U.S. One such portal happened to be located under this house and another had been found in Salem. It was also where my sister was still living in her husband's family home, which dated back to the seventeenth century. A sacrifice upon such powerful land, such as the home of Germaine's coven, would permit me to invoke more energy than I had initially thought possible. Destiny had smiled on me with this revelation. The spiritual and physical planes had opened their arms to embrace and show me the path to unbridled control of all magic.

With the help of Germaine's coven, we scoured the streets of New Orleans with the single purpose of hunting down the one that would open the gateway of ultimate magic. What an invigorating experience it was for me to pursue prey in a city filled with supernatural forces and plenty of tourists too absorbed in the environment to notice us surveying them. It took months but I was finally able to choose a sacrificial lamb for the invocation ritual.

The family's license plate revealed they were from Alabama, *The Heart of Dixie*. I couldn't help but grin. They were staying in an historic hotel located in the heart of the Quarter, which made taking them that much more doable without raising suspicion. The Quarter ebbs and flows with the inane shrill and noise of drunken tourists all day and night. Screams of terror would be easily lost and go unnoticed. I must admit I had considerable difficulty in choosing which member of the family of four I would offer up to the spirits. They were such a wholesome and happy family, completely unaware of the greater purpose one of their lives was destined to fulfill.

After several nights of stalking the family around the city, I made my decision and devised a plan to ensure a successful hunt. The family was enjoying their last night in the Big Easy in one of the many unique restaurants. I could not have hoped for a better place to catch prey than in a city where the libations flow without reprieve. Peering through the window, I observed the parents partaking of various glasses of wine while their teenage son and daughter laughed at the spectacle. The happiness portrayed by this family annoyed and disgusted me. They were living in a world about which they understood nothing. Their mundane existences served no real purpose in their world, but in mine, they would aid me in something they could not even comprehend.

The night continued to favor me in my selection when the parents returned to their hotel after dinner and their children went in search of fun in the streets of the Quarter. After walking around for a while, they entered a jazz bar on one of the many hidden side streets. Smoke drifted into every corner of the club carrying the upbeat and soulful notes with them. The patrons of the club were entranced by the serpentine music of the band and the body of the moody songstress. The rhythmic beats worked just as well as a spell and observing the two of them captivated by the scene around them, I made my move.

"Bonsoir, mes amis."

They looked at each other, dumbfounded. "Barn sour."

"You must not be from around here."

"No, we're on vacation," they responded, relief flashing across their faces.

"My name is Arabella de la Fontaine."

"Hi! My name is Jake and this is my sister Kari."

"Enchantée. New Orleans is such an enchanting city, don't you think?"

Both of them looked around at the other customers, taking in the ubiquitous *joie de vivre* that New Orleans offered before answering.

"It's so cool. There's nothing like this in Alabama."

"I would imagine not. How long are you guys here?"

"Unfortunately, we're leaving tomorrow. Believe us, we don't want to leave."

"Maybe you could just transfer here for college?"

"It's an idea, but I doubt our parents would go for that," said the boy.

"Maybe we could bribe them!" his sister responded, laughing.

As the band starting playing a deeply seductive melody, everyone in the club became consumed. The ambiance changed from one of upbeats and electricity to one of deep and intimate vocal and musical harmonies.

"Do you like the music, jazz?"

"We've never really heard it before."

"It's said that jazz can touch your soul more than any other type of music there is. Once you hear it, you are changed forever."

"You're so right. I can really feel it, but I don't think Jake would feel it even if he was being slapped upside the head with it."

"Eh, it's just too slow and . . .blah for me. I'm going to the bathroom. Be back in a few."

"You and your brother are quite different. Are you close?"

"Yes and no…. it really depends on what we're talking about. I'm definitely more artistic than he is."

"Well, you are in the perfect place to experience an array of arts, from paintings to music. I know an incredible place where you can experience both, if you're interested."

"Um, I should probably wait for my brother."

I nodded at her knowing her brother wouldn't have any qualms about her going anywhere or doing anything for the rest of the night. By now, he had been dealt with by one of Germaine's followers. As we sat there, I noticed a waiter walk towards us and whisper in the girl's ear.

"Is everything okay?"

"Yes. My brother went back to the hotel, so it looks like I'm free to check out the place you were telling me about."

"Excellent."

"I think I'll run to the restroom before we leave, if that's okay."

"Of course."

As soon as she had left the table, I took a special sleep-inducing elixir I had brought with me out of my purse and carefully added a few drops to her drink. Soon her essence would flow through me and give me the power I wanted and needed.

* * *

"Everything is ready for the ritual Arabella."

The altar and table had been set to the specifications detailed in my family's forgotten dark grimoire. I had discovered the book of dark magic shortly after being visited by the inhuman spirit for the first time. Time in the catacombs and tunnels of my ancestral home with the wraith had given me ample opportunities to perfect my casting skills and master the wicked, overlooked legacy of my ancestors. The innards of my family home had contained more about black mystical power than I could ever have thought possible. All of this would culminate in an exacting revenge against those who had dismissed me. I cleared my thoughts and gazed upon the scene that lay before me.

A long solid wood table, which had been meticulously constructed, sat perpendicular to the altar. The altar stood draped in crimson velvet with different colored candles in each of the four quadrants, each representing one of the four elements of nature: fire, wind, water and earth. Various types of herbs were placed in brass bowls atop black candles. Their aroma would call the spirits to our physical plane to assist me in my quest for darkness. In the middle of the altar sat my grimoire, a pentagram traced in blood, which unless hexed and drawn in blood could not be used for evil. On top of the pentagram lay a bowl containing the blood of our animal sacrifice, a dog. Partially submerged in the blood was a large black candle with a flame that burned green and bright, casting a sickly glow over the plush and fragrant garden of the antebellum home.

The virginal offering lay stretched out on the table, her hands and feet tied to the four corners. In the humid glow of candles, all the members of the coven, including the sacrifice, and myself were skyclad, or naked. The night welcomed the casting of such a spell. It was the Esbat of the full moon when magical energy was at an apex and the demons on the other plane yearned for a sacrifice of flesh and blood, like ours. Together, the other witches and I casted a triangle, which as opposed to a circle, welcomes dark and negative energies to enter. With my athame pointed in the direction of the moon, I invoked the evil spirits to come forth and be welcomed into our triangle.

As our chanting grew louder and more fevered, the girl began to wake up and instantly began fighting to free herself from her bindings. She screamed thrillingly loud, but no one would hear her. She flopped around and worked to free herself just like the trapped animal she was. I admired her fighting spirit as I felt the arrival of the energy we had been waiting for. Standing at the head of the table I asked for the spirits to guide me in my task and help me tap into the darkness for which I longed. I held the athame out from my body and over my sacrifice. I moved in measured steps along the border of the table until I reached its head. With one calculated swing of my arm, I ended her fight and watched as her rich blood poured from her neck.

Holding my arms by my side and angled out from my body, I opened my palms and uttered the incantation for summoning and absorbing the dark energy. Instantaneously, the blood from her wound vaporized, and I inhaled the iron tasting fumes deep into my lungs as I became one with my sacrifice and the forbidden magic I had come to New Orleans to claim. My body stirred with a power about which I had only dreamed. Finally having accomplished my objective in New Orleans, I looked forward to reuniting with my sister and Daniel. No one could have suspected the gift I had discovered only months after leaving Salem.

* * *

I felt a surge of excitement and dominance upon returning to Salem and exposing my new powers to my sister and my former lover. No one knew I had left them months ago carrying Daniel's child, a child, which would amplify my powers and help me to destroy those who had tried to bind me from using my gifts.

Feeling perhaps a bit too confident with my new powers, I decided to confront the coven at their gathering near the ancient and sacred rock, the Blood Rock. To protect themselves, they had cast the circle to create a veil through which only magical beings could see. As I entered the forest near the old bridge, their fires burned bright and painted the night sky. They would all be gathered in a circle chanting and praising Mother Nature and thanking her for her bounty. There would be no better nor perfect time to make my appearance.

I knew it would be foolish to appear in flesh and blood to them, so I used my newly acquired power of astral projection to show my face for the first time in months. I projected myself into their circle by putting myself into a trance. They were all stunned when I appeared before them. However, they did not show fear or disgust, they seemed rather glad to see me safe. A part of me struggled to understand their endearing sentiments. I had pictured a much more accusatory scene where I would be expected to explain my reasons for leaving. But I was wrong. At first, they asked nothing about where I had been or what I had been involved with. They only wanted to know that I was okay. However, I convinced myself not to be fooled by the pretense of their reactions. I could only trust one person: myself.

"Oh my god Arabella, you're okay! I, we, were so worried about you," my sister exclaimed.

"I'm fine. I've been away learning from others about other unique aspects of our varied magical heritage, ones I was forbidden to study here."

"We can talk about that later. I'm just so relieved to know you are safe and back home."

The light of the full moon above shifted and the members of the coven got a full perspective of my astral form, my swollen belly where Daniel's child grew inside me no longer hidden.

"Are you pregnant?" my sister asked.

My sister ran forward to hug me, but passed right through my projection of light.

"I wasn't sure how I and my baby would be received by you, so I projected myself to this place."

"Oh . . ." replied my sister as the others turned to whisper to each other.

Astral projection was a very rare gift among witches and only the most practiced and powerful could maintain the concentration for more than a few minutes. I had become one of those very few and I knew it frightened my sister and the others.

"Is the father of your baby with you? We would love to meet him," one of the coven members asked. I scoffed, unable to hide my anger and sarcasm.

"You all know who the father is. He's the only man I have ever wanted to share my life with, yet because of you and your influence, he spurned me. Where is he, where is Daniel?"

My sister's face and body transformed, as if the air had been sucked from her lungs. She looked around at the others, looking for some sort of assistance, but only stone-cold grimaces answered her. She started to speak several times without being able to form the words. She nervously rubbed her hands together and gazed at the ground.

"Tell me, Véronique. What is going on? Where is he?" I demanded.

"I . . . I'm sorry Arabella, but Daniel was killed in a car accident two weeks ago," my sister explained.

He had died the same day as the ritual I performed in New Orleans. My sister crossed over to me and wrapped her arms around me, wetting my face with her tears as she hugged me. I did not return her show of emotion. I stood numb, struck by how much her words had affected me and in an instant, changed the life of my baby, our destiny and me. Her sobs shook my body, but I still resisted surrendering to sadness, weakness.

Daniel, dead? As much as I had wanted to take my revenge on him, I had hoped I could convert and convince him to join me to raise our child and change the world. The universe had decided my destiny would be a solo one and I would not let this change my desire to my oppressors. I could not and would not grieve his death, and I would use his child as a tool in my domination of this coven and anyone else who stood in my way. Having used up her tears for the moment, my sister released me and stepped away from me, but kept her hand on my shoulder.

The leader of their coven and one of the shamans from the Wampanoag tribe came forward and said, "Daniel may have passed, but you and your baby are always welcome here and in this place my dear. Now, please show us your true physical self."

I shifted my aimless stare to look at the man who had spoken to me.

I did not know him, but you didn't have to know someone to kill them for their affiliation with those who conspired against you. As an act of pity or possible fear, everyone who approached me did so with the usual niceties and platitudes, but I was not fooled. Their insides cringed at the thought of what I might have learned during my time away from Salem. However, I knew if I wanted to gain their trust, I would need to play along with them and appear to be thankful about being back.

The members of the coven welcomed me back with food and drink at the ancestral home of my sister's husband's family. I had never met him and did not even know his name, and my sister did not offer to tell me. No worry, I had plenty of time to find out all I needed to know. Their house looked as if it had been taken out of history and placed in the 20th century. The members' pleasantries, fueled by fear, amused and motivated me in what I had come here to do. Small talk bounced around the room as people moved awkwardly from one conversation to another.

In my current condition, I did not drink any wine, but instead had several cups of herbal tea given to me by my sister. She told me it was good for the baby, and myself, but just as everything else was and had always been with them, it was a trick. I should have known better, but the news about Daniel had upset me more than I had thought. Others had always easily manipulated her. She never stood up for herself, never showed the least bit of backbone. The tea contained a mixture of herbs, which slowly made me lose consciousness and before I was aware of it, I had fallen into a deep slumber.

*　*　*

My head throbbed as I regained consciousness. A nightmarish realization came to light. I was strapped to a table, just as I had done to my sacrifice. Blood trickled from my wrists, clever bastards. As I slowly lost blood, my powers weakened. I fought with all the strength I could muster, but the tea with which they had drugged me had also numbed my powers and zapped my strength.

"Let me go! I hate you! I will eradicate every single one of you!"

"Do you have it?" said the man in the long black robe emblazoned with Wiccan and Algonquian symbols.

"I'm looking, but I can't find it," said another, not as highly positioned in the order.

"Find it now! I can't hold her much longer."

"*Liga manus et pes!*"

With those words, a rope further bound my hands and feet and bound my head painfully tight against a frigid stone surface.

Helpless, I laid tied down, as the others chanted and rubbed a mixture of oil and herbs on my swollen belly.

"If this child is born and survives, we will not allow it to be raised by you. Your evil beliefs and gifts can never be permitted to influence or corrupt it. It will be ours to protect and raise far away from you."

"I swear that I will find my baby, and I will exact my revenge on all of you and your generations to come. Your deaths will not be swift and you will feel a pain more agonizing than you have ever known."

In the darkness surrounding me and the others, a man sharpened a hooked knife as he chanted in unison with the others. The sound of the silver blade rubbing against the wet stone irritated my ears and I desperately wanted to plug them. He returned the blade to its ornate sheath as the ten council members moved in a circle around me as they splattered my body with more herb-infused oils. Each of their faces was dipped shadow, the only thing visible, the whites of their eyes as they incanted the memorized words. The constant hum lulled my senses and I grappled with a heavy drowsiness. The dancing flames of the candles and torches strengthened the feeling of sleep. I pushed back and arched my back in a futile attempt to break free.

Tired of my resistance and a desire to complete the theft of my child, the man in the emblazoned robe raised his hand and with one swift slap, I was out. Because of them, I would never see or know the sex of my baby, at least not for several years and not without the blood of many.

* * *

The first thing I remembered after waking up was being cold, wet, and completely devoid of energy, my powers, and without my baby. Whatever they had done to me continued to have an effect on me and I had no idea where I've been exiled. I rolled over onto my hands and knees and lurched violently, spewing a greenish mixture of water and herbs all over the black-brown dirt. In order to completely rid myself of their poison, I stuck my finger down my throat and forced myself to vomit until the only thing coming from my mouth was bitter-tasting yellow bile. I gripped the moist dirt in my weak hands and yelled like a wounded animal into the black void of night. My screams did nothing but echo around me, as I slowly began to realize where I have been sent: shadow realm. I was stuck in the world between the living and dead. I would be forced to watch as they enjoyed their lives and forgot about me, while I rotted away in a void of nothingness.

All of this happened eighteen years ago, and every day since then, I had not forgotten for one moment what they had done to my baby or me. My desire to destroy each of them had grown exponentially during my imprisonment. However, my exile in oblivion had provided me the time to perfect my newly acquired magic and commune with the spirits on the other side. They would be invaluable in helping me prepare for my return to the physical plane. Unfortunately, I could not yet locate where my child resided on the other side of the veil. Despite my best efforts to uncover their location, I had been able to find nothing. Having no other choice, I reached out to the spirits of death. If anyone could find my child, they could.

Chapter 9

The Shadow Realm

SIRENS BLARED AS THE ambulance made its way through the quite streets of Salem towards Salem General. Addy lay motionless on the stretcher in the back, and I sat there feeling unbelievably helpless and angry. The EMTs continued to work on her and check her vitals and the truck bounced back and forth and I sat there useless. I repeatedly ask them if there was anything I could do to help them, and they just told me to continue holding her hand. I wracked my brain trying to remember if she had ever had a seizure or anything similar to this before, but I could remember nothing even remotely similar.

"Addy, I called your mom and dad and I know they are on their way to meet us at the hospital. You're not alone. I'm here with you."

In all honesty, I hadn't been able to get in touch with Addy's mom or dad. Her mom never answered and her dad's phone kept going to voicemail, so I just left messages for them. Thankfully, Principal

McIntyre was following us to the hospital. Even as independent as I was, I appreciated having an adult with us. After Addy began seizing, school had been canceled for the rest of the day and the campus was basically void of human life by the time the ambulance arrived.

The EMT in the back of the rig pulled sterile plastic and paper bags from the numerous cabinets and drawers filling up the sides of the ambulance. Despite the frenetic conversation and the ripping open of medical packets, the female medic worked diligently on my cousin, as she lay there pale and unconscious. Then the beeps on one of the machines pinged rapidly as the thin green line on the monitor plummeted and jumped in no certain pattern.

"Dammit! I can't get her BP to stabilize. It's fluctuating all over the place like I've never seen before."

"What do you mean? Is she going to die?"

"I promise I'm doing everything I can to save her life. I've just never seen someone's BP act crazy like this."

"She's crashing! We're running out of time!"

* * *

The sensation of being disoriented came over me. Was I dreaming? My entire body tingled like when I slept with my arm tucked up under my chest for too long. At first, I couldn't see anything distinctly. I tried rubbing my eyes, but every limb of my body was weighted down and numb. I could just barely make out several voices around me and see some sort of opaque white light, but that was all. Everything merged into a fuzzy, muddled scene. I thought I heard orders being shouted at another person or were they arguing? I struggled so hard to open my eyes and focus on what I was hearing, but it was useless. The fog around my thoughts thickened and I was too weak to clear it. Before I realized it, I had quickly succumbed to exhaustion and drifted into a profound sleep.

* * *

The EMTs were out of the ambulance and pulling the stretcher from the back before I could even let go of Addy's hand. My foot caught on the ribbing around the door and I fell forward and cracked my head on the asphalt. Incredibly, no one saw me and I scrambled to my feet, and ran after the paramedics as they entered the ER. I stood there lost in the confusion of doctors, nurses, and automated intercom announcements. I had no idea what I was supposed to do now that we were here. Consumed in the cacophony of the ER, I was happy to see Principal McIntyre enter the large automatic silver and glass doors. It didn't take him long to spot me sticking out from the sea of scrubs. As soon as he did, he came directly over to me and put his arm around me. For the first time since Addy's episode in the gym, I felt a twinge of comfort and security. Maybe everything was going to be okay.

"Ethan, have you been able to get in touch with Addy's parents?"

"I tried calling them, but neither answered. I left a message on Ed's voicemail, but I haven't heard anything. I never even got through to V's. I'm not sure what's going on."

"I'll try them again. Why don't you just have a sit right over there, and I'll be back in 5 minutes. Okay?"

I nodded and made my way over to the decades old green vinyl chairs. Everything seemed surreal. What was I going to do if she died? How would I be able to face her parents, my parents? I just couldn't believe the chaos unfolding in our small town where nothing even remotely exciting ever happened. I turned and picked up an old crumpled magazine. It was better than sitting here staring blankly into space, but looking around the room, I saw I wouldn't have been the only one. The emergency room presented itself a place of shock and disbelief. Each person sitting in the miniscule baby blue room reflected only the shell of the person they were. They sat longingly, desperate for answers, which would not be as forthcoming as they hoped. They were lost. I was lost. We all waited for some doctor or nurse to tell us the fate of our loved ones, the new trajectory of our lives. In many ways, I hated them for having this power of life and death. I couldn't help but be filled with an overwhelming sense of being ineffective and weak.

"They'll both be here as soon as they can. Try not to worry."

"Good. I feel so useless."

"You did everything you could do. You were there with her the entire time. A lot of people don't even have that. I'm sure she's in good hands, and she'll be as good as new before you know it."

Contrary to Mr. McIntyre's efforts, I didn't feel much better about the situation. For the first time in my life, I had seen the possibility of someone I loved dying in front of me. It was not something that I was prepared for or wanted to experience again. Unfortunately, I had the inexplicable feeling that something was festering around us and before we knew it, would alter our lives while others we loved would be gravely hurt.

Was Addy the first victim or was this merely a sign of things to come?

Mr. McIntyre and I made small talk for what felt like an eternity until a nurse came out to give us an update.

"Are you Ms. Smythe's family?"

"Yes, I'm her cousin. Her parents are on the way."

She said her name was Nurse Lane and that, at this time, they had no idea what had caused the seizure and wanted to know if I knew of any allergies Addy had or if she had been acting strangely this morning before collapsing in the gym. I took a few minutes to think about what the morning had entailed, but I couldn't think of anything I would count as odd, except for the fact two freshmen had been mutilated in the woods near our houses.

The nurse looked at us and said, "How did she react when she heard the news?"

"I honestly don't know. All of this started happening as soon as the principal told us about the deaths. I'm not even sure if she heard it or not. The next thing I heard was a shriek, and when I turned to look, Addy was in between the bleachers shaking uncontrollably."

Mr. McIntyre added that he hadn't noticed anything strange either, but also explained he hadn't seen or spoken to Addy before the assembly. He echoed my statement by saying he'd heard her scream, followed by my shout for help.

The nurse scribbled everything I said on a pad, said "thank you," and turned to walk away.

"Excuse me, Nurse Lane? Can we please go back and see her?"

"I will have to ask the doctor considering she is in critical condition in ICU."

"What do you mean, her condition?"

"As of right now, your cousin is in a medically induced coma to protect her brain from swelling."

* * *

After what felt like hours, Addy's father finally arrived. He ran straight for me and gave me a huge hug. Unfortunately, I had nothing to share with him as far as news about Addy.

"What are they saying? Is Véronique with Addy? Do they know what happened?" He was so distraught that he just kept raddling off questions until Mr. McIntyre put his hand on this shoulder.

"Ed, a nurse came out to talk to us a little while ago. I don't know how else to say this, but Addy is in a coma."

"What?"

"The doctors induced it to try and decrease the swelling in her brain and to save her life."

"I can't believe this is happening. She was fine this morning. What about Véronique? Where is she?"

Ed turned and looked at me for an answer. "We haven't seen her. I couldn't even get a hold of her earlier when everything happened but Mr. McIntyre did. I thought maybe you had talked to her too?" I explained.

"That was over thirty minutes ago and she was coming here from home. There's no way I could've gotten here before her."

"Excuse me, gentlemen, but are you Mr. Smythe?" asked the same nurse from before.

"Yes, I am."

"I've talked to the doctor and he'll allow you and another family member see your daughter for thirty minutes."

All of a sudden, I wasn't sure what to think about going back to see Addy. Were we being allowed to see her because she was better or because she wasn't going to make it? Hundreds of thoughts sped through my mind, and for a moment, I got dizzy.

"Ethan, are you okay?"

"Yeah I'm fine. I just want Addy to get through this."

Ed smiled at me and put his arm around me.

"You know how determined she is. She'll be back at home and studying for AP courses before we know it," he said, but I could tell even he doubted a quick outcome.

"Devon, thank you for staying with Ethan until I got here. I do greatly appreciate it."

"No worries Ed. I'll wait out here for you guys."

* * *

Hospitals are so depressing, and even if I'm not sick, I think I am as soon as I enter one. The light blue walls of the ER waiting room faded into a vomit yellow, which ran along every wall in sight as we made our way down the tiled hall. Everyone who passed us refused to make eye contact and was draped in sterile blue or green garb of various shapes and cuts as if they were walking a sickly runway. Their demeanor and dress did not inspire much confidence or reassurance as we turned right and penetrated the hospital deeper. An array of alarms and announcements violated the air and I couldn't help but recognize I was in the presence of death and dying. They infected every pore and surface of this languid place.

At last we reached Addy's "room," a small area surrounded on two sides by ice blue and white-checkered curtains. On TV and in the movies, I always saw people in comas looking restful and at peace. However, Addy added a stark contrast. Her body lay stretched out and rigid on the mechanical hospital bed, hands clinched tightly in white-knuckled fists. In addition to the inflexible appearance, the features of her face betrayed any sense of her being relaxed. Her eyes were closed tightly and her mouth looked as if she was trying to speak but no words escaped her chapped chalky lips.

Ed moved to sit in a chair right beside Addy, to hold her hand, but he was unable to open her fist, so he held it in his hand. With his other hand, he pushed a few stray strands of hair from her face and caressed his only daughter's face. Despite his strong nature, he broke man's societal "obligations" and tears flowed from his eyes, creating dark wet circles on Addy's gown and sheets. Like me, anger and futility sunk in, as he faced a problem he didn't know how to solve.

I stood at the end of her bed overcome with an uneasy sensation, like someone hidden in the shadows was watching me. But the only people in the room were myself, Ed and Addy. I hated being here and seeing my best friend and cousin fight for her life against something we couldn't identify or possibly even understand. Life was so capricious, and I wanted to beat the crap of it for happening to my family. It wasn't fair.

"Hi, I'm Dr. Ross."

We were both startled by the doctor's stealthy entrance in the room and immediately turned to him for answers. He didn't tell us much more than what Nurse Lane had already told Principal McIntyre and me earlier in the waiting room. All of her blood tests had come back normal and no clues had availed themselves as to what may have caused or was causing her current condition. He did tell us at one point her fever reached 106, and was the catalyst for deciding to induce her coma when nothing else worked to lower her body temp.

"I do want to be honest with both of you. When the ambulance arrived, you daughter did flat line for a moment, but as you can see, we were able to revive her. At the moment, she's stable, but the next twenty-four to forty-eight hours will be crucial."

In that moment, everything became unbelievably real and all consuming. Dying and death changed a person, the white light and all that. I struggled to process this information and I must have shown this on my face because Ed and the doctor led me to a chair in the corner. They asked me if I was all right several times before I was able to respond.

The doctor talked to Ed a little more, before he was paged about another patient. Our thirty minutes flew and dragged by at the same time. We emerged from the putrid hallway back into the blueness of the ER to find Principal McIntyre waiting. We asked him if he had heard from V, but he hadn't. Ed and I checked our phones, but neither of us had received a response from our calls or texts.

I grabbed my phone out of my pocket. "I'll try and call her again."

I dialed the number, but this time it rang until I finally heard a click. "Hello? V? V, are you there? It's Ethan."

Click.

"What did she say?"

"I'm not sure what just happened. It sounded like someone picked up the phone, but all I could hear was some sort of breathing, then the line was disconnected."

"Let me try." Ed pulled out his phone, but was stopped by a police officer that approached the three of us.

The officer nodded "hello" to the principal and myself before he began speaking. "Professor Smythe, I regret to inform you, but your wife has been in an accident out by your house, just before the old covered bridge."

Ed's legs began to buckle and the officer and Mr. McIntyre helped him into the waiting room. I sunk down into the chair beside him and stared through the officer standing before us. How and why in the hell was this happening?

"Is she okay?" Ed asked.

"Well sir, that's the problem."

"What do you mean 'that's the problem'?" Ed asked, his voice growing louder as he spoke.

"We can't find her, or her body. There aren't even any footprints around her car. The only discernible tracks are those of a large deer. The wreckage appears to have been wiped clean of her fingerprints as well. We're not sure what happened. I'm very sorry."

Chapter 10

Hidden secrets

AGAIN THE NOISES PUMMELED my ears without clarity. My senses were discombobulated and fear enveloped me. For some odd reason, I had the sensation I was floating upside down, yet my arms and legs remained locked by my side. With my throbbing headache, it was very difficult for me to concentrate on anything else except for the pain. Every muscle in my body persisted being clamped in a grip I struggled to release. In a way, I felt as if my body instinctively knew of some sort of danger that I had yet to consciously perceive. It was one of those rare times when, despite my self-reliance, I wanted my mom with me.

Where are those voices coming from? It was so frustrating to pick up on the pull of something and not be able to see or clearly hear what it was. I worked to reach out, to move, but my muscles were too fatigued to fight. After struggling against the invisible restraints, I was able to move my hands and then my feet. To my surprise, I wasn't upside down, but rather lying on the ground. The earth was damp, smelling of age and time. The tepid air flowed more freely into my lungs, and I could feel myself escaping the mental haze. My mouth was dry and sticky, and I desperately wanted water. A dull light from above cast transparent shadows of the large and sprawling trees around me as I sat up. The only thing I saw clearly was a bluish grey mist that hovered above the ground as far as the eye could see in every direction. I didn't understand how I had gotten here from the school. Where was Ethan? Where was I? The simple act of thinking produced intense pain that bounced around my head like a rubber ball.

Despite my efforts to ease my headache by rubbing my temples, my brain continued to pound against my skull. Doing my best to ignore the pain, I got to my feet and decided to walk around to find some help, and more importantly, water. Moving around in this unknown environment, I experienced several sensations that struck me as odd and unique from what I was used to feeling. The ground surged in an organic manner beneath my feet as if it were alive and breathing. The space around me weighed down over my entire body, like walking under water. The damp air gave off an energy that stung my lungs, nose, and skin.

My shoulders tensed and my hands and fingers became swollen. A freezing breeze, more like a breath, caressed the back of my neck. I wanted to run away from this place, but all I could do was slowly trudge forward, forcing myself to move. I hoped to find some type of sign that I could get out of this place. The mist surrounded my feet, up to my ankles, as I made my way into the unknown, when all of a sudden I saw something directly ahead of me.

"It can't be."

It was the same road I had ridden down more times than I could count: the road home. My heart jumped and I thought there was hope of making it out of here. I longed to run in the direction where I knew my house would be, but my body refused to cooperate. I pushed onward to get back home, to get back to safety. The dim light eerily illuminated my house, creating a billowing effect, making the red wood siding transform into a cascade of blood.

I stood at the base of the stairs leading to my front door. A mixture of fear and relief held me steadfast for a moment, as I debated whether or not to open the door. What should have felt familiar instead gave me pause. It looked like my house, but was it? After debating with my feelings, and myself I put my foot on the first step. Regardless of these unsettling thoughts, I grasped the iron doorknob and crossed the threshold. I had to look for other signs of life.

"Mom? Dad? Is anyone here?"

Silence. Only the echoes of my calls greeted me.

As I walked through the house, I began to notice the everyday items I was used to seeing were no longer there. The structure was an exact replica of our house, yet the inside contained no personal items. None of our family photos or artwork adorned the walls and my dad's books and papers, which were always scattered around his library, were nowhere to be found. This place was just a shell of the home I knew, which made me wonder where the hell I was. How did I get out of here? Was I dead? I leaned against the wall focused on calming my breathing. I trembled from head to toe and found it difficult to stand. I slid down the wall and sat on the chilly wood floor with my head between my knees. For one of the first times in my life, I had met an obstacle I might not be able to overcome.

I took several deep breaths and stood up. If there were any chance of me getting out of this place, it would be found in my dad's study. I entered the tiny room to see if I could find something that might help me figure out where I was. To my happy surprise, there were a few books on the five shelves of his old bookcase, which normally overflowed with an array of older and newer texts. I grabbed and opened one of his tomes concerning witchcraft in colonial New England only to find the pages were blank. I took another and found the same thing. I was frustrated and felt more anxious when, book after book, I discovered not a single character within its pages. I put my hands on the bookcase to support and calm myself. My labored breathing persisted, and I inched toward hyperventilating.

In through the nose and out through the mouth, I reminded myself as I held myself upright, doing all I could, not to give in to my overwhelming exhaustion and fears. Standing there in the absolute and uneasy silence, a click escaped from the back of the bookcase. I looked up, and in front of me, I saw that a small door had opened in the back panel of the second shelf. Carefully, I opened the door that revealed a hidden compartment I had had no idea even existed. Because of the dim light, I walked over and turned on my dad's desk lamp, but like the books and rest of the house, it was just a shell. I turned back to the hidden compartment and hesitantly reached into the darkness. At first, I didn't feel anything and it took me a moment, as I moved my hand around inside, to touch something. A book.

Without thinking, I knocked all of the faux items off of my father's desk to make room for the book. I put the heavy leather-bound book on the desk, and fingered the intricate designs adorning the front cover. A complex design in gold and silver filigree traced all four edges of the deep green leather book, which resembled a bible in both its volume and gold-leafed pages. Like older bibles, I knew I was looking at something comprising of ancient and far reaching traditions. The filigree created numerous symbols as it twisted and turned and looped along the book's edges. A worn iron clasp bound the book on the right side. An empty keyhole glared at any would be reader who might want to delve into its contents. With difficulty, I blew off a fine layer of dust that revealed writing on the cover of the book. The departing dust uncovered the title *Le grimoire de la famille de la Fontaine* etched into the leather in bold golden script. Below the title laid a symbol, the letter F in an ornate and elaborate calligraphy in the middle of an intertwined circle and triangle. Words adorned the borders of the triangle along its interior and exterior lines. They were so minute and faded that I couldn't read what had been etched in the leather. A small passage in French, at the bottom of the cover, shimmered to life as I stared at the grimoire.

À l'intérieur de ce tome reste la vitalité éternelle et magique de la famille de la Fontaine. Ces sorts représentent l'héritage de notre famille et la promesse de se consacrer à la lumière. Seulement une personne qui possède un cœur et âme de bienfaisance peut entrer et jeter les incantations dans ce livre. Celles qui essayent de corrompre les sorts souffriront des conséquences éternelles.

For the first time in a very long time, I was very glad to have had a mother who required me to learn her native language. Nevertheless, I found it very hard to believe this book contained magical spells and that anyone who tried to use them for evil would be cursed as a consequence. After all, that crap was something only found on TV and movies, right?

Resisting my logical impulses and surrendering to my imagination, I fidgeted with the lock but it wouldn't budge. I reached back into the darkness hoping to find a key, but only managed to entangle my hand in cobwebs and dust. For the next several minutes, I looked in my dad's desk for anything that might help me break into the book, curses be damned. To add to my annoyance, there was absolutely nothing inside the desk. I even went to the kitchen and searched every drawer only to find they were all empty. In frustration, I grabbed the book and shook it before slamming it back down on the desk. I grappled to compose myself by measuring my breath and pacing around the library. I had never been one blessed with much patience. I slid the book to the edge of the desk and squatted down to get a better look at the lock. I tinkered with the lock with two fingers and scrutinized the mechanism that felt so flimsy and brittle. Then, without warning, the lock unlatched itself.

As I opened the book, the interior revealed old, brittle pages, with dry edges and a yellow parchment-like tint. Inside the book my fingers sensed that the majority of the pages were actual parchment. Only a few at the end of the book did not show similar wear and tear or age. Carefully I turned the pages, assuming they would be lacking information just as the others, but, to my surprise, the book divulged pages bursting with colorful and detailed text and drawings. Within the first several pages, I found a detailed and long reaching family tree that was rooted in the thirteenth century.

The ink strengthened in color and vibrancy, as I turned the pages. I was amazed at the amount of information concerning my family. As I flipped closer towards present day, I began to recognize a few of the names written on the tawny pages. On the last page of our genealogy, I read the names of my mother and my dad, as expected, but I noticed two rather odd things, both of which sent a pang of worry through me. My mother had a sister named Séverine Arabella about whom I had never heard anything, and, more earth shattering, my mother and father were childless, unlike her sister. On October 31, 1995, Séverine Arabella de la Fontaine gave birth to unnamed fraternal twins, a boy and a girl.

The world around me pivoted and dipped, as the blood rushed from my head. Conscious thoughts started to elude me, but not before I felt the touch of someone's wrinkled hand on my forehead.

Chapter 11

Necessary means

ONLY MINUTES AFTER ADDY had a seizure, and I had called 911, the ambulance arrived with its sirens blaring. All of the students had been cleared from the gym, and I had decided to cancel school, even though it was the first day of the year. Signs were beginning to appear more quickly than I had anticipated, and I knew the prophecy, if true, would escalate the strange happenings, and unfortunately, the death toll.

As soon as the paramedics were out of the car, I helped them to hoist Addy onto the stretcher and clear a path to the vehicle. I could tell the situation was a dire one when the EMTs worked for longer than I imagined was the norm to find a pulse and hook up their equipment. In the chaos of clearing the gym and the arrival of the ambulance, Ethan never left the side of his cousin, and without a second thought, he jumped in the back of the rig with the paramedic and Addy.

I could honestly say I didn't hold out much hope of her surviving the trip to the hospital. I prepared myself for the worst as I followed them through the center of town. I knew I would have to be there for Ethan if things turned out badly, as I feared they would. His parents were rarely around because of work, and I doubted they would even know what had happened at school.

I sped into the parking lot outside of the ER as the ambulance almost rammed into the entrance. The paramedics burst out of the back of the truck and ran at full speed into the waiting arms of ER doctors and nurses. My fears had come true. I ran after Ethan as he rushed through the doors after the paramedics. When I put my arm around him, he reacted understandably and was visibly shaken at what had occurred in such a short period of time. I asked him if he had contacted Addy's parents, and he told me he tried but was unable to get either of them to answer.

"Go have a sit in the waiting room and I'll see what I can find out."

"Thanks, Principal McIntyre. I really appreciate it."

I pulled out my phone and dialed Ed's number as I walked through the automatic ER doors. I couldn't help but imagine how the earliest settlers of the Americas would have perceived such things as automatic doors. No doubt it would have been considered sorcery, spurring a series of unfortunate and deadly events, not unlike those of the Salem Witch Trials in 1692. I had hoped to never again experience such a time of turbulence and hysteria, but actions had been taken and signs had begun pointing to another such moment in our history.

"Damn."

The call went straight to voicemail, and I didn't want to leave a message of such gravity in a voicemail inbox. Bringing the phone back around so I could see the numbers, I began to dial Ed a second time, but my phone rang instead. It was Ed.

"Ed, where are you?"

"I'm on my way to the hospital. What's going on?"

How the hell did he know to come to the hospital?

"What do you mean?"

"Véronique called me to tell me what happened. I'm making my way there as fast as I can but traffic is a bear."

I had to appreciate the speed at which people could communicate this day and age. I often wondered what America would look like today if there had been such technology centuries ago while at the same time pondering if in today's world we would be better off without information overload.

"Devon, how's Addy?"

"To be honest, I'm not sure. They rushed her back into the ER before Ethan or I could find out anything."

"Ethan's there? Is he okay?"

"As you can imagine, he's a little out of sorts, but I think he'll be okay."

"Does he show any signs?"

"At present no, but you know it can't be long before he does, especially now that her magic is manifesting."

After three hundred years of relatively innocuous magical occurrences, a portal was on the verge of bursting wide open. A world still trying to accept those who were considered different because of their skin color, beliefs or sexual orientation was in no way ready to learn of the existence of witches and other supernatural beings. So many humans claimed to believe in the paranormal, but did they truly realize the white and dark sides of such matters, and more importantly, would they even survive to know the difference?

"Devon, you know as well as I if the prophecy comes to fruition, all of us will be condemned to suffer and die."

"Remember I've been guarding this secret for hundreds of years and I understand what I must do. We will stop the prophecy from being fulfilled by any means necessary, even if that means killing."

"I understand."

Eventually, I returned to try and comfort Ethan knowing I would do a crap job of it, but I didn't care. We both waited in the ER, one of the most ugly and depressing rooms in which I had ever sat, even for a hospital. Ethan was beyond frustrated and I could understand why. It was tough being powerless, and even worse to be in the dark about the health and well-being of a loved one. I sympathized with his position. It was one in which I had been more than a few times throughout my long existence.

When Ed arrived, I followed an agreed upon "script" we had discussed at the end of our phone conversation. If everything went as planned, no one, especially Ethan, would suspect anything out of the ordinary.

Chapter 12

Difficult truths

I RETURNED TO THE shadowy realm in the exact same spot where I had been when I felt the hand touch me. I stood there unable to think, move, or even breathe as I stared down at our *arbre généalogique*. How was this possible? I'd lived my entire life believing in a lie carried out by not only my "parents," but my other family members as well. The disbelief and shock I experienced slowly turned into rage and frustration, pretending to love me while they lied to me at every chance. What about this other child? Where could he be? Did he know the truth or had he been led down a path of deceit just like I had been?

In a fit of anger, I kicked the wall and watched as my foot easily broke through the wood paneling. I grabbed the edges of the desk so tightly my hands have turned pale as several angry tears begin to pool in the corners of my eyes and roll down my reddened cheeks. They fell onto the porous paper and immediately caused the ink of the delicate script to blur. The color swirled into oblong circles and other organic shapes causing different words to meld. The once distinct words become mangled and indistinguishable, like the line between truth and falsehood in my life.

My world was being turned upside down, and I was stuck in an unknown place filled with only the superficial aspects of the world in which I lived and knew. I wanted to yell at someone so badly, but even the chance to do so eluded me in my present situation. To make things worse, I was crying! I never cried about anything, not even when my grandparents had died. I was the strong one who didn't need to rely upon others for help or even consolation.

The continuous flow of tears down my flushed cheeks presented the physical representation of an escalating anger that verged on spiraling out of control. Never in my life had I felt such anger and betrayal. I didn't even know who I was anymore or whom I could trust. Due to the overwhelming emotions provoked by these new truths, I had become even more exhausted than when I entered the house. Without realizing it, I picked up the ancient leather bound book I had found in the cupboard and walked out of the library. In a zombie-like fashion, I climbed the stairs and crawled into the fabrication of my bed.

For the first time since entering the house, something felt real and substantial. My bed smelled exactly as it should. The familiar give of my mattress welcomed my wearied body as I lied down and pulled the fluffy beige comforter up to my chin. I cuddled a feather pillow given to me by my mom, just as I had done since I was a child. She had told me it would ward off bad dreams and any monsters under the bed. In a matter of seconds, I was fast asleep, a deep sleep barren of even a single dream.

* * *

"Addy, wake up."

I rolled over in the bed and tried to ignore the person disturbing me.

"Addy, honey, can you hear me?"

Slowly, I opened my heavy eyelids and saw the blurry image of a person. Who else was in our house? How did they get to this place? My heart leapt at the thought that everything that had happened had just been a bad dream. I opened my eyes wide and jumped back into reality, but my body rebelled against the thought. Tears threatened to return, but I resisted the temptation.

"It's dad. Do you understand? We're at the hospital, and you've been in a coma for a couple of days."

A coma? I was in the hospital?

With great effort and an incredibly dry voice, I managed to ask what happened to me. The last thing I remembered before this moment was getting into Ethan's car outside of my house.

"Don't worry about all of that right now. The most important thing is for you to get better and the very fact you've woken up is a sign that you are."

I heeded my dad's advice as an unwelcomed slumber drug me back into my mind.

* * *

The next day, I had a better understanding of the situation, at least for the parts I could remember before waking up. My nurses and doctor told me they had never seen anyone dream as much as I had during my coma.

"Your brainwave activity was incredibly erratic throughout the entire two days. Do you remember anything?" the doctor asked me.

"I don't remember a thing. It's all a big blank. The last thing I remember is leaving for the first day of school. Everything after that is a wash."

"Don't worry too much about that. It's very common for coma patients not to remember the hours leading up to a coma."

Yay for me! I was now part of a coma-patient statistic. All of this was a pain in the butt for me. A nagging feeling in my gut continued to bug me. It reminded me of when I was taking a test and I knew the answer, could see it in my mind, but I couldn't put it down on paper or explain it for the life of me. Something had taken place during the couple of days I was unconscious and I had to figure out what it was, and why it had happened.

To make matters worse, no one, except my father, was allowed to see me until I was discharged. For some curious reason, my mother had yet to visit me. She was visiting a sick family member in France, but dad told me she would be returning soon, which should have helped to put me more at ease, but it didn't. After what I had just experienced, I wasn't sure where the line between fact and fiction lay. The only thing I did know was that I really missed seeing her even if for a few minutes in the morning or at night. I didn't really realize how very important those few moments were with her until I no longer had them. My entire perspective on life and family was transforming before my own eyes.

* * *

Finally, after a full week of poking, prodding, and my fair share of rancid hospital food, the day had come for me to go home. Having missed the first full week of school bothered me much more than having been in a coma or the causes of my "episode," as we were all calling it. Thanks to a lot of pestering and pleading, my doctors had allowed my father to bring me my books and work from school, so that I didn't fall too far behind. I mean, after all, it was my senior year, and I could see commons of Harvard on the horizon. Also, I couldn't wait to see Ethan. We had never been apart this long before and, like my feelings for my mom, not seeing him if even for only a few minutes was having a toll on me. I missed our frequent conversations, our British sitcom marathons, and our late night chats.

Stubborn as ever, I decided to get ready to leave this god forsaken place before waiting to have a stranger do it for me. I swung my legs off the edge of the bed, but as I did, I pulled out the IV in my arm. The sting from line ran up my arm, and I winced in pain. I hated the sight of blood, and I hoped with all hope it wasn't flowing down my arm. I peeked through my half-opened eye, fearing the worst. Thankfully, only a tiny rivulet of blood trickled from the site.

"I just need my freaking pants, is that too much to ask for?" I had the bad habit of talking to myself out loud more often than most sane people.

As I maneuvered my body, more carefully this time, I noticed my jeans were lying on the end of the bed. I blinked twice to make sure I wasn't seeing things. For more than a week, I had been pumped full of god knows what since I'd been in the hospital, and I wasn't sure I could trust anything I was seeing. At this point, I just wanted to get out of this depressing, drab room and get some fresh air, sleep in my own bed, and, in all honesty, get back to school.

Per hospital policy, an orderly wheeled me out to the front entrance of the hospital to meet my dad and Ethan. When the doors opened, the sunlight burst into the dim hallway and blinded my sensitive eyes. My arm went up to block the sun's rays from my eyes. As we exited from under the awning, into the pick-up lane, my eyes adjusted and my body drank every bit of the vitamin D the sun had to offer. I had forgotten how good it felt to be warmed by the sun on such a chilly autumn day. I could feel my mood improving thanks to the sun, and more importantly my father and Ethan.

"I hope you're ready to get back to the real world, my lady. We sure as hell aren't going to be at your beck and call."

It was so great to hear my cousin's voice, even his painfully bad British accent after more than a week apart. There were no words to describe the exhilaration of normality.

"Oh, please! You know I'm more demanding than the queen herself, so suck it up and get ready."

I jumped, as best I could, from the wheelchair to hug him. It took everything I had not to lose it in front of my family.

"Hi, daddy. Please get me away from this place and home…now."

I should have been happier to see my dad, but after having experienced such a strange dream, I questioned his honesty and sincerity. I hated myself for feeling that way, but something deep inside told me what I had seen in that dream was the truth.

"You got it sweetheart."

I felt as if I were escaping some horrible dungeon as the hospital faded out of sight, and I could not be happier despite the fact I was still weak and confused about my parents. The town passed before my eyes and I relished the everyday activities carried out by the people I had known all of my life. Families taking walks together along the river, kids playing kickball or kicking each other in the park and the sight of the orange, red, and yellow leaves still clinging to the trees, unwilling to give up yet like their fellow fallen comrades. Life and my family's secrets, now more than ever, meant more to me.

"So yeah, your teeth do really look like a beaver's," Ethan said.

"Excuse me?"

"I've been talking to you for the past five minutes and all you can do is stare out the window at the most boring town imaginable."

"You slip into a coma and have to stay in the hospital for over a week. Then we'll see how boring you think all of this is. You're such a butthead sometimes," I responded.

Did I really just say "butthead"? The three of us burst out in a roar of laughter that didn't end until we reached my house on the outskirts of Salem. Yet again, I was reminded of something I had taken for granted before all of this had happened. Was it true what people said? "Home is where the heart is." I wasn't all that sure anymore.

The sound of gravel under the tires welcomed us home as we drove up the driveway to the front door. In stark contrast with the house in my dream, this house looked so bright and inviting in the light of midday. Part of me could not wait to be back in familiar surroundings, however, a larger part of me was uneasy at the mere thought what I had seen could be true and sat hidden in my dad's office. The small windows of the house stared back at me, as I looked out the car window, as if daring me to search for the truth.

When my dad parked the car at the front door, both he and Ethan helped me through the door and to the sitting room to the right of the front door. Stepping down into the whitewashed room I felt more relaxed than I had outside the house. The myriad of family photos and comfortable furniture greeted me and eased some of the apprehension I was feeling. My father stepped over to the hearth and lit a fire that instantly warmed the small, cozy front room.

"I'll go make us some hot chocolate," my father said and I smiled in response.

Ethan told me all about what had happened at school during my absence. It was quite surprising how much drama a high school could muster in such a short period of time.

"So, what exactly happened to me? The last thing I remember is you picking me up for school," I said.

"Are you sure you want to know about all of that? I mean, you did just get home, and I don't want to cause you any stress," he responded.

"I'm fine, I promise."

With a little more pleading, Ethan described the death of the Bower twins who would have been freshmen this year. I couldn't believe everything that happened and I remembered nothing. As far as I knew, we had never experienced such a traumatic and brutal incident in our town, not since the hysteria of the witch trials. Then he got to the point of my collapse and explained exactly what happened at the school assembly that ended with my hospitalization.

"Surely that couldn't have caused me to have a seizure. It's completely illogical and, I mean, I didn't even know those boys," I said, lacking the total conviction I tried to convey.

"I agree, but it's so freaking crazy. All of this started as soon as we found out about their deaths."

Dad entered the room with hot chocolate, my favorite winter drink, for everyone. For a few minutes, no one said a word and we all listened to the crackling fire in the old grey stone fireplace. The joy of the hot chocolate and familiar surroundings was unable to lessen the apprehension hanging in the air. Unwilling to continue to ignore the elephant in the room, I asked my dad the question that had been bothering me since waking up from the coma.

"So when is mom heading back home?"

Ethan choked on his drink, and when I looked over at him, chocolate dribbled down his chin and onto his shirt.

"Are you okay?"

"Ugh, yeah, ugh, I'm fine."

Something obviously wasn't right. Both of them sat there, faces flushed, looking as guilty as someone caught red-handed in a crime, or a lie.

"What's going on? What aren't you telling me?" I demanded.

Minutes passed, and Ethan looked from me to my father and sat completely still, not sure about what he should do or say. My father stood up, looked out the window at the front yard and began to talk very calmly and seriously. He told me the day I went into the hospital, my mom had had a wreck on her way into town. However, they were never able to find her or her body. No one had heard from her since that day, and the police had been unable to discover any sort of credible evidence in the totaled car. My dad, aunt, uncle, and Ethan had called everyone they knew to find out if anyone had heard from my mom the morning of the accident or afterwards. No one had had any luck.

I sat dumbfounded. Was I right to be angry with my dad and Ethan? Deep down I knew they were trying to protect me, but, at the same time, the fact they kept it from me stung more than a little. My dad said the police came to the house multiple times since the accident. They had combed the house, grounds, and the woods around the house. She had simply disappeared. I could tell my dad was very upset about everything to do with my mom, and my situation didn't help.

"Well, I guess we should look at the bright side. They say 'no news is good news,'" Ethan added.

Without looking directly at us, my dad said he was going to run into town to get a few things and would be back later. I knew he was on the verge of tears, and I didn't stop his escape to solitude. Something deep inside me told me I would see my mom again. However, until then, wherever she was, I hoped she was okay.

*   *   *

Later that night, I reveled in getting into my own bed and feeling the welcoming touch of my own blankets and sheets. Everything looked and smelled like home, and I couldn't have been happier, except for the wish of seeing my mother. Where could she have gone and, more importantly, why? Staring at the low wooden beams on the ceiling of my room, I tried to wrap my brain around everything that had happened, but my exhaustion overpowered me, and I was fast asleep within minutes of settling down into bed.

That night, I had vivid dreams of walking through the forest as I followed the voice of someone, who was calling out to me. There was no fear in their voice. It was more of a welcoming sound, a familiar sound. I knew this voice. I started running in the direction of it, the voice of my mom.

"What are you saying? I can't hear you," I screamed into the hollow night.

I continued following the direction of the sound, yet the voice did not become any clearer or louder. Suddenly, I broached the edge of the wood and stood looking at my house. A feeling of déjà vu came over me as I heard my mom again. This time, it sounded as if it were coming from inside the house. I burst through the front door and, in that moment, I remembered.

I sat up in my bed drenched with sweat, breathing heavily, and grasping my comforter. I was staring straight ahead and out of the window opposite the end of my bed. After a few moments, I calmed down and caught my breath before walking into my bathroom to splash some water on my face. Looking in the mirror, the face of my mother flashed before my eyes and with it, I remembered the end of my dream, and the vision I had had in the hospital. Complete and utter doubt clouded my mind as I grappled with the truths staring me in the face since waking up. My life had become a funhouse, warped by people acting as mirrors to protect me from something menacing. Their evasion only made me more determined to get to the bottom of what was going on with my family and me.

I turned and headed downstairs to my dad's library and, more specifically, the bookcase.

Chapter 13

Marked

AFTER I LEFT THE hospital, Principal McIntyre offered to give me a ride home or anywhere else I wanted to go. I asked him to take me to Salem Park. The Porter River bordered the park on its eastern side, and it was a place I would go sometimes when I wanted or needed to be alone. Recent events had forced me to realize the frailty of life, and it was time I faced some of the personal demons I had hidden for long enough. Until recently, I had not even realized the truth about my feelings and myself. Fear had kept me from revealing who I really was, both to my family and myself. I worried what others would think, and if I would be accepted by those closest to me. I envied Addy and her propensity to be herself without worrying about others' opinions. I wished I could be as strong as she was about such matters.

"Are you sure you are okay, Ethan? You know I'm here if you need to talk about anything, no matter what it is."

"I, I know. I just think I need to have a conversation with myself before I talk to anyone else, if that makes sense."

"Completely."

When we arrived at the park, there were very few people taking advantage of the now beautiful weather. The morning fog had been burned off by the sun, which had come to life after a slow start. A slight breeze blew across the mostly treeless green space. Thankfully, the temperature had climbed significantly from the frigid temps of the morning.

Principal McIntyre let me out in the parking area on the opposite side of the park from the river. I reached in the back of his car and grabbed my jacket and backpack before turning to thank him for the ride.

"Ethan, you know if you need anything you can always talk to me," he reiterated.

I nodded in the affirmative and began making my way across the large open field towards the river, towards solitude and privacy.

I felt drawn to a specific area of the park where the river ended and large trees obscured the water from the large vacant grassy center of the park. I was so mentally and emotionally drained that I did not even think twice before changing directions from my usual spot, which was in clear view of the river's shore and the large open field. The fact that no one was in the park today, especially with the weather much improved, surprised me. Generally, on days like today, even during the week, people blanketed this outdoor space. Everything stood eerily still and quiet. Even the breeze had ceased to brush across my face and through my hair as I got closer to the area around the end of the river.

When I reached the river's end at the edge of the park, there were no park benches. It was obvious the city's park service didn't clean or maintain this area of the park. Perfect for solitude and thinking. I was pleased at how much of a barrier a few rows of trees could make between the openness that I had just passed through and where I had ended up. I could barely see through the grove of oak trees obstructing my field of sight back towards the main part of the park.

Without a second thought, I dropped my things on the ground, sat down, and lay back against a tree. I soaked in every moment of this much needed separation from all of the outside noises and distractions. I drew in a deep breath and held it a few seconds before exhaling completely. A mountain of stress and worry escaped my body. Talk about a start to your senior year. I expected to jump into classes, see how much of a slacker I could be to pass, convincingly enough for a university, and dive head first into a year full of sports. Instead, within twenty-four hours, two kids had been murdered and my cousin lay in a coma in the hospital for reasons unknown.

Enough thinking already! I came out here to relax and forget, at least for a little while about the curve ball life had thrown my family and me. I took out my iPod and ear buds from the front pocket of my backpack and queued up my "chill out" mix. My ears absorbed the soulful and sultry voices, lyrics and music of London Grammar, and I cleared my mind of worries, doubts and stress. My entire body relaxed, and I laid into the tree, consuming the fragrant, humid air seeping up from the river. The sun gently warmed my unshaven face. The feeling of serenity was a rarity in my life, and I devoured these brief flashes, when possible.

In that moment, consumed by the music, time became irrelevant until I was awoken by a loud splash in the water. It was early evening. Had I really been asleep that long? Ripples radiated from a spot in the river near the shore, but I couldn't see anything that could have caused it. There were no trees with branches hanging over the water, so I knew it couldn't be that. I looked behind me, but I didn't see anything there either. It looked just like it had when I arrived, deserted.

A sharp burning pain ran up my leg and into my chest. When I looked down, I was completely overcome with terror to see a black snake attached to my calf. I am and always have been deathly afraid of snakes. The slimy scales of the serpent curled around my ankle and foot as it buried its teeth deep into my leg. I attempted to yell out for help, but only a minor squeak came out. Panicked, I leaned towards my bag to grab something, anything, to hit the snake. As I did, the snake bit down harder. Its fangs pierced deep into the tissue of my leg and I could actually feel its venom beginning to course through my veins, like thousands of ants biting the same spot over and over again. My mind searched for information about snakebites from things I might have seen on TV or read for school. Nothing I could remember promised a good outcome, unless I got help now. For the first time in my life, I feared I might die.

However, unwilling to surrender so easily, I decided, at the moment, I was the only person who could help me. In one sporadic motion, I kicked my leg up and down and grabbed my backpack. I began pounding on the snake's head. Sweat rolled down my face, my hands shook, and my joints felt stiff, no doubt side effects of the snake's poison. Fear strangled me as I frantically attacked the snake until, finally, it released its grip on my leg and slithered back into the turbid waters of the river. I pushed my palms into the damp soil and pressed my head back into the trunk of the tree as excruciating pain ran rampant through my envenomed body.

Dazed from everything that had just happened, I groped in my backpack for my phone, until I realized it had fallen out during my attempt to kill the snake. Scanning the area around me, I noticed it was perched on the shore only inches away from the water, and more petrifying, the snake. Out of the genuine fear that I might die, I decided getting my phone warranted the risk. I'd be damned if I was going to die before seeing my cousin again and finishing my senior year. I lunged forward and clasped it my clammy palm. With the phone in my hand, I dialed 911, but before I heard the operator answer, I collapsed. My thoughts and dread washed away into a nebulous, infinite void.

* * *

Feeling the pull of something I couldn't explain, I awoke and sat upright, only to find the world spinning so violently around me that I was unable to make out anything in the fusion of colors. I clasped my head in my hands and, following my instincts, curled into the fetal position, hoping to find the calm I had felt before all of this happened. The topsy-turvy momentum of the world around me slowed and smudges of disproportionate colors and images combined to form a clearer picture of the park, but not how I remembered it. As far as the eye could see, there existed nothing but green pastures of crops and more trees than I had ever seen. There was a complete lack of buildings, streets, signs or any other sign of human life.

I struggled to rationalize the situation. I must have died from the snakebite and this must be some sort of purgatory because it sure as hell didn't look like, well, hell, or heaven for that matter. I had crossed over to an unknown place. I'd never been the really religious type. A deep sadness overtook me, and I thought of all the things I never got to do, or the fact that I was never honest about who I was to myself or those closest to me.

Splash. I jumped to my feet and looked towards the water. A very uneasy sense of déjà vu sunk in. Oddly, I felt no pain in my leg or any other part of my body. At least wherever I was, there was no pain, yet.

"Hello? Is anyone there?"

No response.

I decided to walk back the way I had come despite the different landscape. As I turned to retrace my steps, I heard another splash and looked to face the water. A snake, at least three times more immense than the one that bit me emerged slowly, yet deliberately, from the water. Its glassy, golden eyes were transfixed on me. The scales covering the snake's body rippled a deep mossy green that shifted from lighter to darker shades along its belly and back. Bronze-orange diamonds with smaller yellow circles on the inside them crawled along the entire length of the thick slimy body. Surprisingly, I found the beauty of the reptile mesmerizing and I stood frozen as it surfaced.

Unlike before, I was not afraid or anxious. I existed purely as an observer while the large serpent left the water and coiled its body only a few inches in front of me. When it had finished layering its body into a perfect, loaded spring, I stood face-to-face with the fantastical creature. Its mythical, forked tongue lightly touched my nose as it hissed, exposing a set of massive sparkling ivory fangs, dripping with pearls of liquid death. I admired the shimmering, crystalline beauty of the venom as it oozed from the snake's fangs and teetered at their points before dripping to the ground. I did not experience any fear. After all, I was already dead.

I stood hypnotized by its primal gaze when I sensed the reptile was beginning to communicate with me. However, not a single syllable escaped from its pink salivating mouth. I simply heard and saw the words form in my mind.

"Ethan, do not be afraid. My name is Tesicqueo, and I am your animal guide in this plane."

"What do you mean plane? What is happening? Am I dead?"

"You are far from dead. You were brought to this spiritual plane to experience your vision quest, to discover the truth about yourself and your family line."

"But, I . . ."

" I know you have many questions, yet I also know you sense a great strength within you, telling you to trust me and that you are here for a purpose."

This serpent, Tesicqueo, was right. Somehow he had delved into the depths of my soul and seen my inner most feelings and secrets. All at once, I felt an even greater feeling of calm, and I knew I would be safe and was on the verge of discovering at least some of the answers to questions I had. He knew every part of me, but I wasn't sure I wanted him to know such things I couldn't even deal with myself.

"Ethan, do not worry about those feelings you fear to acknowledge. They are part of you and as such, make you a unique individual. In time these unique aspects will give you great insight and perceptions about a great number of things about which you do not yet fully comprehend."

"How can being gay give me anything, but strife and condemnation from others?"

Gay. I said it. For the first time since putting a name to the feelings I had had since I was a small child, I had revealed a secret so deeply buried, I felt as if I might be sick. Pouring myself into sports had given me the distraction I needed to deny myself who I really was and the opportunity to be *normal*, like everyone else. Now the door had been opened and I wasn't sure how to handle what was to come.

"Do you feel as if the word "gay" is the only word to describe who you are?"

"No, but it's the only word anyone will ever think of when they find out."

"Do not put your future and life in the hands of others who do not understand and accept you. You will find you have more allies on your path than enemies."

"Maybe you're right. I just know what I've seen and heard from others in school and in the locker room. It's hard to believe my athletic prowess will bring acceptance. How many gay athletes do you know?"

Tesicqueo laughed and it caught me off guard. Everything had been so serious up until this moment. But, he had a right to laugh. I doubted a giant snake attending a sporting event would have gone unnoticed and he did know more about me than I even did myself.

"Sorry about that. It's just that I've been suppressing 'me' for as long as I can remember."

"I understand and you will overcome your denial."

I nodded and relaxed the tension from my shoulders and neck.

"Now, it is time to begin. Close your eyes. Look deep into your soul, peel away the calloused, protective layers guarding your true self, and unleash your inner light."

Unleash my inner light? It sounded a little hokey, but I went along with it. So far this snake knew more about me than I did. I closed my eyes and worked to clear all of the other thoughts from my mind. It reminded me of yoga. Addy made me try it one time, and, despite my athleticism, I was no good at it, probably because I kept laughing at the seemingly "ooh ah" ambience surrounding it. Still, I tried to push even those thoughts from my mind so as not to laugh and disrespect the solemnness of what was being asked of me. Interestingly, the stray thoughts bouncing around in my mind were easily released and within moments, nothing distracted my mind from a quiet harmony. For the first time in my life, I reveled in the silence and tranquility encompassing my mind, body, and spirit. I slowly did look inward and bore through layers of scar tissue protecting the center of my soul, my inner light.

"Focus on the purest energy emanating from the center of your being. The answers you seek and your quest for them abide in the brightest part of your inner self."

I sank deeper and deeper into myself until a blinding light, almost like a sun flare, engulfed me from the inside out. Without a conscious thought, I opened my eyes and the soft, warm glow of a fire from a round fire pit welcomed me. The pit had to have had a diameter of at least four feet, guarded by numerous larger rocks of different shapes and colors, some of which contained minerals that sparkled as they reflected the red-orange flames. A dark impenetrable blackness had taken the place of the hazy tree laden environment I had been in only moments ago. The only source of light was the fire, which just barely illuminated the stark nothingness on all sides.

"Where are we?"

No response.

"Tesicqueo?"

Nothing.

A pop coming from the wood in the fire drew my attention to the flames as they danced within the circle. Suddenly, a log came flying out of the darkness, landing in the middle of the fire, and sending sparks sailing into the air. The burning debris floated high above, and when it cascaded down the many different glowing flecks morphed into people, animals, and tents. Within seconds, I was standing in the midst of a Native American tribe.

None of the inhabitants appeared to be aware of my existence. I could touch, feel, and smell everything around me. Except, I could not interact with the people or animals. I felt like an invader as I walked amongst the people and their wigwams for what must have been an hour. On multiple occasions, I attempted to communicate and interact with the tribe without any luck. Frustration had started to take root when I noticed a small child hiding behind a wooden rack covered in drying animal hides. Slowly and carefully, I inched towards the drying rack and observed as the small girl peeked around the corner at me, then giggled, and hid again. I really didn't know what to think, but decided to play along in the hope she might help me in my search.

Near the drying rack, I found a woodpile and hid to continue the game of peek-a-boo with the little girl. After a few more minutes of playing, the little girl ducked back behind her refuge and vanished from sight. I ventured out from behind the woodpile and walked over to look behind the rack only to find nothing or no one, not even footprints littered the sandy ground. I told myself I was losing my mind and stood there completely stupefied at my current situation and what possible purpose could be behind it.

Standing there, looking incredibly foolish and out of place, I became helplessly captivated by the alien landscape surrounding me. The simple, yet wholly enriched daily lives of the native peoples moved forward around me, and I gazed in awe, as they cared for their little ones, prepared to cook and preserve fresh meat, and their eternal devotion to a spirituality I could only hope to understand in my lifetime. Wigwams of all shapes and sizes dotted the horizon creating a harmonious marriage of the full spectrum of colors with their intricate designs and symbols. A myriad of smells tweaked my nose and drew me wholeheartedly in to the life of a people more or less extinct in the present. With my eyes closed, I fully committed to surrendering myself over to the experience promised me by Tesicqueo.

As I continued in this meditative state, a minute electrical sensation manifested itself on the tips of the fingers on my left hand and gently ascended down my fingers before pooling in my palm. I had the oddest feeling of *something* being spiraling out from my palm, almost like a string being extracted from the inside of my hand. The experience was so real I opened my eyes to see what was happening.

To my left holding my hand in her very tiny and silk-like hands stood the little girl with whom I'd been *playing* earlier. She gazed up at me, smiling widely and exposing a mouth full of white teeth except for the two top incisors, which must have been pushed out to make room for her soon-to-come adult teeth. Her face belayed a girl full of giddy, and I had to consciously stop myself from laughing at her infectious good humor.

"Pyas!" she said, tugging on my hand and leading me deeper into the rolling sea of wigwams, the smoke from their fires billowing upwards.

"Kupi," I responded, without hesitation, to this unknown child using a language that I had never heard in my life. Tesicqueo's words reverberated in my mind and I trusted this vision and just went with it.

We methodically navigated the undulating rows of wigwams, making the center of all of the dwellings our destination. The further we penetrated the dense network of tents, one in the distance rose above the others. The size of the central wigwam tripled that of all of the others I had seen. It stood taller and more vividly decorated than any of the other neighboring ones. A striking scene unfolded before the eyes of anyone who looked upon it. A solid thick earthly red encircled the bottom of the wigwam, creating a substantial base to the rest of the picture. A bright ochre sun gave life to a lush field of green plants topped with yellow, corn. Coyotes or wolves and other native New England wildlife roamed the lush fields in inspiring detail as braves rode on horseback, bows and arrows poised, ready to hunt for their survival. In the center of this side of the wigwam, a large pair of hands rested slightly open, in a cup-like position, just above the red line in such a way, they appeared to be supporting the life depicted above them. I assumed the representation of the hands in such a way, portrayed their beliefs about creation.

My little guide did not permit me to linger too long, before she pulled on my hand, guiding me around the backside of the wigwam and around to the front. In stark contrast with the eastern facing slant of the tent, the western delineated a macabre interpretation of death. To say the difference between the two was "night and day" would be a gross understatement. The conglomeration of hides on the western side oozed darkness, broken only by miniscule pin pricks of light representing the stars; however, their light paled in its effort to illuminate the void. The dynamic illustration from before now lay in ruin. Carcasses littered the once lush and vibrant field, drying blood trickling from their gaping mouths. The courageous hunters were now shown as victims, their bodies inverted, heads pointing towards the ground and feet pointing to the sky. The hand so prominently shown open and supportive on the other side had closed in upon themselves to form a fist like an unopened or dead flower. In school, I had learned Native Americans found a great deal of strength in their spiritual beliefs and I surmised this must be some sort of spiritual or religious center for this tribe, where the drawings on the wigwam mirrored the scenes similar to Genesis and Revelations in the Bible. The two books that described the beginning and end of the world as believed by Christians.

Pulled by my little guide, we rounded the corner, and in anticipation of entering the interior, I took a deep breath, knowing many things I knew or thought I knew about myself were about to change forever.

Smoke burned my eyes as we entered the wigwam. At first I found it difficult to see anything and water continuously fell from my eyes. I managed to feel my way around the interior of the wigwam without stumbling too many times over things. With my eyes adjusting and the smoke lifting into the upper part of the tent, I looked down at my guide only to realize, she had once again vanished. "*She's a tricky little devil*," I thought.

Just as it was outside, no one inside the spiritual center acknowledged any observation of my existence. I looked upon and listened to the men gathered around a glowing fire with intensifying fervor, there had to be a reason why I was seeing all of this. An array of men, varying in age and appearance, sat around the fire passing a pipe as they talked exuberantly, making gestures from their crossed-legged positions. Frustratingly enough, unlike before with my small guide, I was unable to comprehend the discussion especially with the electrified nature of the men involved. Even though I lacked an understanding of the conversation, I inferred what I was watching was a debate heatedly protested on two sides. In observing them, I wondered how many great moments in life had been decided after vigorous and soulfully charged arguments, without them, we would probably not be the same people we are today. They were the key to a people, their ideas, and history surviving.

The oldest man of the group, who garnered the most respect and attention of the others, sits silently listening to the debate at hand. His silver braids flowed freely down each side of his head onto shoulders, which betrayed his age. The wrinkles rippling across his face instantly gave him the quality of being wise and thoughtful. His eyes remained shut during the larger part of the fireside discussion until, with great care, he opened them and revealed eyes older than time itself, full of knowledge and experiences. Silence immediately erupts among the other men, who pay full attention to their shaman as he commences to draw several images in the dirt floor between himself and the fire. The only audible sound was of the crackling fire, but even its devouring of oxygen subsided when the old man set to his task.

The meticulous symbols and pictograms scrawled by the man in the dirt remind me of the same sort seen on the outside of the wigwam. He etched a large circle balanced and supported by the same hands detailed on the "creation" side of the animal skin temple, but now a small serpent-like figure rested at the base of them. In contrast with the image, on the opposite side, the figure of the closed and fist-like hands bore down on the top of the orb in opposition, yet they were now topped with the symbol of an intertwined triangle and circle. On the four axis points of the circle, the old man drew what resembled equal signs, and from each of the, now four quadrants, he scrawled lightning bolts working their way towards the center. A fluid line swirling outward obstructed the electric force's progression towards the center and it became clear the pictogram described a battle of some sort. The group of men leaned forward and closely studied the design carved into the dirt in front of them.

Mirroring the actions of the other men, I stepped forward to get a better view of the drawing and in doing so, I accidentally knocked over a small pot of water. In reaction, the old man governing the others, glanced in my direction and when our eyes met, the fire erupted into an all-consuming torrent of light, heat, and smoke. Instinctively, I covered my face to protect my eyes turning my body to protect myself, the flames singing the hair on my arms in the process. When I felt the heat dissipate, I checked my arms to examine the extent of my supposed injuries, but there was nothing, absolutely no sign of being close to an open flame. I circled back around to absolute darkness and no sign of the men I had been watching. *What the hell could all of that have meant?*

Without warning, my attention turned towards a series of deep, sorrowful screams escaping the nothingness. The faint light of torches slowly penetrated the velvet environment and figures were reflected in the light. I did not hesitate to seek out the source behind the screams and the identity of the people walking in the subterfuge of the night. In my hurried approach towards the band of cloaked figures, my body reacted by sending instinctual warning signs throughout my system and in response, I came to the realization that I knew where I was. I was in the woods near my house, near the giant rock bordering the river. The generally docile and tranquil environment has been violated by a group of masked and cloaked figures encircling a young woman who had been tied down to the massive piece of granite. Her screams called to me for help, but just as before, I could not interact with this environment. As I stood stunned at the scene before me, it dawned on me that I must have been witnessing events that had already taken place. My sole purpose here was to observe what Tesicqueo wanted me to see of the past.

My heart twisted and thudded in my chest, my adrenaline pumped more quickly through my body. Despite my wish to free this poor girl, I am helpless in the endeavor. Moving around the periphery of the circle of disguised figures, I noticed the girl is not a girl at all, but a woman, a pregnant woman. One of the robed figures approached the woman and revealed a large sheathed knife from under his cloak. Then, in front of all of the members of this vile group, he drew the dagger and sliced crossways with determination at the woman's belly. I charged forward towards the woman, but my attempt at rescue failed when another flash of light obscured my vision, making the world vanish into an abyss.

"You have seen the events of the past, which have forged the future, your future."

I opened my eyes to see I am back by the river, face-to-face with the giant serpent, Tesicqueo, where all of this began.

"What do you mean? I don't understand what I'm supposed to have learned from all of this. I have more questions now than I ever did before."

"You will. Have patience and look for the symbols, which will guide you along the path destined to be yours, alone. You cannot undertake this journey with another."

"But . . ."

"Awaken and begin your journey Ethan."

A salty breeze tickled my nose and I awoke in the same spot where I was bitten by the snake. There were no indications of any animal life around me, certainly not a giant snake or any snake for that matter. I lifted up my pants leg and saw there were no marks of any sort. *Okay, that was either the weirdest dream of my life or, or . . . I'm not sure what the hell it was.*

Gathering my wits, I stood up, slung my backpack over my shoulder and realized two things: first, my iPod, which had been fully charged, was completely dead and secondly, the mark of a serpent had appeared my left wrist. I rubbed it to see if it could be removed, but it was permanent. My new "tattoo" bore the same striking tribal likeness of the serpent-like symbol I had seen in the shaman's wigwam.

Like it or not, I had been marked for something I didn't yet understand.

Chapter 14

Back from the dead

WHILE I WATCHED ALL of them go about their daily lives unaware of my existence, I thought about what had happened to me and my power. It sickened me beyond belief. An incipient hatred like bitter, churning bile crept up through my being, and I readied myself to break back through to the physical plane. Before long, every one of the people who had banished me to this plane would suffer repercussions almost twenty years in the making. Blood would flood all of Salem, washing clean the impudent, arrogant, and holier-than-thou coven members. To rid the world and myself of those people, there existed no better vicious or nefarious creature than the Widjigo. The demonic creature would seek out and devour those who had wronged and forsaken me.

Many were fearful of the spell used to summon such a creature, but for me it was something with which I was very familiar and comfortable. My interests and control of the dark arts were the reason why I had been sent to this place and my baby was ripped away from me. Through dark magic, I could control nature more aptly and powerfully than those blinded by naiveté, who relied only on natural and white magic: like my sister and her over confident coven.

The sacrifices hung limp with fear and the knowledge of their impending and inevitable deaths. The Widjigo grasped the first of the innocent young boys with his boney, rotting fingers of one hand while slicing open the boy's throbbing throat, draining him of blood, before gutting his helpless and dying victim. The other lay draped over the branch of a birch tree. Behind the transparent barrier separating the physical and spiritual planes, my body shivered with reverence and excitement watching the unholy beast commit to the task that would permit my return to the world of the living. The small puffs of breath seeping from the boy's mouth slowly ceased as his life slipped away from him. His eyes became cloudy, the sign reflecting the end of all that he knew.

Following their deaths, the circle was cast and the incantation recited in order to exhume the necessary power from the blood of the slayed twins. The Widjigo dematerialized into the nothingness from whence he had come. The Blood Rock pulsated with energy that rippled outward distorting the surrounding environment. In concert with the vibrating force of the rock, the fires around the victims climbed upwards, intensifying, and the symbol in blood glowed a deeper, richer red, one not seen for generations. Entranced, I stood poised at the frontier between the two realms and reveled in the formation of a small crack inching down the glass-like barrier. My escape was imminent and I could already taste the plane of the living on my tongue. I let my arms drop down to my sides, palms outward, and concentrated on projecting my magic into the crevice forming in the veil. Bit by bit it increased the speed and size with which it grew. Using almost all of my remaining strength, I pushed against the barrier and broke free of the supernatural chains imprisoning me in the spiritual plan. The rush of the life-giving, oxygen-rich air of the physical plane replaced the stale, acrid air of the shadow realm. Heat from the fire pulled me forward and I savored the rejuvenating power of its flames as they painted my naked body in a barrage of intense shades of red, orange and yellow.

A single-minded goal had brought me back to this place from an excruciating exile, the desire to find my child. The last step needed to consecrate my one true family and supreme power. No one, magical or mortal, who blocked my advances, would survive in their attempts to keep me from what was rightfully mine to possess.

* * *

The first night of my return, I found refuge in a cave hidden deep within the woods, unknown to the inhabitants of the town. Crossing over from the shadow realm had diminished my powers and I would be no match against another witch. Before I could start the search for my child and exact my revenge, I had to regenerate my strength and more importantly my magic. I crawled along the forest floor and collected several herbs native to New England I would need to get back my stolen strength. Determined, I sat at the edge cave and waited patiently for any small animal to pass. The wet, cold night air licked my unprotected skin, and I loathed feeling so vulnerable and exposed to nature.

Sounds abounded in the woods surrounding the cave. The forest was most alive at night, and it wasn't long before a rabbit hopped within reach. Without a moment's hesitation, I grabbed the bunny and tore at its throat with my teeth. It wasn't long before droplets of blood trickled down my chin and the rapid movement of the animal's feet lessened. I sat the small animal's heart on a rock and filled a small divot in the cave with their blood. Using this small sacrificial "lamb," I would be able to prepare, and consume a concoction of the rabbit's blood infused with a mixture of crushed blue violets, birthroot, skullcap, and wild iris, which I had collected in the woods. *The physical plane had welcomed me back with open arms.* I held my hands over the small hole in the ground containing the bloody herbal mixture and warmed it to boiling with the last remnants of my strength. Then, like a dog, I licked the elixir from the ground. The warm potion coated my throat and organs as I lapped up every last drop. The feral essence of the rabbit, in unison with the carefully selected herbs, entered every cell of my body, reenergizing my physical body and magical abilities.

My senses regained their otherworldly acuteness, and I no longer saw only darkness, but a world bathed in lucid hues of yellow, like a cat on a nocturnal hunt. My entire body tightened and yearned with desire as it absorbed the regenerating mixture. I pulled the cracked and dry fingernails from their respective cuticles as blood began to cover my hands. In their place more beautiful and sharper ones grew. The matted and thinning hair covering my head slipped from its roots and floated to the ground, being replaced by raven, curly locks, which rested on my newly toned back and slender shoulders. *Who needed plastic surgery when you had what I did?* Inside and out my being pulsed with physical and magical strength, every fiber poised to set to the task, which lay before me.

Before retaking what was stolen from me and rightfully mine, it was imperative to contact my followers on this side to ensure he had completed all the tasks in preparation for my return. After completing my rebirth, I retrieved the rabbit's heart from the rock. I squeezed the tiny heart between my right thumb and index finger, letting the remaining blood pool in my left palm. Blood was one of one hundred ways to contact those who served more powerful beings. I recited the words in Latin and opened a line of communication with one who had surrendered and dedicated his life to my cause and me. The rich liquid bubbled and foamed in my hands as I called to him.

"Have you procured all that is needed?"

"Everything has been arranged per your instructions. The time is now."

Feeling invigorated, I stepped out from the damp, mold-ridden cave into the virginal glowing light of dawn. First things first, I headed in the direction of the place concealing my family's magical heritage in America, the home of my sister and her family. Today, I thought, would be the perfect day for an impromptu family reunion. Unfortunately, I wasn't sure she'd make it until the traditional, cliché family photo at the end.

Chapter 15

Revelations

MY HEART THREATENED TO leap from my chest by the time I reached the bottom of the stairs. *Was I losing my mind? Had my family really been keeping secrets from me my entire life? Or was all of this a cruel dream, a side effect of my meds and hospitalization?* Hesitation overwhelmed me as I stood at the door to my father's quaint and eternally chaotic office. For a split second, I thought about calling Ethan to have him do this with me, but I didn't want to worry him about something that may or may not be a figment of my imagination. A floorboard creaked and popped behind me and I jumped. This was ridiculous. I took hold of the antique black cast iron doorknob and turned it until I heard a click, and the door opened.

* * *

Another night and I lay in bed with an unending folly of thoughts bouncing around inside my skull, yet again a condemned victim of insomnia. My vision quest experience still didn't make sense to me, even after mulling it over for a week. I would have completely brushed it off as one crazy dream if it weren't for the tattoo on my wrist. Everyone at school had found it "cool" or "bad ass," but that didn't help me to figure what exactly had happened. Tesicqueo had promised me answers, but as I lay here peeved and restless, I felt I had fewer answers now than I had had questions before all of this. It was my last year of high school, and I should have been enjoying all of the benefits that came with being a senior, instead of pondering some sort of metaphysical BS.

Worst of all, I wanted to tell Addy everything that had happened during her brief stay in the hospital, but a part of me, admittedly a small part, feared she would look at me with that face, the one where I knew she thought I was an imbecile without saying as much. Frustrated, I rolled out of the bed and did a set of pushups on the floor, followed by crunches, more pushups, jumping jacks, etc. Something had to clear my mind of all of these doubts and worries. Running. I slid on some running shorts and shoes, stepped out into an unseasonal balmy September night and headed from my barn into the woods.

* * *

For a few moments, I stared into the blackness of my father's academic sanctuary before I tiptoed inside. Being in his study, was like looking into his mind, the inner sanctum of his soul where he came and stayed for hours to recharge his batteries. A part of me, felt ashamed for violating his space, but the desire to validate my vision and prove my own sanity trumped any remaining qualms I might have had. With great care and anxiety, I closed the door behind me, praying I didn't wake up my dad. My parents' bedroom was in the back of the house and shared a wall with his study.

The study boasted an extensive collection of books, papers, pictures and historical knickknacks, so much so, a person could barely see the beautiful natural honey color of the finished mountain ash walls. With the aid of the flashlight app on my phone, I tried to become one with my inner ninja as I strategically dodged the minefield of historical artifacts strewn between the built-in bookshelf, and me that lay on the wall opposite from the door. Behind me, something moved and groaned, and I unintentionally knocked a leather bound book off my dad's desk with my hip. Helpless, I looked on as the book glided in slow motion through the air before dive-bombing an unsuspecting and unsteady stack of papers on the floor, which tilted over and crashed littering the tattered rug in an explosion of paper.

I stood paralyzed with fear, waiting for the sound of my father's footsteps. There was no way he could have slept through such a loud clang of worn leather, paper and wood floors. The air hung heavy as I waited. I listened intently for any sign of him stirring in his room, but there was nothing but silence. I took a deep breath and pushed onward.

After causing that one minor mishap, I reached the bookcase, which for the first time that I could remember stood locked, it's tiny keyhole judging me in my attempt to open it. I cursed under my breath and turned to search my dad's desk for anything resembling a key or other tool capable of opening up the secrets hidden within. Yet again, I heard a sound from behind me, but this time I told myself to ignore it, and instead, stuck to the task of finding a way inside the bookcase. My search of the desk revealed nothing, so I carefully moved to a small curio cabinet crammed into the corner of the tiny room, hoping to have better luck. I had almost reached the small piece of furniture when someone cupped a hand over my mouth and held me tight.

"Don't scream."

* * *

Once I started running, the humid air became a welcome companion causing sweat to seep from every pore. Sweating helped to liberate my body and mind from everything that had been weighing on me earlier. The rest of the world slept peacefully as I made my way along familiar paths. After making a turn at the river, I doubled back towards Addy's house to finish along the wide-open fields on either side of the road leading home. Nothing else moved in the night as I started my trek up the road, complete tranquility.

As I approached Addy's house, I noticed a faint glimmer of light coming from the window of what looked to be her father's study. It bounced around, bathing the window in white. I took my iPod out of my armband to stop the music and checked the time: 2:07am. *Addy and her dad should be in their beds deep asleep, and if they weren't, why would they be using a flashlight in their own house.*

I crept up to the house slowly and tried to peak in the window, but the curtains obscured my ability to see any distinguishing features. All I could see was a dark mass moving around inside. I turned around and grabbed the spare key from under a potted plant at the bottom of the stairs leading up to the front door. As stealthily as I could, I slid the key into the lock and slowly turned it. I carefully closed the door behind me and inched towards his study. Only then did I realize I was only wearing running shorts and shoes. Neither would do much in the way of protecting my body if whoever inside wasn't Addy or her dad.

The door was slightly ajar and allowed a few flashes of bluish light to escape into the entryway as I approached and squeezed inside the tiny room. *This could really turn out to be a bonehead move.* I stood still for a few minutes waiting for my eyes to adjust to the low light, when I realized there was no intruder. *Addy, what in the hell are you doing?*

I knew if I startled her she'd scream and her father would be scared to death, so I tiptoed up behind her and slid my hand over her mouth.

"Don't scream."

Her body tensed, and I could feel her pulse ramp up.

"It's okay. It's me, Ethan."

She spun around and shot daggers at me with her eyes. "What the hell do you think you're doing? You scared the crap out of me!"

"I'm sorry. Wait, what am I doing? What are you doing in here?" I asked.

"I'm, I'm looking for something," she whispered.

"What something? And why are we whispering?"

"A book and I don't want my father to know I'm snooping around in here."

"Well there are more than a few books in here. Could you be a little more specific?"

I could tell from her expression she wasn't sure if she wanted to or could tell me.

"Addy, you know you can trust me," I assured her.

"I know. It's just going to make me sound like a freak of the highest order."

"No more than usual," I said with a wink and a smile.

"Ha ha ha, you're *so* funny!"

"So, I'm waiting for some kind of explanation, no matter what it is."

"Well . . . when I was in the hospital, I kind of had a . . . vision 'thing.'"

"What kind of vision 'thing'? What did you see?"

"I saw my house and when I came inside, I found a book about my family hidden behind that wall." She pointed towards the bookcase and looked back at me waiting to see my reaction.

"Okay. Let's look and see what we find," I said.

"Seriously? You don't think I'm a kook?"

"Not in the least. You're not the only who has had a vision lately."

We locked eyes and said, "Sounds like we need to talk."

"Yes we do, but first, let's look for that book," I added.

* * *

As much as I wanted to kick Ethan in the teeth, I had to admit I was happy he was here and I wasn't going to be doing this alone. It felt right having him by my side as I dove into possibly uncovering a life full of secrets, buried under the guise of the perfect family.

"I haven't been able to find the key. Let's look in this curio cabinet."

Both he and I searched every shelf and drawer for anything looking like the key for the bookcase. Our searched revealed nothing in the way of a key, but we did find a brass letter opener.

Looking at Ethan, "do you think this might work?"

"Well I'm no professional cat burglar, but it can't hurt to try it."

I grabbed the letter opener and walked over to the locked bookcase. I was about to stick the sharp end into the lock when Ethan stopped me.

"You look like you're about to stab someone and you're really shaking. Do you want me to do it?"

I nodded and handed him the improvised key. He was right I was visibly shaking. The fear of finding information that could radically alter what I thought I knew about my family and, more importantly, about my parents terrified me more than anything had ever done in my life. Trying to come to grips with such a realization, if it were true, would be a daunting affair.

Ethan skillfully jimmied the lock with the letter opener and the elderly glass and wood doors creaked open against their better judgment. *Was the house plotting against us?* Now was the moment of truth. *Would there actually be a secret panel in the back of the bookcase or would this all be for not?*

"So, what now?" he asked.

"We see if I'm losing my mind or not."

* * *

The book Addy described from her vision was burned in my mind as I worked the bookcase door open against its will. I had seen these doors opened and closed so many times in the past and never had they groaned and fought against their hinges. Was there something that didn't want us finding a possibly buried secret?

"I don't think you're losing your mind. I believe you and I always will."

With tears in her eyes, Addy looked at me and smiled, "thank you."

I watched her reach into the back of the book-laden bookcase and take a deep breath before pushing against the interior wooden panel. Without explanation, the house quieted any and all the noises revealing its age and in the silence, we heard a small clicking sound come from the back of the bookshelf. The sound of wood sliding against wood followed. We stood motionless looking at one another with stunned and anticipatory faces. *She was right.* Addy leaned her shoulder into the cabinet full of history and seized something from within the hidden the compartment. A leather-bound book with gold decorations and some kind of symbol broke the protection of the case and in the light of our phones the letter F encapsulated within an intertwining circle and triangle shimmered to life.

* * *

From the window, I watched as my sister's daughter pulled my family's heritage from the tiny concealed cabinet. Her cousin stood next to her as they stared down at the book protecting centuries of magic and family lineage. I wasn't sure how they had been able to stumble upon its hidden location, but they had no idea of the power filling the pages of the book they had just discovered. Using great care not to draw their attention, I tried to lift the window, but the frame didn't budge. Suddenly a rippling wave of light and energy radiated outward from the house, and I flew backwards through the air. Damned rowan. I had forgotten the entire house had been reconstructed using mountain ash. The spiritually imbued wood barred all manner of supernatural evil from entering a space. *Looks like I will have to call on him again to help me in my plan.*

* * *

A rustling and whooshing sound came from outside the study window, and both Addy and I spun around to gaze out on the front yard.

"What the hell was that?"

"Stay here. I'll go and see what it is."

"Be careful."

Once again I quietly opened the front door and surveyed the front yard as much as humanly possible, but, at first, I saw nothing. My eyes strained against the dark night sky to bring things into focus when all at once a searing pain overtook my head and eyes. I grabbed the doorframe to keep from falling and waking up Addy's dad. The pain lasted only a few seconds, and when I steadied myself in the doorway darkness no longer covered the landscape of the front yard. All of nature in front of me glowed in the shades of red, blue and green, like someone had spilt the entire contents of a paint store over everything in sight. It looked oddly familiar and after a few moments I realized it reminded me of looking through an infrared or night vision camera, like one of my cameras I use in low light. *Was I really seeing at night?*

I blinked my eyes several times but the view before did not change. I saw everything that lay before me. I saw animals, like deer, pulsing red running through the trees in the distance. I could actually make out distinct details. Tesicqueo's words resurfaced and I decided to just *go with* what was happening to me. I scanned the area outside the window and saw a streak of yellow scarring the illuminated green ground and swooping up into the cobalt air. Someone had been there, watching us. But who would have been watching my cousin's house at almost three in the morning?

"What do you see?"

Addy startled me and when I turned to answer her, the glowing colors illuminating the outdoors faded and my "normal" vision returned as I stepped back into the house.

"Ugh, nothing. At least, I think nothing."

"What does that mean?"

"Nothing to worry about at the moment. Let's open that book."

* * *

Ethan never could lie to me, and I knew there was something weighing on his mind; however, I was dying to dive into the book. The ancient-looking tome mirrored exactly what I had seen in my dream, and I held my breath as I lifted the leather bound and surprisingly heavy front cover. *Would the similarities continue or did the book protect something entirely different from what I saw?*

The book rested on the desk and my heart pulsed rapidly as I carefully opened the protective front cover. I couldn't believe that up until this point, everything had happened just as it had in my vision at the hospital. So far the fear of me being crazy had subsided and the excitement of unearthing ancient family secrets surged. My palms began sweating as I looked down at the yellowed pages.

"You realize you're trembling, right?" Ethan asked.

"I'm excited, nervous, and scared to find out what's inside."

"I'm sure nothing will change. The history of our family is very well known to both of us. Let's just think of it as genealogical research, not trying to catch our parents in a lie."

I nodded. I was sure Ethan was right. Both of our families had always taken pride in their heritage and we had learned about it from a very young age. However, a voice in the back of my mind, told me to prepare myself for what I might stumble upon inside the parchment sitting before me.

"I guess it's now or never," I said.

* * *

I thought reassuring Addy was the right thing to do especially when I didn't really have any idea about what her vision in the hospital had revealed. If it were anything like mine, she'd really have no clue as to what she had seen. Maybe this was part of the process of her understanding what she had been witness to when she was comatose in the hospital. I wanted to believe her concerns were just imaginings in her mind, but a feeling in my gut lead me to take her at her word and prepare myself for some life-altering revelation. But what, I wondered, could actually be so earth shattering to do so.

"Dammit. It's not here," she said, frustrated.

"What?"

"The family tree I saw in the book during my dream. It was right here on these two pages."

"Here, let me see."

Addy held up the left side of the book and pointed to the yellow-brown page, which was devoid of any traces of writing. I leaned forward and scrutinized the crinkled right-hand side of the book before taking the equally empty page between my fingers and flipping to look at the reverse side.

"Ethan, look!"

Tiny capillaries of golden fluid light rippled beneath the two pages resting before us, illuminating a large and extensive drawing of a tree where leaves were replaced with the names of people going all the way back to the thirteenth century. It was true that in her comatose state, Addy had seen the book, and, more importantly, the genealogical history of our family. My body shivered to its core, and the worrisome feeling in my gut became real as the bottom of the tree flashed and shimmered into existence.

* * *

The undulating light from the book illuminated the room as my dream transformed into reality before our eyes. I hadn't told Ethan what exactly I had seen below the names of our parents in my vision, but I knew the secret would reveal itself in a matter of moments. I reached out for his hand and held it tightly within mine as together the past and present of our "parents" came to light. The glow of the book subsided and our lives and the lives of our family line stared back at us from the parchment pages before us.

We stood without saying a word, completely astonished at what we were seeing, for what seemed like hours until Ethan broke the silence.

"Why would they lie to us about this? Why hide the truth?"

"I'm not sure about anything anymore. All the lies coming to the surface and what we just saw happen with the book isn't "right," isn't "normal." What the hell is going on with our family? Who or what are we?"

The book divulged untruths intentionally buried for years by our parents and presumably everyone else we thought we knew well. The falsehoods leapt off the pages of the book, like heated grease popping out of a white hot skillet, showering Ethan and me with familial revelations: our parents were not our biological parents. Our biological mother's name was Arabella, my mother's twin sister, and Ethan and I were not cousins. We were siblings. We were twins.

Chapter 16

Self-preservation

THE SOUND OF SOMEONE pounding on the front door rumbled through the quiet and still air of the house. Ethan and I were both jolted by the bangs and together we slammed the book shut. I hurriedly, but carefully returned the fragile book of secrets to its hidden cabinet in the back of the bookcase. The pounding on the door continued and we stood there frozen with fear and the anticipation of hearing my dad wake up and answer the door, but after a few minutes, he hadn't entered the foyer from his bedroom.

New and muddled thoughts swam around in our heads about the information revealed in the book, reality seemed to be tipping towards a breaking point. And on top of all that, the seriously pissed off person at the door forcibly pulled us from our thoughts only to create more confusion and fear.

"Where's your dad?"

I just shrugged my shoulders and hoped whoever was at the front door would give up and go away, but they didn't.

"Open the door! This is Detective Ayden Malin of the Salem Police Department!"

"What the hell is Detective Malin doing at your house at 3 in the morning?" Ethan asked.

"I have no clue, but if I don't answer the door, he might break it down. How would I explain that to my, my whatever he is?" My whole life had suddenly submerged into a foggy parallel reality without any immediate sign of the lies being cleared away.

We hastily exited the tiny study, but made doubly sure to quietly lock the door, leaving everything as we had found it when all of this began.

"I said, 'Open the door!'"

"I'm coming!"

I wrapped my hand around the doorknob and felt it pulsate in my grasp. Never in my life had I experienced something like this. The world slowed down and I had a "sense" that something wasn't right about the situation in which we found ourselves. Something wanted to hurt us, something wanted to stop us from finding out more about the truth.

* * *

The noise from the door actually hurt my eardrums as it echoed throughout Addy's house. First my vision had acted strangely and now my ears were swiftly giving me a migraine. Everything about me seemed more in tune with my surroundings, exponentially heightened. As we approached the door after leaving the study, I picked up on something I found difficult to explain. The air around us carried warning signals sparking reactions from my skin and my nose. The proverbial hair on the back of my neck and my arms stood up and a strong pungent odor invaded my nostrils. Simultaneously, the muscles throughout my body contracted and poised themselves in what I can only describe as an attack posture. *Why was Detective Malin here and what were his intentions? Or, was this a reaction to what I had "seen" earlier, outside the study window?*

Whatever or whomever it was, my body stood tactfully and instinctively ready to protect Addy and myself against it.

The old black wooden door protested as Addy opened it and Det. Malin came into full view, his fist hanging in the air in mid-swing towards the now ajar door. He had the face of a crazed animal and the light from the light above the front door cast a yellow glow, which reflected off of his dilated eyes. His hot breath reacted with the cool night air and almost opaque white mist surrounded the air around his flushed red face.

"Can I help you?" Addy said doing nothing to hide her perturbation.

"I've been knocking on the door for over 5 minutes. What's the emergency?"

"Emergency? What do you mean?"

"We got a call saying there had been a home invasion and attack."

"Detective we've been talking in Addy's room for around an hour." A little white lie never really hurt anyone and I just wanted him to leave. "I can promise you there's been no break-in or we would have heard something."

He blinked his eyes rapidly and wiped the sweat from his brow with the back of his hand before placing it over his mouth. He stood there in front of us for several minutes without saying a word. His eyes looked straight through us. Addy and I both turned to see if he had seen something behind us, but there was nothing. I tried talking to him; however, I was unable to break him from his apparent trance. Carefully, I reached out my left hand to try and shake him from his stupor, but as soon as I touched his shoulder, he, in the blink of an eye, grabbed my wrist painfully and tightly within his own massive hand.

"What the hell man!"

"Let him go! You're hurting him!"

Our pleas had absolutely no effect on him. All he did was continue to stare through us into the black nothingness of the shadows painting the back of the house. Addy reacted by attacking Det. Malin, punching him in his chest with all of the force she could muster. Nothing. He responded by reaching out and grabbing her around the throat and squeezing so tightly that Addy had great difficulty breathing. I twisted and contorted my body to retaliate. He flicked my wrist backwards, and I fell to my knees as I heard the bone snap inside his vice-like grip. Every nerve in my wrist and arm fired synchronously and I gasped at the amount of pain caused by his hold. Tears formed in my eyes and flowed freely down my cheeks. Doing my best not to be overcome by the intensity of the pain, I pushed my legs out from under me and made contact with his shin with both feet. It was like kicking a concrete block and the backlash ran back from my feet up through my body and exploded in my head. I winced in pain as I saw our likelihood of survival dwindling rapidly.

* * *

Weak gasps for air scarcely escaped my mouth as I glanced down at Ethan and then back at Det. Malin, who remained standing there like someone possessed. His body exhibited an incredible rigidity, almost like a statue. He had not moved a muscle since covering his mouth with his hand, except for attacking and seemingly trying to kill us. I grabbed his wrist with both of my hands and kicked violently against his hold, but it was useless. We were both caught. He had seized us in his steel clutches, and now we were both beginning to succumb to pain and exhaustion.

Mustering the very last bits of strength in my body, I released my grip on his wrist and clawed and pushed at him with both of my hands. For the first time since his arrival, he reacted to my attacks by letting go of Ethan's wrist. His gaze turned towards me, and he raised his hand high into the hair. I instinctually winced and put my arms out, palms outward towards his face and body. A feeling, which I could only describe as a force, grew dynamically in my stomach and swirled upwards through my chest and then surged down my outstretched arms towards my open palms. All at once, this force erupted from my palms in an intense explosion of blue light and energy, which struck Det. Malin squarely in the chest.

His hold on us instantly weakened, and he let go of both of us before he sailed flailing through the air trying to stop his momentum before he landed some fifteen feet from where he had stood only moments earlier. He lay unconscious on the gravel driveway. After I crashed to the wooden floor, I rolled over on my side and then got onto my hands and knees, gasping for air while my throat throbbed with pain. For a moment, I thought he might be dead, but the rhythmic rising and falling of his chest proved me wrong.

"E, Ethan, are you okay?"

"That freaking maniac broke my wrist, but I think I'll be okay. What the hell just happened?"

"I have no idea about anything we've experience tonight." I glanced over at my best friend, my *brother*, and when we locked eyes, the realization that nothing would ever be the same for us finally sunk in and we simply nodded at one another in acknowledgment of that fact. Without any noticeable provocation, Ethan broke his stare and turned his head to gaze into the trees across the road from our house. Like before, his body became rigid and tense, the pain of his broken wrist being pushed from his face.

"Someone's out there. Someone's coming."

* * *

Thoughts ran rampant in my mind as I realized, along with Addy, that there were drastic changes creeping into our lives as a consequence of a life's worth of lies and deceptions. The pounding in my head grew incrementally louder thanks to the pain radiating out from my broken wrist. All of a sudden, the intensity of the pain became almost unnoticeable, and I turned my attention across the road to the tree line opposite the house. I knew something or someone stood at the edge of the forest and moved slowly towards the house. Unfortunately, I couldn't decipher whether or not this was another threat to us like Det. Malin, who lay passed out on the gravel. However, I was certain about one thing, Addy and I could in no way defend ourselves against another aggressor. We barely escaped Malin and that was thanks to something we could not readily explain or even comprehend.

We were sitting ducks.

My stare penetrated the dense trees and underbrush, and like before, my vision shifted to allow me to see more than was humanly possible. Tiny flecks of red and orange disrupted the incandescent blue and purple hues of the forest as small animals scurried around, yet every one of their routes led away from a large, slow-moving bright red and yellow mass.

The glowing shapeless blob of heat headed in a direct path towards the house and us. I blinked my eyes and refocused on the forest, but the figure had disappeared from sight. I scanned the entire length of the forest line and there was no sign of anything, not even the once prevalent scurrying animals.

"What is it? What do you see?"

"I know I saw something moving towards us in the trees, but now it's gone. It has completely vanished."

"I'm ready to wake up from this nightmare. I don't think I can take much more of this."

Hearing this from Addy, of all people, told me what was happening was worse than anything either of us had ever faced in our 18 years. She never let anything affect her to the extent where she felt lost or out of control. Unfortunately, in these circumstances, there was no easy out. There was no waking up and pretending everything was okay. Recent and on-going events conveyed a clear and startling truth: danger and our once ordinary lives were now forever intertwined.

A flash of light crossed my peripheral vision, but faded too quickly for me to distinguish very much about it.

"We have to get help. Do you have your phone?"

"No. It's upstairs."

"Looks like we will have to do this the old fashioned way then." Forgetting the pain, I turn and press my left palm to the ground before yelling in agony along with an accompaniment of several four-letter words.

"Here let me do it." Addy said as she made her way to the cordless phone in the entryway cubby by the front door. "Who should I call?"

"Principal McIntyre." After all, he had told me I could call him anytime I needed him.

"McIntyre?" Addy asked.

"Yes. He's the only one I trust, unless you can think of someone else."

"Looks like we're calling our principal at almost 4 in the morning."

She dialed the number, and I reached out and took the receiver from her. The phone rang several times before a very sleepy and groggy principal McIntyre picked up.

"Hello?"

Working through the pain and the all-too-real fear of someone who was on their way to harm us, I, in very few words, told him we needed his help because we had been attacked. I did not go into details knowing that our attacker was his partner would only confuse things. Through the phone, I could hear him jump out of the bed and get dressed as he talked to me on the phone, making sure Addy and I were okay. Lying through my teeth, I did what I could to reassure him of our safety.

I hung up the phone and turned my attention back towards the front yard, looking, searching for anything that might try to harm us again. Det. Malin still lay unmoving on the ground in front of us. *How had she done that? Did she know she could do that or was it like what happened to me with my vision?*

"He's on his way. I don't think it'll take him very long."

"Good."

"So what happened back there?"

"I haven't a clue. It just *happened.*"

"Well if you makes you feel any better, you're not the only one with things just *happening* to them out of the blue."

We both left it at that and sat in silence for what seemed like hours until we saw the headlights of Principal McIntyre's car coming down the old dirt road that connected our former safe haven to the rest of town. *How in the hell were we going to even try to begin to explain what had happened?*

At the moment, I figured the only person who had our backs might be our principal, our guardian inside of school, and now, outside of it. I mean, he, unlike everyone else, had given us no reason not to trust him, and I hoped that didn't change.

Chapter 17

The ties that break

THE FOCUSED LIGHT OF Principal McIntyre's headlights spotlighted our predicament in an interrogative and somewhat embarrassing manner as he turned into the circular gravel driveway. Like a pair of rag dolls, we sat there waiting for him to get out of his car and help us. He stopped for only a second to check on Det. Malin before he hurried over to us. The panic etched across his face betrayed his usual stoic and controlled manner, yet I felt instantly comforted and safe by his arrival.

"Oh my god, are you two okay?" he asked.

"Um . . . I think 'okay' is a very inadequate word to describe how we're doing at the moment." I said followed by a weak attempt at a chuckle. After all, I was the master of emotional deflection.

"I can understand why," he said as he went to Addy to look at her throat for bruises and any other injuries before stepping over to me, as I lay embarrassingly weak looking on the floor.

"I really feel like an idiot laying here helpless."

"You're not an idiot. Here, let me help you up."

Instinctually, I held out my left arm, forgetting momentarily my wrist was broken. When he grabbed my wrist, I remembered and jerked my arm back quickly waiting to be overcome with another wave of pain, but there was nothing. I felt absolutely no pain.

"Ethan, I'm sorry. Did I hurt you? Is your wrist hurt?"

"It's broken. Det. Malin broke it." I examined my wrist and saw no bruising, no discoloration not a single indication it was broken. It made no sense at all. "It was broken. I swear."

"You guys have been through a lot. I wouldn't be surprised if either of you were a little confused."

"No, Mr. McIntyre, he's right. His wrist was broken. First the book, then the attack and now this." As soon as Addy finished her statement, she realized she had more than let the cat out of the bag. She had revealed something secret to everyone outside of our parents, or so we thought.

"Book? What book?"

"Oh, it's nothing. Sorry."

Thankfully, Principal McIntyre let it go without further questions. I pulled myself up off the ground with only the help of the doorframe and stood leaning against it in continued astonishment at the miraculous healing of my wrist.

The slamming of a car door ripped all of us from our chatter, and we looked as Det. Malin peeled out of the driveway sending tiny rock bullets spraying across the front of the house and doorway. Principal McIntyre spread his arms and acted as a shield for us against the barrage of flying debris. In a matter of moments, the only thing visible thing left of his police cruiser was the glowing trails of red coming from his taillights. Only a blind person would have missed the pang of hurt flash across Principal McIntyre's face after the car faded away in the dark blue and orange light of dawn. After lowering his arms and turning back to face us, Principal McIntyre guided us back into the refuge of the house and down into kitchen.

We all sat in silence around the large kitchen island in the middle of the smaller-sized kitchen. It was an awkward silence born out of exhaustion, hurt, and confusion, each of us not knowing how or where to start the conversation. How could we even try to explain what had happened without delving into what we had discovered hidden in the bookcase? *Would he believe us? Did he already know?*

* * *

Ethan was right, I did feel better now that McIntyre was here with us; however, I still wasn't sure what had happened with Malin and the information detailed in the book. Someone, who we knew, had tried to seriously harm or maybe even kill us, and the worst part of it all was there was no logical reason for it. Even more troubling was the fact all of this had transpired after we found the book. Lies upon lies had been built to hide the truth and now one by one the faulty ground on which they were assembled began to break apart, causing many falsehoods to come to the surface.

The silence grated on my nerves as we all sat there looking blankly into space. I mean, what do you say after everything we've just witnessed. Finally, I had enough.

"How about I make us all some tea or something else if you prefer?"

"It looks like you guys could use something a little stronger than tea." McIntyre said with a wink and a smile. It was exactly what we all needed. The entire kitchen erupted in raucous laughter, which removed the looming dread and pressure staining the environment. My sides hurt from laughing so hard and it was such a relief to forget, even if for a brief moment, the last few hours of my life. I filled the antique copper kettle with water and sat it on top of the billowing orange and blue flame on the stove.

"If you guys could please excuse me, I need to make a phone call."

We both smiled weakly at him and McIntyre stepped up into the entry just outside the door, out of earshot. Ours were not the only lives changed this night, he had also witnessed something that shook the very foundation of a relationship he had spent years building with Malin. Recently, life twisted and turned without warning and a path of destruction lay in its vociferous wake. The water reached its boiling point, and I poured Ethan and myself a cup of my "mother's" homemade herbal tea.

"So . . ."

"Yeah, so . . ."

* * *

My brain worked overtime to try to process what I had just seen and experienced. Ayden's behavior and actions were best described as nonsensical and completely out of character for the man I had known and loved. I leafed through my memories of our three years together and looked for anything pointing to a supernatural reason for what had just happened. Nothing. There was nothing I could pinpoint to account for the abhorrent change in personality we had all just been witness to. One of the only two loves of my life had tried to kill two innocent kids. At least I hope things had not changed since I last saw Ethan. If so, things might be beginning to spin out of control and Ayden's actions were those of someone trying to save the world from a greater evil than it had ever known. *But how?* How would he have even known about the prophecy and subsequent secrets created to shield the truth from the world, Addy and Ethan? It just wasn't possible, unless someone was not who they appeared to be.

I opened the contacts on my phone, selected Ayden's entry, pressed call and waited. The line rang and rang until his voicemail picked up. "This is Detective Malin with the Salem Police Department. Please leave me a brief message after the tone along with your number. If this is an emergency, please hang up and dial 911."

"Ayden, it's me Devon. Are you okay? What the hell was all that? I'm really worried about you. Call me. I love y...'*click*'. Dammit."

The morning sun peaked through the tops of the still bare trees as the dawn took hold of the world and brought light to the world, and hopefully the darkness surrounding current events. For the first time in a hundred years, I felt like having a cigarette, but common sense overrode the desire. I slipped my phone back in my pocket and went back inside the house. Like a persistent mole, self-doubt burrowed its way into my head and I questioned, for the first time since being called as a Guardian, my mission of protecting those in my charge. Above everything else in my life, I was bound by magic and my word to protect Ethan and Addy against the evil of their family and from themselves no matter the consequences. In the end, it was a simple question of life and death where nothing and no one's safety was guaranteed, not even that of the twins.

Stepping back inside the house, I noticed the rug in the entry way had been flipped back, like someone had tripped on it after exiting the study. I quietly checked the door and discovered it was locked, which I thought was odd considering the close relationship between Addy, her mom, and dad. I had known both of her parents for years and never thought of Addy's father, Ed, as being someone who would lock his study door, unless he was suspicious and feared someone had discovered the book hidden in the back of the bookcase. If this was true, a few of the night's events began to make a little more sense, especially after considering this new information.

I reentered the kitchen to find them sitting in silence much like before I had stepped outside to call Ayden. The only difference being that they each had a mug of hot tea wrapped in their hands, but it didn't look like either of them had yet taken a sip. The steam for the hot liquid lingered in the air above the cups before disappearing into nothingness. Looking at them in their current state, I wondered how they were going to take the truth about their lives and families. I had been threatened with life-altering consequences if I divulged anything, but my conscience weighed heavy on me. With everything they had just experienced, now was probably as good of a time as any to try and provide them with answers to their questions.

After almost four hundred years of life experiences ranging from the incredible to the debilitating, I did not envy myself for being the messenger, or them for what was about to become an incredibly unsettling reality.

"Guys, I really think we need to have a conversation about what happened tonight and the night you were both born."

The faces meeting my gaze completely gutted me, and I pulled out a chair and sat down at the island.

"Okay, where do I begin? I guess I should start with your mo..." I was cut off in mid-sentence by a sound coming from the back of the house. *Could Ayden have come back to finish what he started or was it just the old bones of the house groaning against years of support?*

* * *

A sound at the back of the house startled all of us more so than usual, considering everything that had happened since Ethan and I found the book and my vision had been validated. The three of us looked towards the kitchen entry and remained silent. Ethan and McIntyre backed away from the island and stealthily moved towards the door as I stood there, eyes locked on the entry. The sound was familiar, the unlocking of the back door, not by force but with a key. It had to be my dad. No one else had a key and my mom was still in France as far as I knew.

The unexpected visitor would have entered without arousing anyone if we had been asleep upstairs, but we weren't. We were all wide-awake and held our breath waiting to see who might enter the kitchen in a matter of seconds. They craftily walked along the long entryway runner towards the front of the house before stopping. For a moment, none of us heard anything and Ethan and McIntyre rocked onto the balls of their feet, readying themselves for whatever might be about to happen. The sound of another key entering a lock broke the uneasy silence and we all heard the study door give way and creak open on its dry hinges. My patience had run out and I was tired of being shut out of the secrets abounding in my very own house.

"Dad, is that you?"

Both Ethan and McIntyre glanced back at me questioning my decision, but I didn't care. One way or another we were going to get to the bottom of what was true and what was lies.

For a painfully uneasy moment no one replied and all sound ceased. Then, an obviously surprised voice answered my question.

"Addy, honey, what are you doing up?" my dad said as he closed and relocked the study door, a move he unsuccessfully hid from everyone in the kitchen.

He rounded the corner and stopped in his tracks as he came face to face with Ethan and McIntyre. His mind feverishly worked to concoct some sort of what I was sure would be an outlandish reason for his very late arrival home as well as where he had been all night long. As I stood there looking at him, I realized I was hurt, hurt for the fact he left me alone at home after spending a week in the hospital. What kind of caring father would do something like that? A pang of sadness hit me as the memory of what we had seen in the book flashed across my mind: he's not my father, he's a liar and a bastard for lying to the people he supposedly loved.

"Uh, what's going on here? Why are all of you in the kitchen at 5 a.m.?" he questioned as he made a half-hearted attempt at looking at a watch he wasn't wearing.

Visibly shaken, I couldn't produce a single word, which made me angry at myself for letting him make me feel unsure of myself. Ethan, never one to hold back no matter who he was talking to, saw my expression and asked the question I couldn't vocalize.

"Why are we in the kitchen at 5am? The better question would be where in the hell have you been all night? Or better yet, where were you when Addy and I were attacked at the front door?" My father tried to blurt out something but Ethan cut him off with his continued interrogation. "Where were you when we had to call our principal to come and help us because you were nowhere to be found? Tell me that!"

Ethan would have continued to question my father relentlessly if it hadn't been for our principal, who reached out his hand and put it on his shoulder to calm him down before he did something rash. Ethan lowered his head and backed down the steps into the kitchen before he walked over to me and leaned against the island, his back facing my father and McIntyre. He just stared aimlessly out the window. I could hear and see him as he tried to control his breathing and always-short temper.

McIntyre and my father exchanged glances before McIntyre turned to us and asked us to excuse them while they had a little chat. Ethan and I walked directly past both of them without a single look and made our way upstairs to my room where I promptly slammed the door.

* * *

"Who do you think you are coming to the rescue of my daughter?"

"Who am I? I'm the one who has sworn to protect both of them against the forces of darkness, the same ones who want what they have. The ones who will pit them against one another, if they refused to be turned. Something you seem to have forgotten as of late."

I glared at Ed allowing my full range of emotions to show. Not long ago his whole life revolved around protecting Addy and Ethan, giving them both the normal life they deserved. Some had gone so far as to suggest death in the case they discovered the truth and their powers were awakened, something I was fairly certain had happened tonight, if they had found the book. Those same people had drawn a line in the sand and what once was gray had become very white and black for them, and one of those people was Ed.

"You've grown senile in your hundreds of years on this Earth. You're relishing in all of this aren't you? You been living life after life waiting to actually do what you were sworn to do, and now that there is the smallest smidgen of a chance it's happening, you're the knight coming to save the day. It's pathetic."

In the thirty years I had known Ed, I had never seen him act this way or threaten another person. I tried to remember that as I fought the urge to punch him in between the eyes with my clinched fist. Something had happened in the last week, and I very seriously doubted he would give up whatever it was very easily, if at all.

"Ed, stop it. What's going on with you? I've never seen you like this before. We're talking about your daughter for Christ's sake."

"Daughter? You know as well as I do, she's not mine, not really. She and Ethan are the offspring of the aberration of a so-called mother, Arabella. She and Ethan will do nothing but destroy everything our families have honored and struggled to keep secret for generations."

"There is no way Véronique feels the same way. Where is she? I want to talk to her. Maybe she can talk some sense back into you."

"You want to talk to Véronique? Then I suggest you get out a Ouija board and make a fool of yourself like everyone else who uses them."

I did not expect to hear those words come from Ed. Why would he say such a thing? They had been together for as long as I could remember. Since I had known them, they had reminded me of the relationship I had had with my wife so many years ago. Now a great sadness pressed down on me. He was throwing everything away in a single night and it infuriated me that he showed no remorse or honest care for his wife or daughter. I started back at him, demanding some kind of explanation.

"Dead? How was that possible? You had told all of us she was in France visiting family," I asked.

My reaction and questions enraged him, causing him to reveal more pieces of the puzzle without even realizing it. If she were dead, that could only mean one thing: Arabella had found a way to cross back over to the plane of the living: the murdered twins. It must have been some sort of ritual to break through the veil separating the limbo from the physical plane. If she were back, this meant the prophecy was true.

Everything predicted so many years ago crept off the pages and gave life to a power, which could destroy every living creature on the planet. The Blood Rock Prophecy had been set in motion, and we only had one chance to stop it.

"That old and dusty brain of yours starting to catch you up to date on what is actually happening? She's back and there's no way in hell she's going to let anyone keep those kids away from her. She may not know their true identities, but she's ingenious enough to find out before much longer. Just imagine what she'll do when she finds out she had twins, she'll . . ."

Ed choked saying the last part and coughed violently trying to catch his breath. I slapped him on the back a couple of times hoping it would help, but things only worsened. His body crumpled and writhed painfully as he cupped his hands around his throat. His eyes watered as he struggled to breathe.

"Ed, are you okay?" I said as his gasps for air grew more violent and he knocked over a chair as he fell back against the wall. "I'm calling 911." I reached in my pocket and unlocked my phone to call the EMTs, but there was no signal. That wasn't possible. I ran over and picked up the landline, but it was dead too.

Addy and Ethan rushed into the kitchen, when they heard a loud crash coming from the kitchen.

"One of you, call 911 now." But neither of them had a signal either.

Ed banged his head against the wall repeatedly as we stood there like an audience witnessing a macabre scene from a Shakespearean play. Then, as quickly had the choking begun, it stopped. Ed stood there in a haze facing all of us, expressionless. Every blood vessel in his eyes had burst and he stared at us from behind blood-tinted eyes, his black and empty pupils looking like an abyss in a red sea. His hands dropped down to his sides and his entire body unnaturally relaxed in the standing position. His blue-purple bloated face deflated and small bloody teardrops oozed and sluggishly seeped from the interior corners of his eyes followed by similar droplets exiting his ears. I and the two kids watched in horror as Ed's body physically died in front of us. None of us able to do anything to stop the gruesome show before us. Slow and steady gurgles surged up from his throat and into his mouth before escaping as mucous ridden coughs through his lips. At first, we were all too terrified to notice what the coughs actually were until Addy, herself, gasped and explained.

"He's talking. He's trying to tell us something."

Impossible. I thought she must have been trying to rationalize what she was seeing happen to her father, until I heard what sounded like a word too. He was talking and it became clearer as he continued.

"You cannot hide from me. You cannot stop me. They tried to do so eighteen years ago and failed. I have returned, and I will have my revenge against all of you. I am everywhere and nowhere thanks to my followers, like Ed. My dear children, how long I've waited to find you and be your mother. I never imagined twins, but it makes this all the more sweet and delicious. It won't be much longer before we meet at last. Mommy's home."

Arabella. She had put a hex on Ed and made him a Shadowling, a spirit she used to control a person's body, so she could control and manipulate without getting her hands dirty. She could be just outside or miles away watching everything that was happening from behind Ed's blood filled eyes. Finally, the sorrowful pneumonia-sounding gasps ceased, and Ed's once possessed body slumped and rolled to the floor with a heavy, penetrating thud.

"We've got to get the hell out of here now." I said.

I grabbed both kids by the wrists and pulled them with me as I ran out the front door, but before exiting the house, I remember the book. I told both of them to wait as I turned and kicked the solid mountain ash door open and off its hinges, sending wooden fragments sailing through the air. I invaded Ed's privacy and knocked over his desk and other relics between the bookshelf and myself where the book lay hidden. Using my elbow, I broke the glass door protecting his ancient texts and, more importantly, the book, which would reveal everything to Addy and Ethan, if it had not already done so. I picked up a brass reading lamp from the floor and pummeled the wooden back of the bookcase with it until final the panel cracked and released. Hurriedly, I grabbed the book and returned to the entryway. Both of them gawked at me in disbelief.

"But how did you . . .?" Addy asked.

"I'll explain later. Get in the car."

I pressed the accelerator to the floor and for the second time in only a few hours, the old seventeenth century old farmhouse fell victim to an assault of gravel. No one said a word as we pulled on to the road leading to town or when we saw Salem fading away in the rearview mirror. I held the steering wheel firmly in my hands and glanced down at old book resting in my lap as the sign asking us to come back to Salem soon blurred past in the dying pale yellow of a street light.

For the first time in my life, I saw the last of the town I had helped to colonize and had called home for over three hundred and fifty years. The life we had all come to know was over. Now, it would be a fight to survive, a fight that would be pointless unless the two of them were together and learned to use and control their magic. In my mind, I hoped the details of the prophecy weren't as rigid as they appeared or else drastic measures would have to be taken to save us all.

Chapter 18

The Blood Rock Prophecy

FOR WHAT SEEMED LIKE ages, we rode in silence in the car as we made our way along Interstate 93 towards New Hampshire. It was a familiar route and one my family and I used to take when I was little for weekend getaways in the White Mountain National Forest. It was only a little over two hours away but as I stared aimlessly out the window I couldn't help but dwell on what had just happened at Addy's house and this morning in her kitchen. The person we had known, as her father for our entire lives was dead, killed by someone claiming to be our mother who after eighteen years of being exiled to another realm was back to use us in her unending desire for revenge against everyone we seemed to know. For the first time, I became aware of whey I had suffered a long seeded sense of separation between my parents and myself. Since my childhood, my gut had been hinting at the very revelation I had just witnessed. Never again would I ignore such a feeling.

* * *

I felt numb sitting in the back of McIntyre's car as we headed some place far away from Salem, far away from normal. Nothing felt right anymore after everything I had just experienced. Nothing made sense, and I wasn't sure it ever would. How could all of this be happening? Only a couple of weeks ago, I was starting my senior year and getting ready to finish high school on a high note before starting Harvard. Now Harvard looked like a faraway dream of someone who had now become indifferent to the world around her. I knew I had Ethan, but I had the sense of being utterly alone and abandoned by everyone I thought I could trust. My gut had warned me of something I wasn't able to understand until now and as painful as it was to acknowledge the truth, I would rather endure the pain than go back to living the lie I had endured for almost eighteen years. I had to figure out how to make sense of what was happening to my family and me.

* * *

I headed towards the only place I could think of where we all might be safe, at least for a few days. I prayed the refuge deep within the White Mountains still existed because there was no other place I could think of where we could regroup and carry out what had to be done before Arabella found us, which she would do. The speed with which everything had progressed had taken me by surprise, and I desperately tried to sort the over turned filing cabinet that was my mind while also trying to keep the car on the road to avoid someone reporting me as a drunk driver to the state patrol. My focus continued to sway back and forth as we made our way north out of Massachusetts and into New Hampshire. They both needed to know the absolute truth, and they both needed to trust in me and know I would protect them no matter what the cost to me or the life I had built with Ayden. Finally, I looked my destiny in the face, and I would not let Arabella and her followers derail me from the path for which I had been chosen and charged with protecting and seeing to fruition as preordained in the Blood Rock Prophecy.

"Guys, I know you're exhausted, but it's time for you know to exactly what Ed meant back there. It's time you knew about the prophecy, the prophecy foretelling your births and destiny."

At first neither of them said a word. But, knowing the truth triumphed over any level of exhaustion they might have.

"Did either of you know about the book?" I asked.

"Yes, we both did, but before that, I had a dream about it when I was in the hospital," Addy admitted.

"I only just found out about it tonight," Ethan added.

"Did you open it?"

"Yes, after Addy told me about her dream, I helped her look for it, and when she found it, we opened it to see if what she had seen in her dream might actually be inside it."

"What did you find? Did anything happen when you touched it?"

"How do you know about all of this? Who are you, really?"

"I'm someone who's here to help and protect you, now answer the questions, please." Keeping my frustrations and fears at bay proved more difficult than I had imagined. The last thing I wanted to do was alienate myself from them, especially after what they had just learned about the lies that had ruled their lives for the past seventeen years, but I had a duty to uphold and no matter my personal feelings, I had to do what was asked of me so many years ago.

"All we found was a family tree, which changed everything we thought we knew about our families. We saw the name Arabella, who it seems gave birth to us and is our real mother," Addy replied.

"We will talk about her in a moment. Did the book react to you at all when you touched it?"

"This is going to sound really strange. Nevertheless after tonight, I'm not sure what isn't out of the ordinary anymore. When we both touched it, it began to glow and that's when the family tree came to life and revealed the truth," Ethan added as he looked out the window trying to make sense of what he had just admitted out loud.

The prophecy foretold the book, the grimoire of the de la Fontaine family, would recognize and activate the powers of the child born to unbelievable Wiccan and Native magic, which until this point none of us were really sure what was meant by "Native." We had also always assumed there would only be one child born to fulfill the prophecy, but again, tiny details hid themselves in the inexact art of translation and interpretation. No one knew what to expect from twins especially when pondering the distribution of power seeded in the pages of the grimoire. Who would have what powers and to what extent would they reach? We had to get to The White Mountains to know more about how the prophecy might now play out seeing as almost all of our preconceived notions about it were in flux.

"The fact the grimoire, the book you found, glowed and unveiled the truth about your family means you are the ones, the ones described in the Blood Rock Prophecy who would wield immense natural magic rooted in Wiccan and Native beliefs. You both have no idea how long people of both Wiccan and Native American heritage have waited for and dreaded the acknowledgement of the prophecy."

Simultaneously, both Ethan and Addy looked at me. "What do you mean dreaded? We don't even want to be the fulfillers of a damn prophecy. Why would anyone be scared of us?"

"The prophecy tells of a child born of a Wiccan mother and a Native father who would be able to tap into the two sides of natural magic, Wiccan and Native. Having this ability, would allow them to control every magical gift and ability ever known to exist. I'm sure you can understand why someone, magical or not, might be reluctant to embrace such a person imbued with unlimited power. Because of this, no Wiccan-born woman was allowed to conceive a child with a Native man in order to prevent the prophecy from coming to life."

Addy leaned through the two front seats and looked out at the rising sun reflected off the front windshield. "That sounds a little ridiculous, but sure, I think Ethan and I could understand that, but neither of us knows jack about magic and until tonight, thought it was only something used to sell books and produce blockbuster movies."

"Few people have gotten it right and because of that there exist more misinformation than truth about the supernatural. Most mortals see the supernatural every day, but refuse to acknowledge its existence. For centuries, it has been forbidden by all magical and supernatural beings to use magic openly without facing life-altering consequences, like being stripped of their powers or even worse, death."

Ethan chimed in, "Speaking of misinformation, I think we deserve to know who this Arabella woman is, why you seem to be afraid of her and why you say you're meant to protect us."

"As you saw in the book, Arabella is your biological mother and the twin sister of the woman who raised you Addy. Since her childhood, she had a predilection for the more powerful and darker side of magic. She and your mother were very close and when they were eighteen, they left France for the States to focus on the Craft and better control their natural gifts. Against the wishes and warnings of the High Priest of the Salem Coven and the Shaman of the local Wampanoag tribe, Arabella had a secret affair with Daniel, the son of the Shaman and your biological father. She knew of the prophecy outlined from her magical heritage and the traditions passed down by the tribe. She longed for nothing more than to fulfill it by giving birth to a child born of both magical bloodlines, which is what she did by being with Daniel." I shifted in my seat before continuing with the story. The next part had to deal with the night both of them were conceived.

"And?" they both asked. In my concentration on the road and in telling the story, I had failed to notice how intently they both stared at me as I detailed in a very matter of fact manner, their family secrets.

"Sorry. Knowing about the prophecy and fueled by her longing for more power, it's believed, though not certain, Arabella arranged her relationship with Daniel in order to conceive a child born to both sides of magic. She was drawn to the place of your conception hoping she might actually be the person to fulfill the prophecy. Unfortunately, she was right."

"Okay, that's a little bit of TMI, but you can't stop there. Where did they, you know?"

"The Blood Rock on the Achachak River. According to the prophecy, the rock itself holds great energy and functions as a vortex of mystical energy between the realms of the living and spirits."

Doubt and sarcasm dripped from Addy's voice when she ask, "So you're telling me out of all the places in the entire world, Salem is home to a mystical rock? I'm sorry, but that's ridiculous. Where is proof of any of this?"

"Agreed." Ethan shared.

"There are hundreds of supernatural vortices throughout the world, but they are cloaked by ancient magic and finding one requires the spilling of human blood. And where she is concerned taking another's life compares to running to the store for bread. She's evil, manipulative and will stop at nothing to influence you both into joining her."

"Doubtful," they both chided in unison again.

"You say that now, but you'd be surprised at what she can do when she uses just a small amount of her powers."

"And this man, Daniel? Where is he?" Addy inquired with genuine concern on her lips.

I chose my words carefully as I tried to explain the mystery surrounding their father. Basically, Daniel had disappeared after his father and the elders from the coven had helped him to see the deceit being sewn by Arabella in her insidious attempts to draw greater power from the Ether, the magic surrounding both planes of existence. Everyone, including her own sister, believed she convincingly played the part of a woman in love as she carved out her plan in the blood of countless animal and several human sacrifices. For the conception to work, I outlined how she had had to use human blood at the site of the Blood Rock in order to access its power and open a portal between the two realms. The conduit between the living and the dead allowed spirits to ensure the conception of a baby born of both supernaturally gifted familial lines. In an act of complete blasphemy, Arabella had proudly proclaimed her desire to give up the coven's form of magic and focus her talents on the more addictive and darker side of sorcery. She flaunted this to her fellow coven members without any semblance of regret or worry at what she had possibly set into motion. Not even Daniel knew of the pregnancy or her plans to try and fulfill the prophecy. Openly, she belittled and berated their wish to practice what she called "weak" natural white magic and did not shy away from telling them she would find someone to help her in discovering how to perfect the practice of the dark arts. As a consequence, the coven members and even her sister, along with the spiritual leaders of the Wampanoag tribe, exiled her from Salem forever. After that, no one knows where she went until she returned nine months later to publicly show off what she had done and to own the fact she had gotten pregnant in order to become increasingly more powerful.

Ethan looked back at me after having watched the early morning landscape pass by for miles, "they tricked her and took her babies, took us, didn't they?"

"Yes, but how did you know that?"

"We saw it happen in a vision. We saw them restrain her and cut us out of her belly," Addy said from the backseat.

A response failed to form on my lips and for almost an hour, we sat in silence as the flat ground rose higher and higher littered with evergreens and snowcapped mountains accentuated by the sun shone along the horizon. Both of them sat deep in thought, no doubt going over the immense amount of information they had been given tonight, which reset everything they thought they had known about their lives and what their futures would now possibly hold. I wished I could peek inside their minds, know what they needed to hear, but I sat silent feeling guilty for being the one to uproot them. It should have been someone close to them, but no one matching that description existed any longer.

As the sign announcing Pinecrest was only thirty miles away zoomed by outside, Addy, from the back of the car, said she had two more questions she needed answered.

"Seriously, you only have two? I don't even know where to begin with mine." Ethan retorted.

"Okay. Let's hear them."

"One, I'd really like to contact my mom. Do you know when I might be able to do that? And two, you still haven't answered how you know all of this and why you are 'our protector.'"

"As far as your mother, I know exactly what you know from Ed. He said she was in France, but I can't verify or contradict that. Sorry."

"Okay, and the other thing?"

"I was chosen and accepted the role as your Guardian in 1650 by one of your ancestors."

"1650? Are you serious? That would make you almost four hundred years old!"

"Please tell me you're being serious and this isn't another fabrication of the 'so-called' truth," Ethan added.

"I swear on the lives of my wife and children that I am your Guardian and have been since a stormy fall night over one hundred years before the American Revolution when I agreed to be. You guys have been through a lot tonight and heard more than your fair share of new revelations about you and your families. You should probably try and get a little sleep before we reach our destination."

"And just where is that?" Addy quipped.

"A safe place hidden deep within the White Mountains out of sight and the reach of mortals and most supernaturals."

"Like Arabella?" Ethan asked.

"Let's hope so."

* * *

To say I was suffering from information overload would be the overstatement of the century. I couldn't help but think back to my afternoon in the park and my encounter with Tesicqueo. There had to be some sort of connection between what I saw during my vision quest and everything that had just happened at Addy's house. I leaned my head against the window and let my eyes scan the increasingly mountainous terrain jetting by in green and grey blurs. Everything that passed before my eyes brought back memories of a much happier and innocent time. A time before lies tarnished the very life I thought I had. Just at the moment I was beginning to finally accept things about myself, I was bombarded with uncertainties and lies, which threatened to throw me back into the proverbial closet which I never wanted to see the inside of again. I knew I owed it to myself to be honest with myself but that was proving easier said than done. If only I could talk to Tesicqueo and ask him what I should do and who I should trust. Tears of anger and frustration formed in my eyes, which really pissed me off. I did not cry. I did not play to the stereotypes plaguing society about "the gays." Who was I, really? A freaking witch fulfilling some stupid ancient prophecy? A lacrosse player getting ready to get out of a small town and start college? A gay teenager finally dealing with knowing himself for the first time in his life? Or was I simply a "nobody" who was destined to tread water in the sea that is life for all eternity?

My clinched fist gleamed white as it propped up my head against the passenger side window demonstrating to the outside world how very frustrated and "done" I was with all of this crap. I wanted to put my fist through the window and escape into the natural nothingness zipping by outside, but what would that accomplish? Oddly, for the first time in my life, despite the craziness that dominated it at the moment, I felt I was on the right path. And to make things even better, I wasn't as alone as I had once thought. I had Addy, my best friend and recently discovered twin sister, and Principal McIntyre who exuded confidence in his belief he was here to protect us against anything, which might be a threat. Then there was Tesicqueo, who I unquestionably trusted, but didn't really know or even really know how to contact without being bitten by a snake. As I zoned out while looking out the window, I was caught off guard by tears of frustration pooling in my eyes. Hoping to avoid drawing attention to myself, I faked a sneeze and used the sleeve of the borrowed sweatshirt of Principal McIntyre to clear my face of any telling evidence. I felt like a child again and was dying to ask the age-old question, "are we there yet?" but I kept my mouth shut and slipped into a restless sleep.

* * *

Get some rest? How in the world can I get some rest after everything that just blew up in my face and in my life? Ethan had gotten intensely quiet, which meant he was thoroughly pissed at all the "stuff" that had just been dumped all over us like hot fudge on a sundae except in this case, we were the thing melting and suffocating. I should be stressing about some test or essay and not about being endowed with magical powers, which I still found a little difficult to believe. I desperately wanted to talk to my mom, Véronique. Surely, she would know what to say and would be really forthcoming with information about all of this. I truly hoped she was in France visiting family, but something in my gut made me hesitate.

I pushed the thought out of my mind. There was only so much a person could take in the span of several hours and thinking my mother might be dead wasn't one of them. I leaned back and let my body slump into the seat before actually laying down across it. I wanted the answers now or I wanted a way to discover them for myself. After everything we had heard, the book was the first thing to come to mind as far as a source I could use to know more about Ethan and myself. I hoped after we arrived at wherever we were going, we'd have the chance to study the book for ourselves. I mean if we were the ones described in the prophecy, surely we were owed the opportunity to know more about it and more importantly prove to those who doubted our true intentions, that we were good people. In the end, we are just two teenagers who never wanted any of these supernatural things in our lives. Fighting to keep my eyes open, I wondered if going to college was really too much to ask for.

* * *

The road laughed at and badgered me as we continued up Interstate 93 towards Pinecrest and our safe haven buried deep within the forest of the White Mountains. I had made this trip many times, most often with Ayden, but this time it was grueling and like a small child, I was ready to get to our destination. I looked down at my phone for the one-hundredth time to see that I had still not received any sort of message or call from Ayden. I wracked my brain to think of places he might be and what could have been his motivation in attacking. Nothing in recent days, weeks or even months had pointed to anything supernatural being involved. He hadn't shown any signs of being a Shadowling or under the influence of any other type of magic, white or dark. There had to be some sort of logical explanation for his erratic behavior.

Hopefully, once we met with the Rowan Coven and the Pennacook Tribe, things would start to become clearer for all us. In many ways, I was just as in the dark as the kids, which made me incredibly nervous. The la Croix family had known the de la Fontaine family for centuries before establishing the Rowan Coven apart from the older order tied to Salem after the witch trials. Surely they would have an insight into the prophecy and how to better interpret what had been written centuries ago. If not, the very real possibility existed of Addy and Ethan being subjected to interrogation, pain and torture, and possibly even killed if members and believers of other covens discovered the prophecy had been fulfilled and the child, in this case children, had been born. Unfortunately, in my experience, witches had proved to be much more stubborn than their Native American counterparts in looking at the two-sides of any situation before acting or condemning someone to certain exile or death.

Hazy lights and a screaming horn shook me from my thoughts, and I swerved to keep the Tahoe on the right side of the road. Thankfully, neither of them made a single move showing they had even registered the sudden jerking of the SUV. I lowered the window and the crisp mountain air slammed into my face and zapped my dulled senses back to life. With the air swooshing through the window, I breathed in the alpine air deeply and let it fill my lungs completely before slowly releasing a relaxing and revitalizing breath. We were in the middle of nowhere, and I should have felt safe, yet as long as I knew Arabella lurked around basically every tree in Salem and possibly farther out, thanks to her magic, I would not fully relax until we were hidden and safe.

In explaining everything to Addy and Ethan, I had intentionally left out the fact both of them might be forced to separate and learn to use their gifts separately. I wasn't sure what the elders from the coven and tribe would decide in regards to their supernatural education and I didn't want to unnecessarily upset them. Events had accelerated much more rapidly than I had ever imagined, and I struggled to even think about the decision, which may be asked of me after we got there. In all honesty, I had sworn to protect the child born of the prophecy, but I had also been charged with protecting the world from that child, should he or she, or both, follow the dark path to magic and threaten the lives of mortals and other supernaturals.

It would not be an easy choice, but it was one I would make when and if the time came. And in the end, would it truly be a question of life or death?

Chapter 19

August, 1936

UPON ARRIVING AT THE massive citadel, we entered the enormous edifice by crossing a stone bridge, which crossed over a dried up moat and led into a cobblestone courtyard bordered on all sides by the limitless vertical walls of the old fortress. Flowers filled out the lines of the square creating a very colorfully symmetrical and surprising contrast to the hard stony features of the edifice.

A very stern and pale looking woman in her sixties came out of a heavy wooden door located to our right and walked towards us. A terribly simple dress clung to her. A sea of black draped her, exacerbating her skeletal features. My muscles tensed and I carefully stepped a bit closer to my father. Her expressionless spectacle wearing face gave me pause and I instantly thought of my primary school English teacher and the ruler she kept permanently affixed to her hand. For some reason or another, she pulled my father aside and talked to him in private before she even acknowledged my presence. Then the sullen character guided us into the interior rooms and hallways of the fortified stronghold. Our footfalls echoed throughout the medieval corridor and neighboring rooms as we proceeded down the long foreboding hallway draped with a myriad of flags and banners representing the various kingdoms and families in this region of France. The majority of families celebrating and relishing their Protestant roots. Just before reaching the end of the central hall, we stopped and the wrinkled woman drew a heavy iron key from her dress pocket and, with a loud clanking and grinding sound, unlocked the large set of ornate iron studded wooden doors bearing down on us. We crossed the threshold and into a remnant of an ancient world.

The western sun bled through stained glass windows, which were framed by boulders mined from the rocky western French coast, painted the whole of the room in a kaleidoscope of colors. Because the chateau had been built in the fourteenth century, the thick stonewalls worked perfectly to keep the interior of the enormous room cool against the constant heat baking the coast of the port city of La Rochelle. The refreshing air was a very welcomed reprieve after riding for hours in our car across the French countryside in the oppressive August inferno.

The wooden supports had been steeped in a thick concoction of cigar smoke and liquor over the centuries, so much so that one might believe a smoldering fire breathed in the enormous hearth, complete with historically appropriate wrought iron fire tending tools. I hated the overbearingly smoky smell of it, but I had to admit it added to an intangible elegance and mystique perfuming the centuries old library and study. Hundreds, maybe thousands, of books, from first editions of Rousseau and Voltaire to the latest French and English bestsellers, clung to the minute space they had next to one another on the overstuffed wall-scaling bookshelves made of mountain ash.

Ordinarily, visitors were not permitted to search through the varying versions of history lining the walls, but because we were distant relatives of those who had constructed the chateau, my father and I had been given special access to the secrets and enigmas cloistered within the walls. However, we only had two hours, of which, only thirty minutes remained. For months, my father had promised to show me this place and we were finally here. I could barely contain my excitement and curiosity about what might be found.

The both of us had been pouring over books, letters and journals for any clues about our family's escape from a very Catholic France for a Protestant England before finally settling in the English colonies in America. I carefully opened the next to last book in my pile of dusty well-worn books. As I gingerly turned the pages, my eyes fell upon the very information we had come here to uncover.

"Papa, I think I've found something!"

My father left the book he had been scouring for over an hour and rushed to look at what I had found.

"C'est formidable Étienne!"

The once concealed and conflicting truths about the escape of our ancestor Véronique Josette d'Orléans unfolded before us in a series of letters and journal entries.

"Finalement, on va comprendre ce qui s'est passé." My father shook with excitement as he began to read the actual account of what had transpired, every detail written in her own hand almost three hundred years ago. My father was right, after centuries of not knowing, we were about to learn of something the Elders had tried to keep safeguard since the tales and whispers of the prophecy had begun, and the child who might possibly bring an end to all we knew.

16 September 1619

I write this letter from a secret chamber in the home of our neighbor, Guillaume de la Croix. He and his sister have been so kind to me in recent months. After suffering continually, I have taken it upon myself to escape the confines of my home and family with the ancient book, which I discovered outlined my true genealogical history, a history that describes the brutal and incredulous murdering of my entire family. I am the only living member of my family left and I must ensure I would not be the last.

The family who took me does not care to understand me and have made it ever so clear I am not wanted in their perfect and privileged lives. His sole purpose of my abduction, being a necessity born out of the act of executing my true family. Thankfully with the secret help of Guillaume, I have procured a carriage to take me from Paris to the port of La Rochelle. He has assured me I will be in safe hands, but that the journey will be a long and arduous one. I have no doubts, with my talents. I will be able to endure whatever obstacles this journey might place in my path, in my destiny.

His sister and fellow believer, Madeleine, has graciously agreed to accompany me on this journey into the unknown. We are to stay at the home of her cousin, Duc Louis Robert de la Fontaine, while we await passage to England before hopefully continuing on to the new lands across the sea, a land, where I hope to start a new life with others who understand me. As saddened, as I am that Guillaume cannot accompany us to England and beyond, I understand his reasons and find comfort in the part of him I carry with me.

Marie Françoise d'Orléans

22 September 1619

We successfully made our escape from Paris on the 17 of September without commotion or delay. However, I must say neither of us breathed easily until we had left the medieval walls of Paris far behind us. I cannot say enough how much I appreciate the companionship of Madeleine in this endeavor. I do not think I would have been so resolute in leaving had she not been willing to risk her own life and future by coming with me. We had sat hand in hand since we left her home and now, for the first time, we dared to smile slightly and utter a few words for the first time in hours, even though our fear persisted.

We both impatiently awaited the freedom we hoped to find in the New

World, which lay on the other side of the world. We hoped that there, we would be able to openly and freely practice our faith, unlike in the Catholic ruled lands of France. For centuries, people had relied on us for medicine, counsel and as conduits to the other side, but now the Church sought to destroy our peaceful and earthly religion, a religion that predated their Christian beliefs. We did not seek evil nor did we want to harm others. We only longed to continue our heritage as practitioners of white natural magic. Unfortunately, those who had sought to practice and cast dark magic had ruined our peaceful and spiritual reputation and brought the Church's wrath upon us.

For hours as we watched the lush French countryside as we made our way towards Orléans, the origin of my birth name, and the first stop on our journey to the coast. Throughout this first stage of our trip, Madeleine and I conjured images of what we thought might be waiting for us on the other side of the world and how we might be able to freely express ourselves as witches in a new coven. The majority of our fellow practitioners had either already taken refuge or had been violently burned for heresy in accordance with Church law. We deeply hoped and prayed religious freedom would soon find us.

Finally, we arrived in Orléans under the subterfuge of night, which was to be our plan of travel until we arrived at La Rochelle. Most privileged families had relatives living in the principal cities of France like Orléans, Bordeaux, and Tours; therefore, we had to be particularly careful while being in such places. Thankfully, La Rochelle was in a region of France where Protestantism had dominion over Catholicism. Perhaps there we would find a moment of solitude and peace before the next leg of our journey.

* * *

So far, the carriage driver has seen to our every need with grace and kindness. I will never be able to thank Guillaume enough for all he has done for his sister and me. We stop every couple of hours, when the driver believes we are at our safest, so that we may stretch our legs and attend to other business as well as take a few moments to recite a protective incantation. I have continued to read the book while my sweet and dear companion naps off and on in the carriage. I have not yet told Madeleine about the book and I'm not sure if I will. I feel conflicted about divulging its existence to anyone, even to her or to Guillaume. Allowing someone to discover its secrets would most certainly put my life and that of my true family in more danger than we already are.

We arrive in Orléans tonight, and I look forward to resting without being in constant motion.

27 September 1619

I have not written in several days due to an unexpected danger we had the misfortune of encountering in Orléans. One of the stable boys where we were seeking refuge recognized us and informed a member of my extended family, who immediately spread the word of our being in town. It appeared my parents had sent riders out with information regarding my escape. I found their burning desire to hinder me from realizing my path relentless but foolish. I would never again allow them to deny me my birthright. Due to this unforeseen obstacle, we hid for several nights in various barns and stables during the long days until nightfall when it was safer to move about and make our way of out the medieval city. Guillaume had been correct in his assumption of possible danger, one I had initially tried to dismiss.

For our journey through the countryside surrounding Orléans, Madeleine and I found it necessary to disguise us as milkmaids to avoid suspicion, as well as, familial spies spread throughout the countryside. I knew with certainty that they did not care about me, but instead, wanted the book and what it contained returned. It held great power, which could be used to bring about great good or great evil. Toying with such powers would be ill advised for anyone who was not familiar with casting and conjuring, like them.

Our ever generous and protective driver has informed us our next stop will be in Tours, which comes as a relief as neither Madeleine or myself have family residing there. We hope to regain some of the time we have lost during our adventure in the Orléans. The only misgiving for this next step of the journey finds itself in the lack of a reliable road. It may take us longer than we had hoped to make our way across the dense forest and farmland that lie before us.

However, I hope in the knowledge I am fulfilling a destiny from which nothing will keep me.

3 October 1619

After a grueling journey in the rain and along barely visible roads, we have safely arrived in Tours without garnering much attention from the local people. It is the strangest thing, as I do not understand anything being said by the people around us. Never in my life has such a language passed by my ears, like most Parisians, I foolishly assumed the entire country spoke French as we did. Without understanding a single word of the alien language spoken around us, we, at first, panicked in regards to getting food, provisions, and shelter, but our constant companion and driver was thankfully familiar with this foreign tongue, at least enough to communicate our needs. It appeared only the wealthiest people of Tours spoke French and knowing this, helped us to stay within the confines of the village.

Despite the lack of effective communication on our part, the people of this village, with their strange customs and dress, were delightfully pleasant and accommodating, and a part of me hated to see their unique concept of culture fade away behind us as we left their borders. The heavens yet again rumbled and presented us an unsteady sky, which soon pelted us with large heavy droplets of rain.

The farther we leave Paris behind us, the happier and freer I feel; however, the seed of uncertainty as to what drastic measures my family might explore plagued my thoughts and dreams. I meditated to rid myself and aura of these nagging thoughts, yet every day they returned to taunt *me. To further steady my mind and spirit, I focused on reaching La Rochelle, then England and finally the Americas in my mind's eye, knowing freedom and happiness lie in my future. As for now, I marvel at a France I never knew existed.*

Even in the rain, every blade of the green grassy fields vibrated and exalted life, reveling in the replenishment they received from Mother Nature. The animals in the fields gazed upward in instinctual amazement and I appreciated the simple lesson of thankfulness at what our Mother gave us each and every day.

Perhaps one day in the future, I could return to my native country, if things progressed and the Church no longer extorted its domineering prejudices and . . . .

"Just what do you think you are doing?" The stone-faced woman bellowed as she stormed through the impenetrable looking doors.

Shocked by the intrusion, I looked at my father. He remained calm and composed despite the continued verbal attacks by the woman as she stomped her way over to us and our pile of books.

"How dare you disturb priceless books and artifacts in such a blasphemous manner! I want you both to leave this very instant!"

What in the world was she talking about? We had been invited and given permission to look through the library. I was profoundly confused by her tirade, and the accusations she was throwing at us. We weren't destroying anything. We were doing simple research on our family's heritage.

As soon as she reached the table where we had been reading the letters, she reached for the book I had found, but my father wrenched it away from her. He gave it to me and told me not to let go of it no matter what happened. Hearing this infuriated the woman, and she stepped back and raised her hands in the air, creating a gust of wind that blew loose papers and pages in all directions around the room and up into the rafters. She was a true witch, like us, but not of light and natural magic. Her power came from a place of hate and darkness.

Her eyes erupted in a shade of red so deep they appeared black.

"Étienne, go over there and hide under that table. Protect yourself my son and avert your eyes from this whirlwind of debris. Do not for any reason try and get involved with what you are about to hear. Protect the book and its secrets at all cost."

"You are a fool, François. Neither you nor your child will leave this room alive. As a member of the Sabbat du Cercle Noir, I will take back that book and the information contained within its pages about the prophecy."

My father looked back towards me and said, "Je t'aime. Close your eyes, mon cœur, and run as far away from France as you can when this is over."

I said nothing. Fear choked my words back down into my belly, and I closed my eyes as tightly as I could. The next minutes were filled with screams and explosions, which rang out like bombs in my tiny ears. Tables crashed onto the hard rock surfaces and books flew off the shelves banging into the furniture filling the rest of the room, their pages flittering through the air. I fought so hard not to cry, but failed miserably. I thought the blaring noises would never stop until suddenly there was nothing but silence. I was so scared to open my eyes that I almost ran for the door blindly, but I had to see my papa, no matter in what state he might have been.

However, I wasn't prepared for the carnage that lay before me. As the massive room came into view, all I could see was a battlefield populated with demolished books and splintered furniture. In the middle of the room, was my father, his motionless and bloody body facing in the opposite direction. For a terrifying moment, I did not see the woman, until a dripping sound drew my gaze upwards. There, I saw her, impaled on a long thick wooden spike, where a medieval banner had once hung. Thick rivets of blood oozed from her nose and belly splattering and staining the silvery rock floor and the delicately woven carpets beneath her.

I raced to my father's side, but it was too late. He lay there dead. His cloudy eyes wide open focused upward towards the wooden chapel-like ceiling. To my surprise, his face belayed no trace of fear. He just looked like my father. The strength and kindness of the same man I had loved throughout my thirteen years still shone through his lifeless eyes. I couldn't bring myself to look at the rest of his body, as I knew it was severely mutilated and contorted like a spring. I simply kissed his forehead and closed his eyes before getting to my feet and beginning what he had told me in the last words he ever spoke. Not a single tear escaped in that moment, and in a few short minutes, I went from being a teenager to a man. A man, dedicated to protecting the secrets of our family and destroying every last member of the Sabbat du Cercle Noir. In that moment, I committed myself to uncovering everything I could about a prophecy so dangerous to supernatural and mortals alike that my father had been murdered.

Chapter 20

Rowan

THE FRIGID WIND RACED through the tops of the pines surrounding the consecrated enclosure buried deep within the White Mountain National Forest of New Hampshire. The invisible force of the wind beat out childish musical tones against the pane of my window, as I sat crossed-legged on my bed with my back against the wall reading an article on my MacBook for a paper I was writing on the transition of pagan worshippers to Christianity in Constantinople. My bedroom in the Pinecrest house exhibited the angst of my teenage years when I hated the entire world. Posters of death metal bands plastered the walls and all of the furniture had been defiled with paints varying in hues from grayer black to darker black. I didn't technically live here anymore, but I owed it to my parents and myself to take the room back to a more innocent and less aggressive me. Throughout all of the existential teenage crap in my life at that time, I never stopped loving my parents or telling them everything I was up to when I wasn't at home, unbeknownst to my friends. After all, I couldn't have been too bad, considering I graduated as the valedictorian of my class. Now, my room at our coven's encampment reflected the newer, more educated, and worldly me. The one who dedicated his life to the Craft and his welcomed familial obligations. I loved our home deep within the mountains more than the one we kept in Pinecrest, which was used to pacify the humans who were increasingly clueless about all things supernatural. Our home at the coven's encampment was a truer picture of who we were as individuals and as a family. The coven gave us life and our entire family a sense of belonging and faith.

Our coven, the Rowan Coven, had established a "home" here late in the seventeenth century after the explosion of hysteria and subsequent witch trials, which killed numerous innocents until they ended in May 1693. The word rowan comes from the Sorbus americana, or American Mountain Ash, which provides us with protection because it keeps dark magic and those who would do us harm from entering the protected circle outlining the coven boundaries. This is why we adopted the word Rowan to the name of our coven, as a sign of safeguard and a warning to others.

Our ancestors had escaped to this area and these woods to create a new coven far away from the troubles abounding in Salem and start a new life masked by the building farms, trading with the Abenaki peoples and working in the sawmills, which would appear in force in the earlier part of the 19th century. The coven's close relationship with the Abenaki tribe dated back to when we first came to this part of New Hampshire. The coven founders and the Abenaki people quickly established a long standing and deeply rooted friendship based on the love of the natural world and magics. If it had not been for their guidance and knowledge of how to survive, everyone would have perished soon after arriving to this place and none of us would be here to tell about our ancestry.

In order to maintain secrecy, most of us lived double lives: the mortal-side in Pinecrest and the Wiccan-side deep in the forest where we could be protected and safe to practice our Craft. My father, Victor de la Croix worked as the town doctor as well as serving as a leader of the coven alongside my grandfather Étienne. My mother, Martine, taught in the local elementary school as well as teaching young witches about their heritage. She also kept a detailed account of all of the familial lines, which had created and sustained the coven over the centuries. My younger sister Julie, had just graduated from high school and unlike me, never cared for school and only ever did the bare minimum to pass her classes. Let's just say her collegiate focus and outlook was less than stellar, which was in stark contrast with her sometimes overzealous dedication to all aspects of the Craft. More often than not, she allowed herself to overindulge in her gifts for the short-lived glory of showing off to others. I, on the other hand, was a junior, studying religion and theology at Dartmouth University, just over an hour away in Hanover. As much as I loved school and university life, I visited my family as much as possible due to the rapidly failing health of my grandfather. All of my friends continually interrogated me about why I could never stay and party like I had freshman year, but, of course, I could not tell them it was because I had to practice my witchy powers with fellow witches. I had learned to come up with some pretty awesome excuses to satisfy their questions and sneak off to spend the time with my parents, grandfather, and fellow brother and sister witches. Above everything else, family has always come first and represented the most important aspect of my life and overall happiness.

My family's heritage reached back through the centuries to the beginning of the Renaissance in France where they used their influence and position to educate and open the minds of others. However, some people will never open their minds to inherent differences in people, and my ancestors found it necessary to immigrate to the English colonies via England in the mid-16th century, after fleeing from France with other Protestants, or Calvinists, during the backlash propagated by the Catholic Church after the revocation of the Edict of Nantes. After that, there were no longer any safe places in France for non-Catholics. For centuries, people like us were persecuted and suffered from discrimination or worse without reprieve, whether it be for being Protestants or Wiccan.

Upon arriving in the New World, we thought we had finally discovered a refuge in the Salem colony. The village was surrounded by exquisite natural beauty and magic nourished by a powerful supernatural vortex concentrated in a rock along the banks of a river the native peoples called the Achachak. However, less than seventy years after arriving in our supposed utopia, accusations were made and all supernaturals were thrown into the light for all to see. The majority of these claims were untrue, yet the damage had been done and we were forced to again flee a home and friends we had grown to love. After a month of surviving in the wilderness, we made it to the White Mountains. The Abenaki peoples and our lives had flourished for longer than they ever had before in the entire recorded history of my family and coven.

I truly consider myself fortunate to be part of something with such a rich history. Something I didn't appreciate when I was younger and something my sister still did not fully recognize or appreciate it. Now as a twenty year old, I sat here on my bed feeling like a frightened child. My granddad, Étienne, and Standing Bear, the Abenaki shaman, had guided our coven through dark and difficult times as well as helped us grow and hone our magical talents and gifts along with our deep relationship with the Abenaki people. Suddenly and without any apparent cause, my granddad had fallen very ill a couple of weeks ago in the middle of the night. Despite our knowledge of countless herbal remedies and potions, and my father's extensive medical background, nothing had been able to pinpoint the cause or alleviate his rapidly deteriorating condition. The laws created and passed down by our coven elders forbade the use of magic in healing the sick and bringing back the dead. For them, it was a way to keep us in touch with our very human and mortal sides of life. Anyone who attempted such blasphemous acts would be immediately excommunicated, but only after an elder had bound their powers. I understood the rules and abided by them, but they really blew when you were the one affected by a situation like that.

I both wanted to be with my granddad and wanted to stay away and forget what was happening to him. Lately, he had become delirious and did not even recognize us when we went to visit him, which hurt me more than the fact he was terminally ill.

Lost in my thoughts about him and what was going to happen, I realized I had read the same sentence more than five times and had no clue what it had to say about paganism. I closed my MacBook, set it at the end of my bed, and laid back. I stared at the ceiling until someone knocked on my door.

"Quinn?" my mom said as she slow opened the door and stuck her head inside. She was such an amazing person, and I was struck by it every time I saw her. She had shoulder-length straight brown hair with the kindest eyes of anyone I had ever met in my life. She had always told me "there's nothing we can't get through if we talk about it," and I believe it with all of my heart. Her smile always made me smile back even when I thought I hated the world or school stressed me to the edge of sanity.

"Come on in."

"We're going to go see your granddad. Do you want to come?"

Isn't that the million-dollar question? I didn't want to see him again wasting away and helpless after knowing him for twenty years as a strong and prominent man, but I owed it to him and myself to face my fears. The point of life is living it, and I had to do this for my family and myself.

"Yes, I'd like that."

She smiled at me and asked if I knew where my sister might be. Unfortunately, I had no idea where she might, which was more often than not the case for all of us.

"Maybe she's already there," I said trying to inject a little hopefulness.

I'm pretty sure it didn't work.

"Okay. I'll see you downstairs in a few minutes."

I sat up on my bed and decided to just stay at the haven for a couple of days and spend the time with him I wasn't able to do because of school. I grabbed my computer, books, notes, research, and my craft book. I really couldn't safely practice at school, so this would be the perfect time to multitask while visiting with my granddad. Some might say multi-tasking was a way to deny what was really going on with him and they would probably be right. Before walking out my bedroom door, I glimpsed at my desk and saw a family photo from when I was fourteen and my grandmother was still alive. I picked it up and put it in my bag. Maybe it would trigger his memory and make him lucid, if only for a minute.

The ride from our home in Pinecrest to the coven's haven took around forty-five minutes depending on the traffic, and by traffic, I mean moose and other large game that often used the roads to pass from the base of one mountain to the other, especially in the spring. Neither of us said much during the ride into the woods. What was there to say really? What would small talk accomplish? We were both too preoccupied with him to spit out meaningless words about more or less meaningless goings-on in our lives.

Without warning, my mother slammed on the brakes, and we both watched as hundreds of animals, big and small, darted from right to left across the road. The fear in their eyes created a fear in us. We have never seen animals react in such an extreme way and in such large numbers. They tripped over one another as they hurriedly bounced and leapt across the road in front of us. None of them even acknowledged the car when, all of a sudden, a buck crashed through the back passenger-side window. Shards of glass flew through the cabin of the car, and I quickly lifted my hands, palms outwards, and concentrated all of my energy and thoughts on the single action of repelling whatever came near us. Rippling waves of green energy and electrified air radiated from my hands and the broken glass changed direction and moved away from us. My mother, seeing an opportunity, slammed her foot on the gas and her hand on the horn and plowed through the raging torrent of wildlife without hesitation. Thankfully, my spell worked and protected us as we passed through the bizarre herd of animals to the other side.

I lowered my hands and the energy lessened, and reentered my exhausted body. My body caved into the seat, sweat trickling down my temples and brow.

"Oh my god, Quinn! Are you okay?"

"What was that? Why are they so freaked out?"

Behind us the flow of animals continued to pass over the road and into the woods on the other side. Our brief intrusion had done nothing to stop the unimaginable stampede of hooves, fur, claws, and antlers. I assured my mom I was fine and we continued, albeit a little more quickly, to our destination.

Our safe haven sat in the middle of an open field protected by various evergreens and mountain ash trees. It was also shielded from the outside world, aka mortals, by a continuous flux of magic, which created an invisible barrier that reflected the image of the forest, basically like a mirror. No one had ever been able to break the barrier and enter without being permitted by one of the members or Abenaki tribesmen. We finally reached the hidden entrance to the camp and faded into nothingness as we crossed the barrier.

Upon entering the encampment, I was always struck by the way it resembled a Swiss alpine village. The mountains soared upward in every direction one could see. Snow gripped the top of the mountains conspiring with nature as the temperatures began to lower and winter moved southward from Canada over the rolling lush green mountains. The wooden cabins, each unique to the family who lived there, spiraled outward from the center of our meeting places, a circular amphitheater protecting a deep fire pit, which consistently crackled and sparked with fiery purpose. The fire had been burning continuously for as long as I could remember. It had never been extinguished because it marked the very nucleus of our coven's power and spirituality.

Several people stood outside in various places talking amongst themselves as we passed through the veil protecting us. We were our own self-sustaining village, tucked away from the mortal world. My mom parked the car and several friends, after seeing the back window, walked over to make sure we were okay. All of the members worried about each other and were the extended family of each other, especially for those who no longer had parents and were younger. Just because we were magical did not mean tragic events had not marred our lives and, at times, taken away our loved ones. Even if it were too soon.

While my mom described what had happened on the road, I grabbed my bag and computer and headed across the meeting space in the direction of my granddad's house. He was bed-ridden and had been that way almost since the beginning of his curious illness. No one could understand the symptoms he was having. My aunt, Terre, had been taking care of him. Most of the cabins in the Rowan were earthen colors, shades of browns and greens that melded with the natural surroundings. However, my grandfather's cabin stood starkly different among the sea of natural colors. All four sides of his house were white washed and reminded me of Aunt Polly's house in Mark Twain's "The Adventure of Tom Sawyer." Like Tom, I had been tasked to help white wash my granddad's house during one of the hottest summers New Hampshire had ever had.

That summer the sun beat down on the ground with such veracity, my bare feet sizzled as I ran from my parent's cabin to visit my granddad. Like most spring and summer days, he stood outside the house in his garden taking care of the multitude of herbs and vegetables. I could always smell his house before I reached it. The smells floating over the fence and out from his house were always a great indication of the season and what might be served at our monthly coven meetings. He would spread his arms, and I would barrel into him, almost knocking him down. He had a solid, yet slim, build, and he would lovingly wrap his strong arms around me to toss me into the air. I had loved it when he did that, and I would scream and laugh loudly as my body broke free of gravity, and for a brief moment, I flew. Every visit found him smiling from ear to ear, happy to see us, even if we had seen him earlier in the day. That was my granddad, happy and always possessing a good and caring spirit. He and I had always been inseparable and looked so much alike, a lot of people, in the mortal world, thought he might be my dad. We both had wavy dirty blond hair, mine longer and shaggier than his more respectable coiffed look, that framed our round long faces and dark brown eyes. Our bodies were tall and lanky, both a blessing and a curse, especially when my legs grew faster than my body and I tended to be clumsier than I would have liked. That day, we whitewashed the entire house and then worked in his garden until it got too dark to see. Our hands were so soiled from the fresh dirt that they looked invisible in front of faces. We laughed and cajoled for hours until I passed out while looking out the window of my very own room upstairs. That summer of my tenth year was one of the best of my life. One I would never forget.

Walking up to his house now, the white had faded and his garden showed the signs of neglect. I took a deep breath and took a moment to prepare myself as I opened the door. Various lamps dimly lighted the inside of the house and only magnified the sadness my family, and I was already suffering. His small rustic kitchen smelled of nothing, just stale air mixed with the acrid odor of sickness. The furniture in his sitting and dining rooms sat listless from inattention. Nothing seemed vibrant or active as it had before all of this. It created an environment and space that was uncomfortably silent, and I feared I was too late to say goodbye to the most important man in my life. A small creak at the top of the stairs alleviated my fears as I saw my aunt coming down from his room, a smile on her face.

"Hey Quinn," she said as he hugged me. She always smelled of lavender and appropriately so, as she was never angry or out of sorts.

I smiled and asked how he was doing.

"He's actually having a fairly good day today. You should go on up and see him."

"Thanks. I will."

I climbed the stairs and crept into his room, being careful not to make too much noise in case he was sleeping. The image I saw of him as I turned from closing the door, sucked the life from my very soul, and I fought hard against the tears fighting to burst from my eyes. He lay in his wooden bed ashen like a weathered statue, his eyes fixated on a point in the ceiling, one I could not see. An old quilt held him down, pointless considering he couldn't move, and his long frail-looking arms extended down to his waist. He breathed steadily, but the time between breaths hinted at the lack of time he had left. I stepped over to the edge of his bed and sat in the chair next to him. It was still warm from aunt Terre, the only warmth in the entire house.

"Hey granddad, it's me, Quinn," I said as I reached out to hold his hand. His large, now aged and speckled hand rested in mine. His skin felt like fragile vellum paper, so delicate and thin. I feared holding it too tightly and hurting him. Everything about him was so vulnerable in this moment, and I told him I was here for him, and that I was so happy to see him. We "talked" for over an hour about school, my research (he was always interested in what I was studying), and a random assortment of other things, none of which was too important. Glancing over at the nightstand, I noticed he had the same photo of our family I had always kept with me. Everyone was so happy in the photo, and I, childishly, wished for the power to go back in time and relive all of the moments we had had like that.

"Quinn."

I turned my head to the door, but there was no one there.

"Quinn, my boy." It was my granddad.

"Granddad. But I thought you were, I mean I thought…"

"No need to worry about all that right now. You're here and that means more to me than anything in the world."

"I thought you were going to die. I thought we were going to lose you."

"I am dying, and I've made peace with that, but there are things you need to know."

"Don't say that. You can't die."

"We all die, my boy. Immortality is not natural, and no one should ever strive for it. It is our responsibility to make the most of this life and leave a legacy for those we love so that we actually never really die, but leave on in the memories of others."

All the strength in the world couldn't stop the tears that began to pour from my eyes. I didn't care if anyone came in and saw me crying. It didn't want him to die, to leave me and us.

"I need you to be strong and listen to the things I have to tell you. You must carry on my work and be there for those who are approaching. They need our help."

"What? Who's approaching? A threat?"

"They are coming here to seek protection from a great evil that could destroy everything we know and hold dear."

"Okay. I'm listening."

"Unfortunately, this old body and illness has stolen the physical strength I need to vocalize everything, so I'm going to perform a Merging in order to integrate my thoughts with yours."

"I've never heard of that. How's that possible?"

In as few words as possible, he explained to me a tradition and gift only few every generation possessed. These select people hold the power to cast the Merging and transmit their thoughts, knowledge and life experiences with another, but only at the end of their lives. However, after the "information" was transferred, the person casting the spell would slip into a deep coma and die within a day.

"You won't understand everything you hear and see at first, but with time and the help of the Elders and Abenaki shaman, you will know what you must do."

"But why me? I haven't even mastered everything I've been studying."

"You will and much sooner than you think. Guard and protect the Guardian and his charges. It is your destiny."

"Guardian…"

Before I could get another word out from my lips, the once resting hand of my granddad grabbed mine with such vigor and intensity, I could not budge. Our joined hands pulsed and a blue aura surrounded them before spreading out and encompassing his entire bedroom and us. Flashes of light began to explode in my mind's eye, and I quickly became overcome with a rapid stream of a life's worth of knowledge.

Arabella…blood…rock…grimoire…Guardian…twins…end… incredible…power…escape…family…death…warlock…Dane.

My grandfather's grip loosened, and his hand dropped to the bed. I gasp for air. I felt like I had been underwater for too long. My lungs burned for oxygen. I sat back in the chair completely exhausted and overwhelmed by emotions and memories. My granddad lay motionless in the bed with his cloudy, opaque eyes gaped open. I collected myself and leaned over and closed his eyelids. It was better this way. The Merging had robbed him of the very last of essence of life contained within his sickly body. Unexpectedly, I felt relieved to know he was no longer suffering and he now rested with our ancestors on the other side. I knew he would always be at my side, a guiding spirit throughout the rest of my life.

I leaned over and placed my wet face and throbbing head in his lifeless hand and put my hand on his now still chest. For the first and only time, I let go and completely broke down. For the first time in a very long time, I didn't care if my sobs reached downstairs. Now was not the time to hide my feelings. I wanted this time to grieve by myself. After only a few minutes, my tears stopped and I sat up and just stared at the family photo on the nightstand.

A knock at the door broke my meditative stare, and I turned to see who was there. The door slowly opened and a head poked around the frame of the door.

"Hey, man. You okay?"

My best friend since childhood quietly entered the room. Without saying a word, he walked over to support me. He put his hand on my shoulder and asked his question again with just a look.

"It's tougher than I had imagined, but I know I'm not alone and that will help me move forward."

"We are all here for you man."

"Thanks, Tesicqueo. I really appreciate it."

Chapter 21

A warm welcome

THE WOODEN GREEN AND white welcome sign for Pinecrest, New Hampshire, whipped by as we sped down Interstate 93 N towards Pinecrest. After passing through the town, we would take another highway deep into the White Mountains before slipping into the woods towards the Rowan Coven & Abenaki camp. Only a few more miles until we would be able to stretch our legs and stop having to look over our shoulders every few seconds.

As we passed through, the people of Pinecrest moved about doing their normal mid-morning activities. Mayberry had jumped off the television screen and come to life here. It made me envious of the life the townspeople led. Farmers stood alongside their freshly grown and harvest produce, which glistened in the still present morning dew. Primary school kids walked in a line holding hands as they went on a fieldtrip. Almost every individual stopped to wave or say "hi" to fellow townspeople as they made their way along Main Street. I envied them and their blissful ignorance. They didn't have to worry about the evils of living in a larger city and suburb of a major metropolis. It was times like these when I flashed back to my life with my children and my wife, and the joy they brought me before I had to worry about once unimaginable realities. Supernatural forces had taken them away from me and now I protected those same forces in order to avert the deaths of other innocent victims.

In a matter of minutes, we had passed through the town and made our way along the Kancamagus Hwy into the White Mountains National Park. Only members of the coven and tribe knew the signs pointing the way to the turn off and path to the camp. I hoped I remembered them clearly enough not to get us lost in the woods. That's the last thing we needed at the moment. I looked forward to seeing Étienne again after so many years. I knew he would have the answers Addy and Ethan longed to know. I believed he would also be able to explain, perhaps more clearly, the prophecy and why they were at a critical crossroads in their young lives.

The car slithered through the mountains on the black asphalt surrounded by an unparalleled natural majesty that calmed the soul and replenished hope. I tried to call Ayden but my call went straight to voicemail. If Arabella had taken him, I prayed for a quick death for him, rather than have his soul be blackened by her immoral sorcery. Looking up from the phone, I slammed on brakes throwing both Addy and Ethan onto the floorboard. Both of them grumbled and moaned as the car screeched to a sliding halt.

"What's the deal?" they croaked.

The road ahead of us became almost impassable due to the bodies of dead animals strewn for what seemed like miles ahead of us. It looked like the apocalypse had come to greet us head-on. Silence pervaded the entire car as all of us attempted to assimilate what we were seeing.

"Why would they do that?" Addy asked, trying to shake the sleep from her eyes.

"It's like they barreled over and killed one another," Ethan added.

"Animals don't do things like that unless they're extremely sacred of something. I've never seen anything like this in all my years on this Earth. We have to push forward and get to the camp."

* * *

Worry and uncertainty quivered in my gut, and I wiped my wet palms on McIntyre's back seats while we passed by a horde of dead animals. McIntyre maneuvered around their still bloody bodies. Flies had already invaded their wounds and buzzed happily over their mangled corpses. I wondered what Ethan was thinking. None of us had the courage to comment on what we were witnessing outside the vehicle. The gorgeous and towering mountains populated by thousands of evergreens and wild flowers stood deformed by this animalistic carnage.

Once we cleared the animal wasteland, we didn't follow the paved road much further until McIntyre turned directly into the woods. There was no road or indication any person or vehicle had ever entered the woods at this point. The unknown had now invaded our lives with a vengeance, and I didn't see it giving up too easily or any time soon. We had both put our faith in our principal, our Guardian, who promised to take us some place safe where the answers we had would be answered and where we would begin to learn about our "gifts" as he called them. The sarcastic part of me died from laughter thinking any of this could be true, but the rational part of me had seen too many things lately to deny that something else was at work, something intangible and extraordinary.

Ahead of us, a grove of trees came into view, but the car did not slow down. We just kept moving forward at the same pace. Surely he was going to stop or, at least, slow down. Ethan yelled out from the front seat demanding to know what McIntyre was doing. However, nothing either of us said registered with him. Pine branches scratched and clawed at the side of the car as it crushed saplings and fallen branches. Ethan lunged for the steering wheel, but it was too late, and we collided with trees standing in the path of the car.

* * *

My reach for the steering wheel had been fruitless, and we crashed into the massive pine trees directly in the path. As strange as it may sound, I expected to "wake up" dead, floating above the grisly scene of the accident before seeing the so-called light. However, death had not come to me, and I definitely wasn't flying above the wreck. Smoke didn't invade the cabin. Glass hadn't shattered and showered all of us. In fact, nothing had happened. The SUV simply drove through the massive trees and sat parked at the edge of a village. I had seen a lot in the last several days, but to say this event had blown my mind was an understatement. What would be next, flying monkeys?

I looked in the passenger side mirror and discovered a dense and undisturbed forest flanking us on all sides from behind. Nothing gave evidence of our off-roading trek through the woods. Honestly, I didn't even see the road or anything else that looked familiar from our journey just minutes earlier. Embarrassed, I realized I was suffocating the door handle in my grip, and, not so slyly, I released it and looked into the backseat to see Addy huddled in the floorboard. Her arms were protecting her face from what ended up being nothing.

"Addy, it's okay. You can get out of the floorboard," I said as a chuckle escaped me without warning.

Principal McIntyre turned to face us and said, "Like I told you guys, as your Guardian, I'm here to protect you. I'm not here to put your lives in danger."

Addy climbed up from the floorboard and back into the backseat, looking a little worse for wear. "Please don't ever do that again. I'm not sure how much more I can take today."

"This is just the beginning for both you. It's important you get ready for things much more stressful and dangerous for that matter."

We both let the word "great" slip sarcastically from our white, chapped lips.

"Well, no reason for us to stay in the car. There are lots of people you guys need to meet."

The three of us slid out of the SUV and looked at something out of a travel book about mountain villages. It made me think of the fabled utopia, Shangri-La. I told myself if this were the famed mystical city, I was going to go to the closest mental hospital and check myself in. When would all of this stop? When could we go back to being "normal"? However, my fear quickly evaporated when Principal McIntyre welcomed the both of us to the Rowan, a place where the Rowan coven and the Abenaki people had lived for hundreds of years. Now, it was to be our home as well, for the time being. As we walked towards an amphitheater encircling what looked like a fire pit, he explained we would be protected from anyone not belonging to the coven or tribe by an invisible protective barrier that covered and hid the entire village. He added that the village continued to be home to both witches and members of the Abenaki tribe, a group of Native Americans who had lived in these mountains for over a thousand years.

I couldn't help but be relaxed and at ease with all the natural beauty of the surroundings. The wooden cottages, all of varying sizes and natural colors, dotted the landscape in a thought-out yet free flowing formation, which worked its way outward from the center fire pit. Something inside told me I would truly discover myself in this place and everything, in some way or another, would work out for both me and Addy. I just hoped this resolution came about without any more bloodshed or death, but the very same inkling told me not to hold my breath about that.

* * *

I had to forcibly swallow several times to get my heart out of my throat. My hands still felt numb from being clinched to protect me from the expected, yet, thankfully, unrealized debris of the crash. For a moment, I was sure I was going to die before reaching eighteen, which would have royally sucked. I wanted, I needed, something good to happen after so much bad. Where were my senior year and a future at Harvard when I needed it? I seriously doubted many of my former classmates would have agreed with me on this point, but at this moment, I would have given anything and everything to have it all back in my, once very planned out, life.

Where was my mom? I desperately wanted and needed to talk to her. She had always been honest with me, or so I thought, and wanted to hear her side of this sordid story. Something wasn't right. She would have tried to contact me by now if she were just visiting family. *I need you, mom.*

People appeared from nowhere to come and greet us as soon as we stepped out of the vehicle. Their eyes conveyed genuine concern and care. I immediately felt better and knew we had reached a safe place at last. Standing amidst the coven members, I was shocked to hear a number of people speaking French, as well as other languages. There were also several Native American peoples, the Abenaki I assumed, who greeted us and used their native language among themselves. Most likely to describe the crazy scene of an SUV entering their hidden town, and the comical entrance of two petrified kids who basically tumbled out onto the ground as they got out of the car.

I had the oddest sensation as I watched the unfolding actions of these people. Not a single person revealed surprise, anger, or astonishment at our arrival in this place. Many gave me the impression that they had been waiting for this day to happen. Was it the prophecy or something else that had prepared them?

* * *

It was so good to be back with the Rowan Coven and the Abenaki peoples. I had not been here in more years than I cared to count. I had witnessed the earliest beginnings of this coalition of these two groups in my earlier years. I had known the ancestors of many of the faces I saw before me. It felt comforting to be back in the company of people who cared for others selflessly and endlessly. A trait not often found in modern times.

"Devon, is that you?"

Martine. She had been a little girl the last time I had seen her here. Her family, and that of her husband Victor, had been instrumental in casting the spell that created and sustained the barrier, which now protected this sacred spot.

"Martine, it's so great to see you!" I said as we hugged one another. "You've really grown!" As soon as the words bounced off my lips, I regretted saying them. They sounded patronizing and a little creepy coming from me when I still looked thirty-five. Thankfully, she dashed my fears with a hearty laugh.

"Well, thank you, but we're closer to the same age now. I'm actually older if we focus just on the number."

"Touché."

"Where are Victor and Étienne? I really need to talk to Étienne about Ethan and Addy."

The smile of her face melted and way, and the faint sign of tears grew in her eyes. She lowered her head and stared at the ground for a few seconds before meeting my face again. No sign of tears present.

"Victor is on his way from Pinecrest now. He should be here within the hour. However, Étienne became very ill a couple of weeks ago, and his health has been deteriorating ever since."

"Martine, I'm so sorry to hear that. Is he accepting visitors?"

"My son, Quinn, is visiting with him now. He went straight to his house after we arrived. We can go there now if you like. I'm not sure he will even acknowledge your presence, but you should see him."

I let Ethan and Addy know I was going to see one of the Elders of the coven and that they would be in good hands until I met up with them again in Martine's cottage in an hour or so. I thought they would both appreciate some alone time away from the constant danger with which they had been faced as of late.

"If you need anything at all before I get back, I will be in the whitewashed house over there."

"I think we'll be fine. It'll be nice to rest and meet some new people without have to constantly look over our shoulders," Addy affirmed.

We parted ways, and Martine and I headed towards Étienne's house, which had not changed in forty years. Martine and I walked in silence as we crossed the open air space buffering the cottages that housed the members and tribesmen. The air smelled fresh, tinted with the scent of fresh pine needles mixed with the purified waters of the melting snow. For as far as the eye could see, nature showed her resilient muscles and beauty, one of her last refuges from overuse and destruction. It was easy to see why the Abenaki and the coven members alike had chosen to come to this ancestral and sacred area buried within the White Mountains. No one could deny the awesome presence felt here, fed by the mountain streams and everlasting green landscape. Just being in this place of natural beauty renewed my spirit and soul. For the first time since seeing the warning signs about the prophecy, I found peace and assurance with my role as Guardian.

* * *

I had never had a better friend than Tesicqueo. We had grown up together and enjoyed a friendship that allowed for us to be completely honest with each other about our gifts. The majority of witches my age did not know what it was like to have people in their life who understood what it was like to be a supernatural. Most mortals feared us, and those who were more conservative believed we worshipped the devil and drank the blood of infants, or worse, ate them. Some people could be so damned closed-minded and blind to the facts.

Tesicqueo's grandfather, Standing Bear, was the Shaman of the Abenaki tribe here and his father, Running Fox, had recently ascended to the role of Sakom or leader. The spiritual life of the Abenaki rested in the very capable and experienced hands of Standing Bear; however, his son was the one who helped the people to reach a consensus on the practical routine matters. Much like our coven, the Abenaki people relied on strong family ties to create a functioning society. This had been one of the primary reasons for the harmony that existed between our two peoples for centuries. Our individual families formed one large family unit grounded in beliefs and customs.

"I'm really sorry, man. Your granddad was a really awesome man. Is there anything you need?"

"Nah, it's okay. I'm actually glad to have been here for his last moments and say goodbye. He's not suffering anymore and that's a good thing." Hundreds of thoughts and memories tumbled around my brain and ricocheted off my skull. I attempted to narrow my focus in order to make sense of what I was seeing in my mind's eye, but it was a futile task. If anything, it made everything in my head string together, creating more confusion and mental cloudiness.

We headed downstairs to let my aunt know my grandfather had passed. I didn't know if I should mention what else had happened, and if I did, whom I should tell. I felt so far outside my depth of understanding, like a child learning to spell. Somehow my aunt knew about my grandfather as soon as we looked at each other. We were incredibly sad but at the same time, relieved the suffering had ended before continuing any longer. No one deserved to suffer as my grandfather had.

"We have to find out what the hell caused this. There has to be something we can try, something we can cast to discover the root of this disease, if that's what it actually was." Anger took over my voice as my words came out, and I felt compelled to apologize to my aunt and best friend.

"Quinn, there's absolutely no need to apologize. I agree with you and we will find out how all of this happened and why it happened to him."

"Does anyone know where my mom is? I'd have thought she'd already be here by now."

"That's right. I guess you haven't heard, but a Tahoe containing a Guardian and two high school kids came through the barrier about fifteen minutes ago. Your mom is out there talking to the Guardian, a man named McIntyre," Tesicqueo answered.

"Wait, that's what . . ."

"That's what, what?" Tesicqueo inquired.

"Nothing. It's not important." I blurted in response, but my deflection had failed miserably. However, now wasn't the time to delve into a spell I'd never heard about and was a rare occurrence even for our kind. "I think I'll go and get my mom. Do you mind getting him ready for the Ascendance, aunt Terre?"

"Not at all. I'll see you guys soon."

Soon was actually sooner than either of us expected because as I reached for the door, my mom and the Guardian opened it. The Guardian had very strong and distinctive features, which I couldn't help but think were, in some way, familiar. He stood at least 6'4 and carried himself with a commanding yet compassionate presence. Somehow I knew him, but from where?

"Hello everyone, I'd like you to meet Devon McIntyre. He's a very good, old friend of Étienne."

The exchange of greetings was sincere yet brief. How do you break the news of someone's death without just saying it in a very matter of fact way?

"He'd . . ."

"Mom, I'm sorry to come across as rude, but granddad has passed away."

There were tears. Lots of tears. Where was all of this coming from now and why had it taken almost thirty minutes to finally happen? I found myself looking foolish in front of my very non-emotional best friend, my strong as an ox aunt, and a perfect stranger who I had never met before in my life. In this moment with my mom, I had what I needed to really exercise the gnawing ball of emotions ripping my insides to shreds. It felt cathartic, deeply invigorating, yet exhausting, and it was over. Without warning, the tears stopped, the well of sadness, for the moment, bone dry and void.

I opened my mouth to say something, but this stranger, this man named Devon McIntyre, this Guardian, put his hand on my shoulder and with tears in his eyes said in a single look that there was need for such a thing. When all is said and done, even the most hard-ass people reveal their humanity from time to time.

My mom decided to help my aunt Terre prepare my grandfather for the Ascendance and went upstairs to gather a few things for the ceremony, which had to be held within forty-eight hours of his death. For my part, I made the decision to talk with McIntyre and meet these kids who had arrived with him. My granddad's final words pulsed in my mind, and I felt I owed it to him to investigate his final message, or warning.

The night air provided a welcomed change as all of us stepped out of my grandfather's cottage and stepped down into his once vibrant garden. Hordes of insects buzzed in chorus in the trees encircling the camp and a distant bird called out into the night high in the mountains. I loved being here, and I knew dealing with my granddad's death would be easier here than in Pinecrest or at Dartmouth. Thank god for breaks.

Now, I wanted to meet these two kids who had come through the barrier with Devon. Something told me things were about to amp up around our normally peaceful, hidden community.

Chapter 22

Introductions & recollections

THE NIGHT AIR FELT amazing after being stuck inside the car for almost two hours. My muscles greatly appreciated the opportunity to stretch. My whole body reveled in being free from the vehicular confinement. An overwhelming desire to run around like a five year old overtook me, but I was able to subdue the desire to act like a child in front of people who I had only just met.

Everyone greeted us with such overflowing care and sincere politeness. It made this place feel like home like a surrogate for the one in Salem, which had been violated and destroyed by my biological mother. I could tell McIntyre worried about leaving us when he went to meet his friend, but we were happy to be on our own for the first time in a while, in a place free of conflict and fear.

The people asked about us, but not in a pervasive manner. They genuinely wanted to know about us and if we possessed any magical gifts. I looked at Ethan when I heard these questions, not sure of how to respond to them about something we had only very recently discovered. I held the grimoire tight against my chest under my jacket and the fleeting thought of asking them what they actually knew about it, and possibly us, came to mind. I mean, after all, they had been raised with magic, a concept far away from the preconceived notions of our lives.

"We are so happy to have you both here with us."

"Thank you so much. We really glad to be out of the car," I said as we all laughed.

Laughter really was the best medicine. I didn't know about Ethan, but I continued to feel more at east as time passed.

"So, have the two of you been practicing your magic for a while?" asked an older woman with a kind and gentle face. Her amethyst eyes reminded me of my granny in France.

"Um. We actually just discovered we had gifts last night," Ethan responded. The faces of the small greeting party flashed surprise and intrigue. We were like a primetime soap and they were our dedicated audience. "What we know about all of this is mostly thanks to our Guardian."

"Oh. You have a guardian?" a middle-aged man inquired completely showing his keen interest in the subject.

In the back of the group, I heard a small child ask someone what a Guardian was. Was it really that big of a deal? I assumed all new witches had one. Just thinking the word "witch" sounded so weird and foreign to me.

"Yes we do. He's the man who came with us through the, the . . ."

"It's called the barrier dear," said the old woman with violet eyes as she put a comforting hand on my forearm.

"Thank you. Doesn't everyone have a Guardian?"

"Only the most special and powerful witches and supernaturals have Guardians who are dedicated to their protection and guidance," she continued.

"Oh" was the only word that slipped from both of our mouths, simultaneously. The prophecy. Did these people know about it? Should we tell them? Now I wanted McIntyre back with us to clarify our confusion and field the questions coming from the people greeting us.

"And have you only known your Guardian since last night as well?"

"Um, yes, that's right."

"I don't think you guys could be any nosier if you tried," a deep and booming voice announced coming from the direction of the homes in the distance. In the distance, I could see three people walking towards us. Thankfully, one of them was McIntyre, but the others were faceless figures, shorter than McIntyre, striding forward.

* * *

Around fifteen members of our coven and the Abenaki tribe surrounded the two kids who had arrived with McIntyre. We rarely had visitors, especially ones who were unannounced. Excitement perfumed the air and had rather quickly infected the young and old alike. Memories transferred to me by my granddad continued to act like emails shuffling themselves around into mental folders in the inbox that was my brain.

"So what are you expecting from this first encounter?" Tesicqueo asked, being sure to put unnecessary emphasis on the word "encounter."

"Who says I'm expecting anything? I just have a feeling about this," I answered, keeping my eyes fixed on the group ahead. "That's the thing about meeting someone for the first time, it could amount to absolutely nothing or it might just change your life."

"Always so philosophical about every damn thing."

"Why do you think I'm studying theology and religion?" I snickered in reply. We both laughed and grinned at each other as we reached the small group gathered around two teenagers. They both looked a little lost and very glad to see us approaching. A few of the scanty group of members chatted amongst themselves while others continued asking the two teenagers questions about who they were and what their gifts were. As their faces emerged from the shadows covering them, I came face-to-face with two visages vibrantly vivid in my new memories. Their names were Ethan and Addy, and I all at once knew things about them, the prophecy, and their possible destinies.

"Hey now everyone, let's not smother our guests. Let's give them some space and possibly some food, if they'd like that."

The tiny group moved along and dissipated back into the homes from where they had come as they continued to mutter about the excitement of the night.

"I'm sorry about that. We don't get many unexpected visitors here."

"It's fine," the girl, Addy, said.

"Ethan and Addy, I'd like to introduce you to Quinn and Tesicqueo."

After the introductions, Ethan face reflected shock and fascination.

"I know you. I had a vision about you, you guided me through a visit to the past," he said as he stared at Tesicqueo.

"What do you mean a visit to the past?" Addy interjected.

I was completely clueless about what he was saying even with my recently acquired and still simmering memories. I looked at both Tesicqueo and McIntyre. It was McIntyre who intervened.

"I think it might be a good idea if we take these introductions indoors and talk somewhere less public."

* * *

Upon first seeing him, completely dumbfounded was how I saw myself. Even with everything that had happened, including the realization of having gifts, whatever you wanted to call them, seeing Tesicqueo here, in the flesh, made my brain do somersaults. Now, after letting the moment sink in, I felt validated and a little less crazy than I had been feeling since that day in the park. Almost, as if by reflex, I looked down at his wrist, and saw that it was embellished with the same serpent tattoo mine now carried. However, his was more ornate and complex. I made a mental note to ask him specifically about my mark when we had the chance to be alone and talk.

However, the recognition I felt was not reflected in his face. I wasn't sure if he was playing dumb in front of his friend and McIntyre or if he truly had no idea who I was. Surely, the former was the case. I thought to myself, how could he not know me? I know the vision was real, and I had the mark to prove it. The same one he had.

As we followed the three of them, Tesicqueo, Quinn, and Principal McIntyre, in the direction of someone's house, Addy and I lulled a little behind to chat about what we had experienced in the last twenty-four hours. We still hadn't had the chance to discuss the news of our new lives and the secrets kept from us for almost eighteen years. I knew she wasn't too thrilled by my revelation of having already seen Tesicqueo in a vision. But there hadn't been any time during the past day to dish on my own personal freak show in the park. Wasn't trying to deal with high school enough without having to grapple with magic, witches and god-only-knows what else?

"So, I really do consider myself a fairly observant person, but how the hell did I not see your tattoo?" She wasn't wasting any time one this.

"Hey let's be fair. It's not like we've had a lot of chat time recently and besides you know I would have told you when I had the chance. I wanted to tell you right before we found the book, but in the moment, that kind of took precedence over my new and miraculous tattoo."

"I guess I'll accept that."

"You don't have a choice," I said as I gave her a slight slap on the back. One thing in my life was a sure thing and that was the friendship and connection I had with Addy would endure anything thrown at us. No matter if that something came from our recently discovered biological mother or a normal, mortal person. Did I really just think that without feeling completely freakish?

"We both have a lot to share, and it isn't fair we haven't been able to do that. I still can't believe my father tried to kill us. I don't understand how someone could change another person to such an extent their entire being would be completely changed."

"It's just freaking screwed up, that's what it is. I know you're trying to find a logical explanation for what happened, but after everything we've been witness to during the last day, I don't think logic is something that applies to our lives anymore. It's unfortunate, but a glaring, pain-in-the-ass truth."

The wind had picked up slightly and wafted through the small quaint environment. I loved smelling the crisp mountain air as opposed to the smell I had grown accustomed to in Salem. Since we were mainly a fishing village, the only smells I had grown accustomed to, were those of bait and fresh catches. I looked back over to Addy to ask her about reading more of the book, but her gaze rested fixated in the growing light pushing over the protruding mountains protecting us from the outside world. I knew she was shedding a few tears for her father, despite her desire not to do so, and wondering where her mother might be and if she were okay.

"I'm sure she's fine. Your mom was always one of the toughest people I have ever met. You'll see her again and probably before you know it, you'll be hugging her like when you were little."

Addy just looked at me and smiled, a few glistening droplets of water slid down her face and reflected in her eyes. I threw my arm around her and drew her close to my side and we walked together, heads resting against each other, knowing we would get through all of this as long we had each other.

"We're lucky to have one another, Ethan, and I never want that to change."

"No worries. It never will."

As we approached a whitewashed house, a man in his forties stood outside talking to a woman around the same age. The resemblance was immediate. They must be Quinn's parents. They both stood tall with darker hair than Quinn, but their facial features screamed of the genetic link between the three of them. Seeing these biological similarities reinforced the lack of mine with the two people I had called "mom" and "dad" for the past seventeen years. Embarrassingly, it angered me, and I was immediately ashamed of my thoughts.

"Addy and Ethan, I'd like you to meet my parents, Victor and Marine."

"Hi, very nice to meet you."

"Where's Julie? I thought she be with you dad."

"I thought she was already here. I haven't seen her since last night."

Quinn exhaled forcibly doing nothing to hide his frustration with this person named Julie.

"Julie's my younger sister and . . . and I'll leave it at that."

Point taken, and I couldn't' wait to meet Julie if and when she made an appearance.

"Why don't you guys spend some time together getting to know one another? I'm sure Quinn and Tesicqueo can explain your gifts to you much better than I, "McIntyre suggested. I could tell he was ready for us to have some time with other people around our age. I think he thought we had grown tired of his company, which wasn't true in the least. However, I did have to admit it'd be nice to be around people closer to our age and I really wanted to talk to Tesicqueo.

"Sounds like a plan to me," Addy chimed in.

"There are a few things I need to discuss with Quinn's parents anyway."

The three adults said their goodbyes and entered the whitewashed home and closed the door behind them. For a few moments, we all just looked at each other in silence. We obviously didn't know where we should go to chat, and I supposed the other two were trying to decide on a place that would be out of the way and private from curious eyes and ears. In a very short time, we had become the talk of the town, so to speak, whether it is for better or worse.

"Do you guys mind if I have a moment with my sister?" the word tasted strange as it escaped my mouth.

"Sure, no problem. Why don't we all meet back at the center fire pit in say, thirty minutes?"

"Perfect. See you guys in a bit."

The two them strolled off in the opposite direction of the center meeting place as Addy and I began our talk. We walked towards no fixed point along the tree line surrounding the village. We had so much to say, but at first the conversation struggled to come to life and sustain itself. Where do you begin to jump into the storyline that had been our lives not only for the past twenty-four hours but the past several weeks? We had both seen and experience things unnatural for our once mortal world, but, at the time, neither of us had had an eye to dissect and understand what was actually going on around and to us.

"I think we can both agree all of this craziness began when you passed out in the gym the first day of school."

"Agreed. No one still knows what happened and why it all happened. Everything was fine and then it faded to black. The deepest and consuming blackness I've ever seen in my life."

"Do you remember anything from your time in the hospital?"

"I'm not sure. I could swear I woke up at various times while I was there, but . . ."

"But what, what is it?"

"At one point I thought I saw a man in my room. A man I've never seen before in my life. He didn't scare me, quite the opposite. I felt safe, like he was there for me, to protect me."

"Well that just shot the freak factor up a couple of notches. Did he say anything to you?"

"Not so much in the forms of words but more like images in my mind. But I'm not sure because I also had that crazy dream or whatever it was while I was there."

"I say we don't discount anything we've seen or think we may have seen. Can you remember these images?"

"No." she said sounding frustrated and defeated.

"It's all right. What about your dream? What do you remember?"

"It was the strangest and most real dream I think I've ever had in my life. I woke up in the mud, and my senses were electrified by everything around me. It was like I was connected to everything."

She continued and described in detail the trees looming large and abundant around here and then the appearance of her house in the distance. However, the house solely mimicked her actual house and the few pieces of furniture lying around it where brittle and hollow, except for what she found in the bookcase.

"It's like you told me. You knew where to find the book."

"Yeah, exactly."

"Did it show you anything more than what we saw?"

She furrowed her brow and closed her eyes in focused concentration. I reached over and put my hand on her wrist and her back instantly straightened and she sat inflexibly upright.

"Are you okay?"

"Yes, don't let go. Everything is coming into the light and becoming clearer."

Could this be the prophecy, the combination of our magic? McIntyre told us some believed it to be too much for someone to possess and those believers wanted us dead. What did it all mean?

"I see the book. Just like with you, the names are becoming clearer. I see our parents, but they have no children, the print is vibrating and blurry."

I grabbed her wrist tighter and a pulse of heat and light flowed from my hand into her wrist, a glowing rippling flash traced the length of her arm before centralizing in her chest.

"It's Arabella, her name, it's there. There is a line draw for children, but we're not there. They didn't want her to know anything about them, about us."

I was about to push further when the glow moved from her chest back down her arm and pulsed back into my hand and towards my chest. In an instant, everything around me evaporated to black and I found myself standing next to Addy in her vision. We looked at each other, but said nothing. We each put a hand on the book and the room around us and our bodies were bathed in rays of bright orange and yellow warm and tingling light.

Looking down at the book, every page glared back at us with writing, drawings, and further information regarding our family's history and beginnings. The pages turned on their own accord showing us what looked like recipes of various topics, spells. The words etched on the parchment floated up from the pages and infiltrated our minds, at first slowly and then so rapidly the words were colorful blurs racing across the air. When the book reached its final revelation, a warning eyed us in a bold and intention laden blood red script. No one, not even those foretold in the prophecy were to use their gifts for personal reasons without suffering the life-altering consequences. We were also warned that if we, the ones prophesied, used our powers too much, the one banished from our plain of existence, Arabella, would gain the ability to locate and come to us. Nothing could guard us from this happening. Then, without warning the book exploded in a revolting wave of blood and mud. The room and us were covered in seconds as the repugnant mixture chocked us. We both brought our hands up to our eyes and mouth, and the next thing we saw were the faces of Quinn and Tesicqueo standing in front of us and shaking us, as if we had been asleep.

"What's going? Are you guys okay?"

Addy and I looked at each other before answering.

"I think so. Why are you guys here? It's hasn't been thirty minutes yet."

"It's been almost an hour and a half. You both sure you're all right?"

We both nodded. Both of us were much more than fine, for the first time, we understood. Somehow we had discovered the answers to almost all the questions we had had about our family and the book. Finally, some light had chased away some of the darkness overshadowing the truth about our lives and us.

My joy of being more in the "know" about our lives gave way to anger. We were blessed with the gifts, yet the very same gifts, if over used, would bring the one person who wanted to corrupt and use us for her own diabolical desires. What a crock! How was that fair? I desperately needed a run.

"You guys look like you've been through something pretty rough."

"I guess you could say that." I answered.

"What that?" Quinn asked pointing at Addy's shirt.

The grimoire peaked through the bottom of her shirt and the leather and gold leafed bottom right corner glistened in the pink-yellow morning light.

"Ugh, it's, it's my . . ."

"It's your family's grimoire, isn't it?"

"But how did you know that?"

"All Wiccan families have a grimoire. It contains our family's spells and family history. You know, you really shouldn't really be carrying it all over the place under your shirt. For each family, it's a very sacred tome that shouldn't be lost."

"We had to leave in a hurry, and I did the only I thing I could think of to get it out of my house safely. You have no idea what we've been through."

"You're right. So why do you guys tell us?"

They were right. We had to tell someone besides McIntyre. After what had just happened, we knew more about our situation than he probably did. Since we weren't experts on all things magical, Quinn and Tesicqueo might actually be able to help us with deciphering what we had just learned.

"Sounds like a plan. But I'd like to ask a random question?" I asked.

They waited and Addy looked at me suspiciously.

"Do either of you like to run by any chance?"

"That's definitely not me," Quinn said and he pointed at his best friend. "T's your man if you want to do some physical exercise. Although freak might be a better description," he finished with a smirk.

"Well, what are you waiting for? Let's hope you can keep up," Tesicqueo said as he darted off into the woods bordering the barrier behind us. I shed the sweatshirt I'd been wearing and fell in pursuit of him.

"Well, A, looks like it's just me and you."

"My name is actually Addy."

"I got it, A. Don't get your magical panties in a bunch."

"Well this is just going to be fantastic," Addy blurted sarcastically as she stood and looked Quinn in the eyes.

In response, he gave her a wink and a smile.

Chapter 23

Mutual understanding

I COULDN'T BELIEVE WHAT Ethan and I had just "seen," if that's what you would call it. I guess we had finished what we had started back at my house when we both touched the book. Admittedly, it was amazing to think magic existed, and, even more so, we both had the ability to use it. On the flip side, if we used them too much, we might bring about our end. Why would someone prophesy our lives and then create such a restrictive curse on us. Were people really that scared of us, and what we might do? Sure, we both had tempers, but we would never do anything to hurt another person.

"Hey A, you coming?"

"Stop calling me that. My name is Addy. Every time you say that, I think of 'The Scarlett Letter.'"

"Well, you are a witch after all, just hopefully not an adulterer. I think you're a little young for that," he shot back at me.

I seriously wanted to reach out and slap his face or better yet, do whatever I had done to Ayden to him. It'd be nice to see his face after I knocked him on his butt. I laughed out loud, and he looked back at me.

"You try that on me ,and we'll see who's the one left standing and laughing."

"What? How the . . .?"

"Supernatural here, or did you already forget that?"

"Stay out of my mind."

"Damn. It was just starting to get juicy."

"You're an ass."

"It's my most endearing quality."

He was so annoying, yet there was something about him that made me want to know more despite his jackass attitude.

"Where are we going?"

"Hold your horses why don't you. Are you always this impatient?"

I didn't even make the effort to offer a response except for the overstated rolling of my eyes. I decided it would be better not to flame the fire of his ego. I just followed him behind a row of houses and down a worn path, passing through some underbrush, before entering a tiny clearing, which gave upon a small rocky stream flowing down from the mountains. The day-to-day noises created by the village ceased and silences abounded in this apparently secret spot.

"It's so quiet here."

"It's great, right? We are just on the other side of the barrier, outside of its protection. I often come here to get away from all of the voices buzzing around me."

"I can definitely see why."

"Don't get me wrong, I love being in Rowan with my family and friends, but from time to time, I need silence and solitude. What better place to achieve both."

Somehow, by passing through the barrier, Quinn had changed, the way he carried himself, the way he spoke even the way his facial expressions revealed his feelings and thoughts. I wondered if he felt he had to "keep up appearances" while within the barrier for the sake of his family. I could sympathize, to a certain extent, with that feeling. I had often seen myself in the same situation even if I had been the one creating the undue stress and expectations.

"Still worried about someone getting your grimoire?"

I hadn't realized I had been holding it like my life depended on it since being with Ethan on the other side of the village. I loosened my death grip and let it slide from under my shirt. I held it out and offered to Quinn so that he could look at it.

"I appreciate the offer, but I can't open it."

"Why not?"

"When it comes to grimoires, only the family members it belongs to can open them. It's a type of protection against its contents being used improperly."

"What if I want to show it to you?"

"As long as you are the one who opens it, we'd be good to go. But don't feel like you have to do that for me. I was just picking at you back there."

"I know, but something tells me I can trust you."

"So, tell me what happened back there with your, brother, right?"

"Newly discovered brother, yes. For the past seventeen years, we believed we were just cousins and close friends."

"Wow. Who needs reality TV when you have that?"

I couldn't help but laugh. He was right after all. We had been unwilling participants in one crazy family drama perfect for reality TV. It felt good to laugh and be around someone who understood me even if I didn't really know him at all.

"To be honest with you, I'm not really sure what happened. I was trying to remember something from when I was in the hospital a week or so ago and then all of a sudden I flashback to a dream I had while there. Before I knew it, Ethan was there in my mind standing beside me in my vision. We were in my house and we saw the grimoire, touched it, and then we were bathed and light and words and symbols from the book flew off the pages and seeped into our heads, like memories."

"To me it sounds like your powers were activated when you both touched the book. Was it the first time?"

"No. Before we had to escape Salem, we touched it in my house after I found it, which was only possible because I had had the dream."

"Did you both touch it for very long that first time?"

"No, we were cut short by a crazy police officer pounding on my door. But how could us touching it in my mind be the same as physically touching it?"

"As a supernatural, you have a certain amount of psychic energy and power. You took what you absorbed in your house into your being and when you both touched it again in your vision, the energy was reactivated and the completion of the magical transfer, so to speak, occurred. I would bet you money he was touching you when he appeared in your mind."

"How did you know that? How do you know any of this?"

"Remember, I've grown up being supernatural, and I've learned a lot over the years. Your powers are probably complimentary and intertwined, and you are more than likely stronger together I would imagine, just like it says in the prophecy."

"What do you mean? How do you know about any of that?"

For a moment, he looked off at some point in the distance before turning back towards me. He sat right in front of me on a rock bordering the creek. The only sounds filling the air where those of distant birds and the soft and billowing flow of the cool mountain stream. If you were going to bare your soul, what better place to do so, right? Following his lead, I made myself comfortable on a fallen tree which put me in his line of sight, his face told me he was carrying something that was eating at his soul. A secret he wanted to share with someone. It was nice to have further proof of our similarities and not the validation of great differences. He waited a few seconds more before he started talking.

"So, you've been pretty straight forward with me, and I feel I should return the favor."

"Please don't feel like you have to share anything with me if makes me you feel uncomfortable."

"No, it's not that. A lot is going on in my life right now. Something happened late last night and I haven't told anyone anything about it yet. I still don't know if I fully understand it."

I sat there and relaxed into the log without saying anything. It was one of the moments where I wasn't sure if I should say anything. If I decided to, what exactly I would say. The crisp mountain air flicked across my face and made my hair dance right into my mouth and I had to spit it out without a single shred of elegance. In the process of doing so, I leaned back a little too far and tumbled off of the log. Quinn jumped to his feet and looked behind the log. I couldn't help but laugh heartily at myself for being clumsy and making a complete fool of myself in front of him.

"Oh, my god. I'm so embarrassed," I managed to say through deep shrieks off laughter.

"Okay, so since you're laughing, that was freaking hilarious."

For a few minutes we just laughed until he helped me back onto my former seat on the log. The impromptu comical slapstick cut the tension and I felt so much more comfortable. I think he did as well.

"So I hope you enjoyed my little display there. I planned it out pretty well I think."

"Oh yeah, pure comic genius. You should take that act on the road."

"My tour starts next week actually," I retorted.

"My grandfather just died early this morning."

He just blurted it out and I shifted on the ground. With just a few words, the lighthearted atmosphere evaporated. I guess he had reached the point where just saying it out loud was what he needed and made it real.

"I'm really sorry to hear that. Were you guys very close?"

"Very much so. I spent all of my time with him when I was growing up. He taught me almost everything I know about magic: casting, history, genealogy, as well as being responsible with the craft. He was even one of the Elders of Rowan."

"I'm sure it was amazing having someone there to teach you about all of this and guide you through using your gifts. I would have really liked to have met him."

"He was an incredible grandfather, guide, and friend. We shared everything with each other, even at the end."

"What do you mean?"

"It's how I knew about you and the prophecy."

"Sorry, I still don't understand."

Quinn proceeded to tell me about something called the Merging, a ritual where the memories, experiences, and knowledge of someone can be transferred to another, typically a family member. However, performing the Merging came with a consequence, death of the person telepathically conveying the information. At the moment of his death, Quinn's granddad, Étienne, had fulfilled the ritual and died almost instantly. A long life's worth of memories and knowledge imparted to Quinn in a matter of moments, almost becoming one with his grandfather who now lay dead in his bedroom in the whitewashed house were we had been earlier. I had never known or experienced such a sacrifice in my life, and I was honestly startled at the way Quinn talked about it with such nonchalance and distance. He reminded me a lot of Ethan and a little of myself. All three of us liked to compartmentalize "uncomfortable" things in our lives. I hadn't yet made up my mind about whether that was a good or bad trait to have.

I told him he didn't need to feel obliged to be here with me with what had happened to his grandfather, but he assured me he was where he needed to be. In the Rowan Coven, it was the task of the parents to prepare a person's body for what he called the Ascendance. He didn't go into detail about the ritual and I didn't want to pry, but I gathered it was their form of burial.

"My grandfather knew you and your brother were coming to Rowan. He actually knew you were close. He told me it was my destiny to help you survive the coming storm."

"Well, that doesn't sound ominous in the least," I joked anxiously.

He didn't laugh at my attempt to lighten the mood and continued in a rather informative and dry demeanor. I had a flashback of my AP Chemistry class during my junior year.

"Something more evil than anything we or the Abenaki people have ever faced is coming. Thanks to my grandfather, I can see something rippling along the horizon of the near future. Many people will not survive what is drawing nearer with each passing hour. She's gathering strength and advancing."

"You mean Arabella?"

"Yes, your mother."

"Just because she offered up some genetic material, does not make her my mother."

"It doesn't matter. She will reach out to you and your brother to join with her."

"There's no chance in Hell I would ever even think about doing that and neither would Ethan."

"I know you feel that way now, but when the supernatural is involved, the lines between good and evil are not so well defined. Your best friend, your brother can be the same person to slice open your throat and watch you bleed out."

I opened my mouth to protest, but stopped myself. Who was I to contradict him? He had lived his life entirely immersed in the supernatural world. The implications would be mind boggling if he were right. Who could do such a thing? My mind darted through the people I knew and wondered, if any of them, might turn against me and do what Quinn had so graphically described.

The sound of twigs and branches snapping on the other side of the stream caused us both to jump to our feet, senses on high alert. For several seconds, nothing appeared from the thick green and overflowing undergrowth surrounding the thick trunks of the evergreens. The sounds got closer and more pronounced. Whoever it was did not care about making their arrival a secret one. Finally a hand emerged followed by another and then an entire body came into view. It was a teenage girl with flowing deep golden locks and deep brown-black eyes that scanned us with surprise once she had broken through the natural wall on the other side of the creek.

"Julie? What the hell are you doing?"

"I went for a hike, like it's any of your business."

"You're out wandering in the damn woods when our grandfather has just died and mom and dad are looking for you to help?"

"Don't get your mightier-than-thou boxer briefs in a bunch! I'm eighteen years old, and I can do whatever the hell I want to. I don't have to answer to mom or dad and certainly not to you."

"What's your deal?"

"That I'm so over you and the way mom, dad, and the entire freaking coven, for that matter, just love you as their supernatural poster child of perfection and success."

"Julie, that's not fair. I didn't ask for any of that."

"Well you sure don't deny it. Now get out of my way!"

Quinn didn't move and muscle and stared at his younger sister in defiance of her little tantrum. Continuing her pigheadedness, she raised her right arm and flicked her hand at Quinn, who reacted by thrusting his right shoulder backwards, as if an unseen fist had punched him.

"Julie, are you kidding me with this crap?"

Without so much of a verbal response, she now swung her arm up and around her head and thrust her palm violently forward at her brother who took the brunt of her magical assault. Quinn flew backwards through the air until his back made bone-crushing contact with a large rock bordering the stream. I ran towards him on the ground when Julie recreated the same move and thrust her plan towards me. Everything occurred before my eyes in slow motion with no conscious thought on my part. In response to her threat, I lifted my arm and drew a circle in the air just before the water-like energy leaving her palm reached where I stood. Her attack vibrated in mid-air and returned to its source, knocking her back into the undergrowth where she had first appeared. In the blink of an eye, it was over and I had no idea what I had done or how I had done it. I didn't care. I continued over to Quinn, who lay on the ground where he had rolled over to one side. His face winced at the severe pain inflicted by being flung against the solid stone.

"Oh my god, are you okay?"

After a few heavy and steadying breaths, he said, "yeah, I think so. Where did Julie go?"

"Um, I'm not sure. I somehow knocked her back into the tree line, and now I don't hear or see her."

"Looks like you're a quick learner. Mind helping me up?"

After getting Quinn to his feet, we crossed the creek and scoured the trees and bushes to see if we could find Julie or a clue to where she had gone, but we found nothing. Wherever she had gone was a secret, and if my first confrontation with her was any indication, I didn't think she'd make it easy for us to find her again, unless it was on her own terms. I didn't understand how someone practically my age could have so much pent up anger and hate. There were some crazy kids in my school, but no one had ever acted like that, at least not that I knew about.

"I've never known her to have that much power. Something's not right."

"Please don't say that. The last time something didn't feel right, my father tried to kill me and my biological mother tried to abduct me."

"I think we'd better pass back through the barrier and head back to my granddad's house."

Carefully, we both crossed back over the stream and reentered

Rowan and hopefully safety against crazy bio moms and sisters with severe teenage and supernatural angst. Once back inside the invisible dome, I noticed several trees had been placed near the center fire pit of the village. Many of them still lay unused on the ground, but several had been used to create what I could only describe as some sort of altar.

"It's for the Ascendance. It'll take place tonight at midnight."

* * *

They shimmered back through the protective wall and faded from sight. Glaring from behind one of the massive trees to hide my presence, I had to admit I had underestimated both of them. Their powers were growing at an astronomical rate and soon would be fully realized. Did they even know the greatness they possessed? They could easily decimate anything and everything, which stood between them and total control of all of magic. No one had ever witnessed such potential and command of supernatural elements.

Using them would be to my great benefit, and I looked forward to corrupting any good nature they may have left. The barrier was formidable and I had not yet discovered a way to penetrate it, but, in time, I would. When I did find a way through, they would pay for harboring what was rightly mine and no one, no matter who they were, was guaranteed survival. It was mine to fulfill and release. Their end would be my beginning, my domination of all things supernatural.

Chapter 29

Self-realization

TO MY CHAGRIN, TESICQUEO had not been kidding when he asked me to try and keep up with him. He shot off into the trees lining the perimeter of Rowan, and I lost sight of him within seconds. I struggled not only with the terrain but his speed. The terrain had quickly transformed from more or less level dirt paths to one that was rocky and becoming increasingly steep and perilous. I knew I was a good runner, but I was actually having difficulty maintaining my balance as I chased after him going deeper into the sky-seeking pines and the undulating prickly bushes and other flora. For the first time, I saw nature in a less than meditative and calming light. This was definitely not the sparse forest behind my house in Salem.

My ankle rolled on a loose rock, and I looked down to check my footing, but when I glanced back up at the "trail" ahead, Tesicqueo was nowhere to be seen. What the hell? I had no clue where I was, and I knew there was no way I'd be able to find my way back to Rowan without getting more lost than I already was.

"Not too bad for your first time," a voice echoed from behind me.

I turned around and found Tesicqueo standing behind me on the trail with his leg propped up on a boulder looking at me with a bemused look. It wasn't exactly demeaning, but I felt small in any case.

"But how?" I protested.

"You don't have to be a witch to play with perception and the world around you. Things are not as black and white as you might think. Basically, throw anything you learned about physics in school as far as you can out the proverbial window."

"That's perfectly fine with me. I hated physics anyway."

"So, I guess things have been a little crazy for you lately."

"That's more than a tiny understatement. I am still trying to assimilate everything into some kind of cohesive picture, but so far, it's proving to be a little more difficult than I'd like."

We both sat there for a few minutes, me to better catch my breath and he out of respect for my difficulty with the leisurely jaunt into the woods.

"What do you mean I realize more than I know?" I asked.

"Huh? I didn't say anything."

"But I swear I just heard you tell me that."

"Damn Wiccan psychic abilities. Get out of my mind!"

"Ugh, could you explain please?"

He proceeded to explain to me how all witches possessed varying degrees of psychic abilities. Some would only pick up on emotions while others, like me it seemed, could read the thoughts of others, sometimes without warning. He informed me the more I practiced and the more I learned about my abilities, the easier it would be for me to control it. Hearing that from Tesicqueo was a huge relief. I definitely didn't want to be wandering around hearing the random thoughts of people just passing by me on the street.

"But you have something your sister doesn't?"

"What do you mean?"

"I don't know why, but you have an enormous amount of Native American energy flowing through your *Manitou*, or spirit. There's a very rare and powerful balance of this native energy and the Wiccan essence surrounding your inner being."

"But how is that . . . Daniel. He is my biological father, and he was part of the Wampanoag tribe before he died, a full-blooded member."

"That explains the existence of this energy then. You mother, I assume, was Wiccan."

"Yes. She rebelled against the wishes of the Wiccan followers and the tribal members when she became pregnant with my sister and me."

"Ouch. What happened to her if you don't mind my asking?"

"They cut us from her belly, literally, and banished her to some place between life and death. However, they're not sure how, but she found a way to cross back over and as soon as she did, she tried to take both of us."

"That really sucks, I'm sorry. And all of this because of the prophecy?"

"How does every else, but us, know about this god-forsaken prophecy? It's changing and ruining my life, and I don't even fully know anything about it."

"One of the perks of growing up in the spiritual and supernatural community. I assumed it had to do with the prophecy when I sensed the presence of both Wiccan and Native American energies within you."

"And my sister is the same?"

"I don't really know. I don't think so because I haven't felt the same things I feel when I'm around you."

"There seem to be so many freaking 'rules' with magic."

"Yes and no, but the big "no-no" rule says no Wiccan man or woman can have a child with a member of the tribe." I guess my confusion shone through and he continued to explain. "It all has something to do with a balance of power and someone not having too much of it, yadda, yadda,

yadda."

"Yet, you all live together?"

"Yes, and it actually works. We are all very close, it's just that members of the opposite sex can't, you know."

"That sucks."

"Yes, it does, but that's one of the perks of being gay."

Flabbergasted. Completely flabbergasted was the first word to come to mind when Tesicqueo made his very unexpected personal revelation. Had he said this because he knew I was and if so, how did he know?

"That make you uncomfortable?"

"No, no not at all. I just mean, I never, I'm . . ."

"Still coming to grips with being gay?" I nodded, but didn't vocally affirm his question. "Don't worry man, it'll get easier. My dad freaked a little when I told him, but he told me something that I will always remember, 'there's nothing you could ever do that would make me not love you.'"

"That's pretty amazing." I answered realizing I'd never really heard that from either of my parents about anything in my life. It had always been go, go, go and do this and that.

"And, if I could give one other piece of advice, it would be this, 'The key to being happy starts and finishes with your own self-acceptance, and not by denying who you are in order to be accepted by others.'"

For some reason, I wanted to cry and hit something at the same time, something I had been feeling more often lately. Sitting there, I squeezed my fist as hard as I could to fight off my polar opposite emotions, when we suddenly heard a loud pop.

"What was that?" Tesicqueo asked.

We both looked around for several minutes before he looked at me, "Holy crap man!"

I followed his stare and saw that the rock beneath where my fist rested I had completely split in two. A jagged and aggressive crack had run completely through the solid mass. I lifted my hand and one of the halves rolled over and down the mountain a little ways before resting against a tree.

"How did you do that?"

"I have no idea. I was just clinching my fist to keep from doing something stupid when it happened."

"You emotions connect with your powers on a very primal level. It's difficult, but really important to try and control them if they go too far one way or the other. You see what can happen if you don't." He told me with a smirk to cap off his explanation.

Being around Tesicqueo, my self-doubt and the preoccupations I had about my family and current situation eased, and I felt more in tune with abilities and myself. I told him how much of a calming presence he was for me and how much I appreciated his help in better understanding who I was as a supernatural and a human being. He laughed graciously and begged me to stop because he was starting to feel like a therapist, something I would never want to do to anyone, so I promptly desisted with my therapeutic praise.

"So, I do have a question for you that has nothing to do with emotional support."

"Shoot."

"You know I'm completely new to all of this supernatural stuff. How can I practice it if I don't know what I'm doing? I mean our Guardian has helped tons, but he's not technically in the know when it comes to magic."

"That's a fair question. But I have one to bounce back at you. What do you know about your gifts and the prophecy at this point?"

The episode with Addy roared back into my mind. What had actually happened in that vision? Was it real or had we just imagined everything?

"I guess I should start at the beginning. It all started when I got bitten by a snake and had what you told me was a vision quest."

"I told you that? But I've never met you before today."

"My guide was named Tesicqueo, and he showed me visions from the past. I never saw his, your, face. He always appeared to me in the form of someone else or as a massive snake. I can't really remember specifics other than what I've told you."

"It sounds like my spirit self-connected to your Native American energy and came to you in order to show you your Native ancestors and past. I swear I had never seen you before I met you today."

"The more I learn, the more confused I get. Like the tattoo. The snake tattoo appeared on my wrist when I woke up from the vision, and I don't know why."

"It's true. It's a lot to take in, but you'll get there, especially with my help and the help of your sister and Quinn. The fact that my spirit-self came to you in a vision, means we are in some way connected."

"Thanks for that. It does help to calm my frustration about being in the dark."

"As for your tattoo, we are both guided by the snake totem, that's why we have been marked with their figures on our bodies. Our totems help guide us and show us our true self. In our case, the snake signifies the power of healing and transformation as well as our natural ability to lead others spiritually."

Being told I had been born to be a natural leader resonated with me because I had always been able to work with and coach my teammates in lacrosse and in other team type situations. I could see how the signs of my gifts extended further beyond what I had originally thought. Maybe throughout my entire life, small things had been alerting me to what the future would hold. The time I disappeared into the woods came to mind along with all the questions I and many others had surrounding it, nothing had ever been definitively proven.

"Would it be possible for you to help me recover lost memories?"

"It's possible, why?"

"Something happened to me when I was around five years old, but I can't remember what happened and the police were never able to find any kind of evidence."

The sound of thunder echoed in the distance where dark gray clouds had begun to accumulate and sparkle with lightening. The bright green of the forest melded into a deeper, more sinister shade of green, which only helped to highlight the approaching storm. The tops of massive evergreens swayed from side to side along the horizon.

"I'm game for trying, but not out here in the open. There's a cave nearby where we can build a fire and try a ritual our ancestors have used for centuries to reveal memories lost in time."

I stood up and told him I was ready to try anything he thought might have the slimmest chance of success in hopefully helping me to regain a past I had never been able to visualize in almost fifteen years. The once distant winds had already reached us when we arrived at the mouth of a craggy and gaping cave carved into the mountain of solid granite. A cold dampness dominated the interior of the cave as we breached the opening. The only sounds were nocturnal creatures that inhabited the various nooks and crannies surrounding us. Not the most hospitable environment, but I was willing to try whatever I could to retrieve my memories.

By the time we had penetrated the cave opening, the storm was upon us and raging with hurricane force for as far as the eye could see. Despite the eerie conditions of the cave, I very much preferred to be out of the torrential clash of rain, hail, and lightening exploding from all directions outside the relative safety of the cave. The only foreseeable problem came in the utter and far reaching blackness consuming the interior of the cave. It was so dark I could not see my own hand in front of my face, much less Tesicqueo.

"Tesicqueo?"

"I'm right here, in front of you. And please just call me T."

"Not on the top of my list of things I'm thinking at the moment, but thanks." I shot back with a slight laugh. "Any ideas about shedding some light on our situation?"

"Yeah, you."

"What can I do?"

"If somehow you've forgotten in the last few seconds, you are a witch."

"That is true, but I don't know how to access or use my abilities."

"See the fire and light in your mind and superimpose that image in the spot where you want the light and fire to come from."

Following his instructions, I conjured the image of both fire and light in my mind until I could actually feel the heat and illumination emanating from within my head. Then without any other focus on my part, I felt the same feelings coming from above me on the ceiling of the cave. I opened my eyes to see the entire cave bathed in light and a comfortable, welcome glowing heat, which poured down from above us. The many different minerals contained within the rock around us shimmered in reaction to the flowing ceiling. It was as if the walls around us were studded with precious stones, and more importantly, it was just freaking cool that I had been able to make it actually happen. Perhaps, ultimately, this magic thing wouldn't be too hard to master and control.

"Interesting choice for conjuring a fire, but it works," he responded using air quotes around the word "fire."

"At least we can see. Now what do we do?"

"Now we sit down and see if we can actually make this happen." He remarked as he kicked away some rubble from the cave floor and squatted down into a cross-legged position on the ground. He looked up to me and waved me down, so I too, sat in the same way across from him on the damp, cold rocky bottom of the cave.

* * *

As I looked at him seated across from me, I hoped I had not overexerted myself and my abilities in more or less promising to help him retrieve those memories lost so long ago during his childhood. I had only seen elder tribal members perform the ritual on others who had been in accidents or attacked by something supernatural. Despite my limited knowledge of the ritual, I knew I had to help him connect with his past, especially if we shared a spiritual connection. I had never heard stories of one's spirit making contact with another person without being consciously aware of it. I made a mental note to discuss such an experience with my father once we returned to Rowan, hopefully he had some answers not only for me, but also for Ethan.

"Okay, the first thing we need to do is call upon our spirit totem, the snake, for guidance into the past events of your life. He will guide us to the point where your memories have been buried too deep for you to access."

I held out my arms, palms facing upward and asked Ethan to extend his arms in the same way but have his palms facing downward on top of mine. The second the skin of our palms touched, there was a literal spark of energy, which rippled outward from our hands. So far so good I hoped. Nothing like that had ever happened in the rituals I had witnessed.

"Was that supposed to happen?"

"Yeah, it just means we've made a connection to the natural world around us," I postured without much confidence. "Now focus on your tattoo and the snake."

The force sparking from our connected palms spun outward and into the middle of the square formed by our arms pooling on the floor of the cave. Slowly, the liquid force contorted and undulated into the form of a two-headed serpent, one hand looking at Ethan and the other looking at me. It was incredible. I had never experienced such a phenomena, even with other tribal members or witches. I watched as the creatures transformed in front of me while Ethan's eyes were closed, his face showing his deep concentration. The fluid two-headed creature of pure energy writhed and moved about within the confines of our arms, until stopping and splitting into two separate reptiles. Each of them poised themselves directly in front of us. I could not shake my gaze from what I was seeing. The snake coiled in front of Ethan lunged forward as if it were striking prey and dissolved into Ethan's chest just as the my spirit totem launched itself into my chest.

Ethan's eyes opened revealing steely, shining gold eyes, which I could only assume reflected my own eyes. The cave around us began to spin violently, so fast that our hair flapped and moved in the wind. The rocky surface of the cave dissolved and a path along a river appeared around us. An enormous rock, or more aptly called boulder, sat dipping slightly into the river from the rocky and tree laden shore. A small child trotted out from the trees and towards the rock. He was talking to a, as of yet unseen, person. As he got closer, I realized it was a young Ethan. He did not show any fear in being alone in the woods. The vision faded and reappeared several times before a stable image fully materialized and played out before us.

The white trees danced as the wind blew through their tops and down towards their trunks and across the ground before returning to the midnight blue sky looming overhead. A soft and perversely childlike voice bounced around from between the trees without giving away where it was actually coming from. The child version of Ethan quietly and calmly inched closer towards the large rock before the same unseen force led him on to the top of the boulder. Then, the source of the voice appeared and sat right beside him.

* * *

At first, the memories stuck like spider webs running from limb to limb until finally one threadlike series of images broke free and then the rest followed until they formed a complete account of that night in the woods. A sliver of fear crept into my mind, but quickly disappeared as I realized I was not alone. T was there with me, and this was only a memory, not an actual event, taking place. I watched the toddler version of myself making his way to the Blood Rock, the magical vortex Principal McIntyre had told us about. For some unknown reason, I could feel every sensation the younger me felt, the sand and rocks giving way beneath my tiny feet, the crisp breeze brushing against my red little cheeks and my long locks flipping back and forth.

The voice guided me to the rock. Ever since getting lost, I had tried to remember the voice, to pick out something specific, which might help me recognize it. Until now I had never been able to do that. Now, something in the voice resonated with me. I knew the voice, and the man who it belonged to had just materialized next to me as I sat there in childish innocence. How was this possible?

The clarity of the scene wavered as I grappled with the realization of who had tricked me into following him into the woods and to the river. Before long, the vision shattered into a thousand pieces of reflected light, impacting with every surface of the cave. The force was so great that it pushed both T and me backwards against the ragged rocks behind us.

"I don't understand. How the hell is that possible? How was he there back then?" T exclaimed.

"I have no idea. It doesn't make any sense at all. We have to get back to Rowan now. Everyone is in danger of not only Arabella, but him too."

The storm continued to pummel the once calm and tranquil natural beauty of the White Mountains. Hail stones created a false sense of winter before the season had arrived. Nature rebelled against the natural order of things, and we dashed from the mouth of the cave in the general direction of where we had come.

"Stay close to me!" T screamed from several feet in front of me.

The wet and heavy branches of trees slapped me in the face and attacked my arms and legs leaving stinging red scars which were continually washed clean because of the large raindrops. T's drenched form fought against the same forces of nature as we retreated to Rowan as fast as possible. I feared what we might find when we reached the barrier. We had been lured into a trap and a damn good one at that. Our once safe haven had turned into possible burial ground.

Would anyone be left standing? Would they still be alive?

Chapter 25

Unnatural phenomena

I SAT TWIDDLING MY thumbs in Quinn's grandfather's cottage as he told his parents about what had happened just outside the barrier only a few hours before. His family had been shocked to hear the account about Julie, especially when no one had heard from her in almost a day. His father had told us she had gone to a friend's house to study and spend the night, and he had not seen her since then. Everything was beginning to look uncomfortably similar to the events that occurred in my last night in Salem.

Getting bored with my current situation, I stepped outside while Quinn and his parents were discussing both Julie and the burial of his grandfather, Étienne. He had explained the ritual to me after we arrived back at his grandfather's house from our confrontation with his sister. The members of the Rowan coven believed a spirit could only be released from their earthbound form through the purity of fire. The altar, which was being constructed, was for Étienne, who would be "buried" this evening at midnight. The entire coven as well as the Abenaki tribal members would be present to give their final farewells to a man who had been described to be as one of the most important and influential Elders these people had ever had. I wondered what exactly he, and now Quinn, knew about me, Ethan, the prophecy, and the predicament in which we found ourselves in at the moment. I desperately wanted to discuss with Quinn further, the information he had received from his grandfather during the Merging. I considered asking him if the Merging would be a possible remedy to my lack of certain things pertaining to my powers and the prophecy, but the thought of risking either of our lives didn't seem worth it to me.

A thundering boom penetrated the evening sky behind me, which made me jump. The weather had been so peaceful of the entire day, but now a rolling and bursting storm forged its way down the huge valley funneled on its tirade by the green and brown mountainous walls. Giant bolts of lightning electrified the air in the distance and cast a spectral glare on everything below the gray-black storm clouds. Never in my life, I had seen such a violent storm form so quickly in New England, but I also knew from school the weather in the White Mountains was some of the most unpredictable. My nerves were on edge and it helped to try and take a logical approach to such a strange phenomenon. However, logical thoughts couldn't entirely help to squash my worries that something else might be gathering strength off in the distance.

I just hoped Ethan was okay. I would have thought he'd be back by now with Tesicqueo. If they had been caught in the storm, I wasn't sure they could make it back to Rowan safely or any time soon.

"Hey, my dad would like to talk to you for a few."

I looked back and saw Quinn hanging his head out of the sitting room window. "Please be okay Ethan." I whispered to myself as I walked back inside the whitewashed cottage.

* * *

Hailstones fell from the sky like ice missiles in an air strike. Even when taking cover under a tree, the tiny bullets found their way to us and belted our flesh. Huge red welts covered almost every inch of our exposed skin, which was a lot considering both of us were wearing t-shirts and running shorts.

"This is insane! We've never had a storm like this," T yelled as he futilely protected his head with his arms.

"I've never seen anything like this before especially in New England," I said in support and surprise.

A bolt of lightning struck the earth to our right and the soil around us steamed, popped and trembled as the accumulated hail detonated in a spray of tiny chards of ice.

"We've got to get away from here and back inside the barrier. I don't think we can last much longer out in the open."

He grabbed my arm and we charged back into the full force of the wild storm brewing and intensifying above our heads. The wind churning behind us came close to lifting us up off the ground as it ripped through the unnaturally turbulent environment. I didn't think it would be possible, but the weather deteriorated further, as we got closer to Rowan. A sudden gust of wind whipped through causing T to trip on a rock and begin tumbling down the mountain trail we were following. I did my best to dig my heels into the muddy terrain but it was useless. I stumbled and followed him down the scraggy muddy trail as we both rolled towards an ominous ledge in the distance.

* * *

The all-wood sitting room of Quinn's grandfather's house looked like a throwback to a simpler, more tranquil time. You couldn't help but feel cozy in the space, even after everything I had witnessed in the last couple of weeks. I sat down in an incredibly comfortable leather chair that gave in and allowed me to sink down into its softness. I heard people coming down the stairs, but I was too exhausted to stand up and do what would be considered polite. McIntyre was with them as they came into the warm sitting room and all sat opposite me on another comfortable-looking leather couch and chair. All of their faces looked rather serious, but not enough so as to make me nervous that some new and unexpected event had necessarily happened.

"Addy, we need to have a little chat with you if that's fine."

"Sure, is everything all right?"

"Yes, we think so we just want to make double sure that that's the case."

"Okay . . ."

"Has anyone hear acted strangely or asked you questions you thought were out of the norm?"

"Um, no, I don't think so." So many people had come to greet us when we arrived and my mind flipped through each of them trying to remember anything that might have been out of the ordinary. The only "weird" thing was how the people reacted when they found out we had a Guardian.

"Nothing said worried me or made me think something might wrong."

"But?"

"Well, the people were really interested when they found out we were with you, a Guardian."

"But that's it, there was nothing else?" Quinn's dad probed.

"No, I don't think so."

"No you don't think so or no, nothing?" he pushed.

"What is going on?" I remarked a little more loudly than I probably should have.

McIntyre intervened and assured Mr. de la Croix that I would have told them if there was anything out of the ordinary especially after the past day's events. I was confused by his pushiness about whether or not I had heard anything weird. Should I be worried about something? I didn't think I wanted to pursue such a thing with him at the moment. He seemed stressed and a little out of sorts, but I just assumed it was because of his father's death.

"Thanks Addy, we really appreciate it."

With that, the two men left the room and exited the house. Quinn just stood there and looked as confused as I about what had just happened between his dad, McIntyre, and me. Was it too much to ask for more than thirty minutes of normalcy?

"I really want to apologize for my dad's really odd behavior."

"No worries, it's not your place to apologize, but I definitely don't like being interrogated about something when I don't even know the reason for the questions."

"That's completely understandable. You wanna get out of here and go check on the preparations they're doing for my granddad's Ascendance?"

"That would be great."

We stepped out of the house and outside where the sky was as black as coal and threw an oppressive midnight hue on everything protected inside the barrier. I asked Quinn if we had anything to worry about since we were in the barrier, but he assured me we were completely safe from any sort of weather phenomena. A loud and sudden clap of thunder and lightning directly above us didn't help to give me a completely reassuring feeling.

* * *

The world rolled and tumbled by me, like something out of a home video, as I rapidly descended the rocky side of the mountain we had hiked earlier. Only controlled by the force of gravity, we both quickly neared the ledge of a cliff that opened to the large, deep valley below. There was nothing that I could clearly see to stop me from meeting my death in a matter of moments. I desperately scrambled to grasp something with my hands and fingers without success in a pointless attempt to save my life. I felt several of my fingernails being ripped off as I grabbed for rocks and branches too weak to slow my progression followed by a severe stinging sensation leave where my nails had once been and shoot up my hands. In the few distinguishable flashes of clear sight I had, I looked death in the face and closed my eyes as I went over the cliff towards the deep crevice below me.

A sudden jerk on my wrist sent me careening into the saw tooth side of the cliff. It was the same wrist Detective Malin had grabbed during our confrontation with him at Addy's house. It snapped loudly even above the thrashing noises produced by the storm, and I yelled out in pain, an agony that rendered my arm numb and useless. I hung there, my face wincing, for several seconds until I heard the familiar voice of T telling me to hold on and that he was going to pull me back over the side of the jagged ledge. Fighting through the intense torment, I helped T to pull me up by using my legs and one good arm to climbed the side of the mountain.

Finally, I reached safe ground and rolled over on back and rested my head on T's chest. We were both breathing so heavily, I thought we might drown from taking in so much rainwater between breaths.

"Are you okay?" He asked between deep exhausted breaths.

"I'm just peachy. You?" I laughed and the pain in my wrist throbbed vigorously, but I didn't care because I was alive and, for the moment, out of danger.

Without any sort of warning, he kissed me on the lips. My first kiss from a guy. His lips were soft, and it lasted for less than a second.

"You know this could be considered one hell of a first date, but could we please keep the life threatening experiences to a minimum."

"Agreed."

We slowly got to our feet and by the time we did, my wrist had almost completely healed, just like before.

"It's pretty cool to be able to heal that quickly, isn't it? I think you're going to need that gift more than you know sooner rather than later."

As he finished saying this, I looked in the direction of Rowan and noticed the storm had moved and centered itself over the invisible village. Hail, rain and lightning bombarded the bubble protecting the coven and tribal members. This was no freak weather event. It was a deliberate and concentrated attack on Rowan. But by whom? Arabella? And was she working with whoever was behind all of this?

I followed T as he resumed the trek towards Rowan. At least now we wouldn't have to contend with the weather, which had almost just killed both of us. My gut told me I was about to face something I wasn't prepared for, and in the short time that lay between now and when we reached Rowan, I would have to prepare myself mentally and magically, whatever that meant, in order to protect myself and those I loved. Did I have enough energy to do so?

"You might not think so, but you're ready Ethan. You'll know what to do when the time comes."

"I hope you're right."

For the first time since we began our hike back, Rowan grew closer in the distance, the cataclysmic storm serving as a menacing and unmistakable beacon looming large and deadly for anyone who lay in its path.

* * *

Several people busied themselves with final preparations for Étienne's ritual as we approached the area. Many of them hurriedly worked with tears in their eyes, the weight of losing their Elder after so many years of service and guidance couldn't easily be hidden. I was still surprised at Quinn's composure regarding his grandfather's sudden illness and death. I thought about asking him about it, but I figured it would be rude of me to delve into his personal life.

"You know I don't mind if you ask me about him."

Damn psychic witch stuff.

"It's just, you seem so calm and stoic. I'm not sure I would handle something like this the same way."

"What about your dad?" He shot back at me.

He was right. I wasn't moping around or sobbing constantly, I hadn't thought too much about him since he died right in front of me.

"I guess the weight and importance of everything else has kind of taken over and given me something else to focus on."

"Exactly. I'll deal with all of that after everything else is over and done. If I take even second to grieve him now, I feel like I'll lose it and be no help to you or anyone else if we are attacked by your mom."

"Arabella. I'd prefer we not refer to her as my mom. It makes me want to vomit."

"Point taken."

The violence of the storm overhead made us both look to the black, cloudy sky above the barrier. Unlike before, it now hovered directly above Rowan and unleashed its full fury. Every time the lightening clashed with the invisible barrier, energy rippled down the sides of the dome towards the ground before it dissipated into the earth. No one else seemed to pay any attention to the raging event except for Quinn and myself, probably because they were so involved in the preparations for the night.

"So, for the Ascendance, does everyone help prepare the altar or is it done by specific people?"

"No, it's an honor to build it. There are a select group of members, called the Divineurs, who prepare every detail of the ceremony. According to legend, they can see the window to the other side and know how to maintain the portal so a spirit can pass safely."

He told me the Divineurs used certain herbs and spells or chants to open the portal between the planes of the living and dead. Doubt must have run rampant across my face because he assured me the Divineurs had been doing this for centuries and could protect against anything crossing over from the dead. I sincerely wanted to believe him, but knowing my biological mother had done that very thing gave me a sense of anxiety. My thoughts wandered and conjured images of what would happen if she tried something like that again here in Rowan. Maybe she would meet her match here and be defeated. I mean, there were a slew of witches and tribal members here, all of which could surely defeat her, right?

"Hello? Earth to Addy."

"Sorry, I must have zoned out."

"As far as I've seen since meeting you, it seems to happen more often than not."

"Shut up. Aren't you worried about Tesicqueo and Ethan? They should be back by now, don't you think?"

"I'm sure T has everything under control. However, it is a little odd he'd stay outside the barrier when the weather is so malicious."

As if the storm were listening to our conversation, the booms created by the thunder and lightning highlighted the word "malicious" as soon as Quinn verbalized it. It remained centered above Rowan and still no one reacted to the tempest rampaging the barrier. I figured if no one else was worried about what developed around us, I shouldn't either. They knew more about these mountains than I did and I decided to focus on other things rather than be the only one stressing about a storm.

* * *

"What the hell was that, Victor? It wasn't supposed to be an interrogation."

"Your father's not the one who just died Devon."

"You're right. Mine died centuries ago, but that doesn't give you the right to pressure a girl who has been through what she has in the last several weeks and especially the last twenty-four hours."

"Don't try and give me some sob story. Just because you're a Guardian doesn't mean crap to me and gives you no right to try and sanction me from doing whatever I want."

"What the hell has happened to you? And don't use your father as an excuse," I responded.

"How dare you even utter the name of my father! You strut around here like this is your home. It's not! You haven't been back here in decades, and we all know why."

"Don't talk about things you know nothing about, Victor. You weren't even born the last time I visited Rowan. I've made peace with my decision and it's none of your concern."

Victor walked towards me, so close so that I could smell his acrid breath. He looked me dead in the eye and pointed his finger into my chest.

"Typical pompous response from you Devon. I suggest you leave again before you ruin lives like you did before."

Victor turned away from me and stormed out the door. I ran after him, but by the time I reached the front steps of Étienne's cottage, he had vanished. As I stood there scanning the village, my phone came to life and began vibrating in my pocket. I pulled it from my pocket and saw it was Aiden.

"Aiden? Are you okay?"

Static answered back intertwined with garbled words that I couldn't fully understand. I repeatedly said hello and asked for him to repeat what he was saying, but nothing coherent came through the line. Then with a sudden and dark clarity, I heard a voice, which was not Aiden say "Prepare for the coming end of what you hold dear." Click. I redialed the number, but there was no answer, not even his voicemail picked up. What the hell did that mean, and what could I do to prepare to stop whatever it was that was coming? It was in times like these, I wished I were not simply an immortal, but a being with magical gifts.

I needed to find Addy and Ethan and not let them out of my sight. The foreboding message worried me about when this supposed end might become a reality. I walked out of the house and noticed the rumbling storm overhead. In the world of signs, I felt this was one of the most clear I had ever seen.

We were all of us on the precipice of something life altering and dangerous. No matter what happened in the looming hours, I would sacrifice my own life to save and protect both of them. Death might be a welcome respite from a full four hundred year life. I had seen enough death and suffering that my own would complete my existence on this Earth.

Chapter 26

Ascendance

THE DIVINEURS HURRIEDLY FINISHED the preparations for Étienne's Ascendance ceremony that would take place in less than an hour. Despite being a ceremony for the death of someone, the altar evoked a beauty and serenity about the end of life. Nothing about the many adornments made me think of death or sadness. Every detail perpetrated the importance of the enjoyment and appreciation of life, no matter how long or short it might be. All four of the natural elements, earth, wind, fire and water, surrounded the wooden bed-like structure constructed of mountain ash, each of them marking the four points of the compass, north, east, west and south. All of which were important aspects in the Wiccan religion and tradition. Learning so much so quickly gave me a higher confidence in my newly discovered gifts, and it was all thanks to Quinn and his patience in explaining all of this to me.

The various herbs and flowers softened the hardness of the wood jutting out of the ground to form a platform. They flanked all sides of the pile as well as creating a circle traced in the ground around it where the four elements were placed equidistance apart from one another. There was another white substance lying underneath the flowers and herbs, but I couldn't tell what it might be from my vantage point. Ever since becoming consciously aware of magic, the image of the circle recurred with frequency and always in moments of protection or honor, like when I instinctually protected us against Julie's assault.

"I've noticed the presence of the circle a lot since learning about magic."

"Great observation. For us the circle is a sacred shape because it protects against evil and represents the life cycle, which is never ending. Even after death, we are reborn."

"What's that underneath the greenery?"

"Salt. We believe it to be pure and it adds to the protective power of the circle. It also does a damn good job against ghosts and demons should the need ever arise."

I laughed at the words ghosts and demons, but Quinn didn't join in the laughter.

"Are you serious? Demons and ghosts?"

What else was I going to have to worry about? Human dangers were bad enough already.

"See what fun it is to be magical and see all the special little fun things life has to offer?"

"I feel like the luckiest girl in the world." I offered when I noticed someone who looked like Quinn's father storming across Rowan near the center courtyard and headed towards a group of houses near the edge of the barrier.

"Is that your dad over there?" I asked, directing Quinn's line of sight with my finger.

"Yeah, I think it is. I'll be right back. You gonna be all right by yourself for a bit?"

"Sure."

He left in the direction of his father, and I wondered if what had happened earlier between the two of us had caused some sort of unnecessary frustration with our presence here. We all deal with loss in different ways, but his father's anger towards me about what I might have seen or heard when we arrived pushed beyond any sort of normal irritation. I just hoped he was okay and wouldn't take out his frustrations on Quinn.

"Addy, there you are," a voice said from behind me.

I turned to see McIntyre rushing towards me. For the first time since saving us earlier, he looked distracted and concerned about something, which was exactly what I didn't need.

"Is everything okay?"

"Yes."

"For having lived almost four hundred years, you're a pretty bad liar."

He apologized with a very welcome smile and explained the exchange he had had with Quinn's father, Victor, after the two of us had left the cottage. Even McIntyre thought his actions were odd for someone who had just lost their father. He had known Victor since he was a boy, and he had never known him to act so erratically. It was very much out of character for the typically calm, small town doctor. I felt like there was something that had happened after their confrontation, but for some reason I couldn't read his thoughts like I was able to do with others. Instead of images or sounds, my mind was confronted with nothing but a blank wall. Maybe it was because he was an immortal, a Guardian. Some sort of safe guard against people stealing his memories about events he had witnessed throughout his long life.

"Have you seen Victor?" His question brought me back to reality and I quickly answered.

"Yes. I saw him walking off in that direction and Quinn just went to find out what was going on with him."

"Good, maybe he can talk some sense into him. I sure wasn't able to do so."

Part of me believed Quinn would be able to do just that, but the other side of me doubted anyone, no matter how close they were with him, would be able to talk Victor down from the rampage he apparently was hell bent on undertaking.

"By the way, where is Ethan? I haven't seen him in hours."

"Me either. I'm starting to get worried about him especially with the storm. Quinn assured me T would take care of him, but I'm still concerned."

"I'm sure Quinn's right. Hopefully they'll get back soon, at least before the ceremony begins. It looks like they're almost ready to begin." He added.

"I hope so. I'm not sure I want to face another death or a celebration of it unless he's here with me."

Not matter where we were lately, death confined us and more or less laughed in our faces.

* * *

The rain ceased to assail our faces and body as we drew closer to Rowan. However, the wind gathered strength and blew with a veracity we had not yet seen since the storm appeared. The full force of the storm centered on Rowan itself and more specifically the magical barrier protected the coven. The flashes and cracks of lightning struck the rippling surface of the protective dome giving the false notion they were powering it. Sheets of rain outlined the surface of the dome and gave the feeling of an unsettling optical illusion of the village, which lay on the other side, like an impressionist painting accidentally doused with water.

Even though we struggled to maintain are footing, we finally reached the border of the barrier. I moved forward to walk through the invisible wall when the undulating shield ferociously repelled me. Because he had no choice as I was propelled backwards in his direction, T caught me and stopped my fall. For someone who had been playing sports his entire life, I felt like a fool for coming across as a clumsy weakling. My competitive nature had always driven me to be a better athlete, but now when I needed it, I failed miserably.

"Dammit!"

"Are you okay?"

"I'm fine except for feeling like a weak fool."

"Don't be so hard on yourself. It's not like this is something you are used to dealing with in your life."

T was right, but my stubbornness refused to let his words provide me with any consolation. I punched a tree bordering the edge of the dome and yelled out in exasperation. Blood trickled from the scrapes scarring the knuckles of my clinched fist as I gritted my teeth and closed my eyes. As soon as I opened them again, my vision had changed like before when we were confronting Det. Malin. Everything around me changed into shades of green, blue, and yellow, again like a heat sensor or infrared camera. The full scope of the dome came into full view and for the first time, I could see its curvature and the places where it entered the ground.

"Ethan, are you all right?"

I turned around and faced T. He stared out me with an astonished expression, which intensely studied my face.

"Dude, what's going on? Your eyes are completely white!"

"It's like looking through an infrared camera. I can see the heat and energy coming from everything around me."

I could see every vein, artery and system in T's body, even the tiny electrical impulses sent from his brain throughout the rest of him. It was a fantastically impressive light show, like nothing I had ever seen before in my life, the human glowing and full of life.

"The electrical force of the lightening can actually weaken the effectiveness of the barrier. I think I know what I need to do to get us inside."

* * *

Filling the center meeting place, the amphitheater and surrounding area, was a sea of solemn faces highlighted by the dancing orange and yellow flames of numerous torches positioned throughout the sacred ground. It was an awe-inspiring sight to see so many people present to celebrate and remember the life of someone who had been a kind and benevolent leader of the Rowan coven and friend and ally to the Abenaki peoples. Tears were already being shed by many of the attendees, both ones of sadness and relief that his sudden and debilitating illness had passed. McIntyre and I stood side-by-side, back behind the others so as not to invade on their time with their fallen Elder.

The cream colored heavy robes of the Divineurs created an elegantly engaging contrast with the brown of the timber used to build the altar. The white, light greens and purples of the herbs planted around the entire ceremonial space gave a quieting softness in comparison with the backdrop of the earth floor and browns of the cottages. I expected all those present to be dressed in similar gowns and robes, but it was a preconceived notion. The men, women and children wore their normal everyday clothes and stood or sat quietly as the funeral procession made its way from Étienne's simple white cottage towards the central meeting space.

"I'm going to go and look for Victor and Quinn," McIntyre whispered as he quietly moved off into the darkness.

Quinn and his father should have been here by now, but they were nowhere in sight. His mother and the other Elders had postponed the ritual as long as they could without breaking the strict rules of the ceremony. Now, as the party approached the altar, everyone stood and bowed their heads as the body of their fallen leader processed towards the remarkably intricate altar built for exclusively for him. How could they be missing such a ceremony?

* * *

My dad appeared and disappeared as I chased after him towards the edge of the coven grounds. Every time I got close to him, he vanished into thin air. Why would he be using magic and where and when did he learn to teleport?

"Dad!"

He stopped and stood unbending with his back towards me and without saying a word. He raised his left hand and clinched his fist tight in the air. Immediately, I felt a surge of pain erupt in my chest, and I leaned over unable to breathe. From my vantage point, I saw his feet turn so that he was facing me, then suddenly, I flew into the air before he violently slammed me back down onto the hard sandy ground. My head bounced as it made contact with the solid earth, so much so my vision blurred and I struggled to maintain consciousness.

I don't know if the memories were activated by my head pounding the ground or as a consequence from the magic my father used against me, but I saw a memory from my grandfather's childhood in France. I saw some kind of fortress or castle on the coast where he and his father were searching through mounds of books and papers. There was a fight between his father and some evil witch in which both of them perished. Smears of blood flew across the picture in my mind followed by papers dancing in air stamped with various words and passages. At first they passed by too quickly for me to read them, but then I focused my mind's eye and brought them into view. The words "Sabbat du Cercle Noir" materialized across the face of the woman my great grandfather had been fighting. Then, two small hands held up a piece of parchment detailing the treachery and betrayal of the first son born to the autumn blood moon. It would be my dad his birthday was October 31.

With great effort, I rolled over onto my side and tried to pick myself up off the ground, but my father planted his foot deep into my gut and another memory surfaced. No, it couldn't be true. He would never have done that to his own father. Rage overtook my body and my senses and I kicked my father in the stomach as he moved in for another physical onslaught. My countermove succeeded in knocking him off his balance and giving me the opportunity to get to my feet. I hurled concentrated orbs of white magic at him, but it did nothing to further throw him off his guard. The capillaries in the whites of his eyes gleamed red and he bared his teeth in a sadistic and seemingly delightful smile when he scowled at me. Pure hate and disdain oozed from his entire being, he was not the man I thought I had known my entire life.

"How could you?"

"It was my destiny, my son. We cannot escape what fate has laid out for us."

"But he was your father. You could have at least tried to be a good person and change. Nothing is ever written in stone."

"Out of the mouths of babes. You have no idea what I have been able to achieve thanks to my destiny and her help."

"It's Arabella. You've been working with her. You both knew McIntyre would bring them here if something happened in Salem."

"Well, just you look at my Ivy League scholarly son. It's just too bad you didn't see this coming. Unfortunately, you won't be able to warn your friends about what's about to happen."

"You're a sick bastard. There is no way you will get away with this. They are the ones described in the prophecy, they'll defeat you."

He laughed and moved even more uncomfortably close to me, so close, in fact, I could feel and smell his foul breath. He clasped my shoulders and squeezed so tightly the circulation slowed so much so both of my arms began to tingle. I tried to squirm out of his grip but he held me too securely and increased the pressure in response to my attempt to escape.

"Nothing is as certain as you may think. After all, I was thought to have been the one detailed in the prophecy, but alas, it appears fate had something more important in store for me. Working with Arabella to obtain what is now rightfully hers."

I couldn't believe what I was hearing. It was completely discombobulating and I tried to use what my grandfather had imparted in me to find a way out of my current predicament. However, everything was jumbled and nonsensical.

"Quinn, my son, it's no use trying to file through a lifetime of memories. You'll never find the one memory you need to defeat me and stop the inevitable."

With that said, he released my left shoulder and placed his hand on top of my head before slamming the bottom of his foot into the side of my lower leg. I heard the bone in my lower leg snap under the force of the pressure. I dropped towards the ground, but he clasped both sides of my head between his hands and lifted me as high as he could off the ground. His fingers tingled with an energy that trickled into my head. The last thing I remember before losing consciousness were his gnashing teeth and rancid breath whirling into my nostrils.

They had to be stopped, both of them, but no one knew except for me. I desperately hoped all was not loss to the licentious intentions of my father, Arabella, and the others I feared followed the convictions of the Sabbat du Cercle Noir.

*   *   *

"Excellent work, Victor. Be sure to hide your son so that he doesn't arouse any suspicion amongst the coven and tribal members."

"Yes, Arabella. Your plan is unfolding just as you wanted. The power foretold in the Blood Rock Prophecy will be yours before the end of the night."

My loyal follower spoke the truth, and I could not wait to take what was rightfully mine. They were my children and any and all power they possessed owed itself to me. There was nothing they could do to shield my blood kin from me. Destiny had provided me the opportunity of meeting Victor during my time in New Orleans. He was nothing but a puny believer in all that was innocent and weak in the world of magic. He had blindly followed the traditions of the Rowan coven, until I showed him the infinite possibilities that lie with following the teachings of the Sabbat du Cercle Noir. He had been there the night I made the ultimate sacrifice that showed me what I needed to take my revenge. He had been the only one after my exile to the shadow realm to contact me and do all in his power to free me from that place. He had proven himself more than once and I knew he would do whatever I asked of him, even it required the sacrifice of himself.

"Julie, there you are. Help your father and prepare the others for our surprise. I will arrive soon."

Thanks to my and her father's influence, she had willingly followed our plan. She had always been interested in a more powerful and satisfying magic. Unlike her father, Julie was strong, and I saw great potential in her desire for more power. She, in many ways reminded me of myself. In a show of her dedication, a trail of dead witches littered the eastern seaboard, serving as a bleak and bloodstained reminder of what was needed to take the powers of others. The girl had known about her father for years and together they had fooled everyone, even those closest to them. She had been so timid the first time I made contact with her through her father, but thanks to my selflessness and the guidance of her father, she had gained more power and learned to control it.

Now, everything I had envisioned was coming to fruition more quickly than I had imagined, and I couldn't wait to see the faces of those who had been betrayed when they discovered the truth. The Sabbat du Cercle Noir was poised to invoke my family's magic concealed within the ancient pages of the de la Fontaine grimoire and turn the twins of the prophecy against one another before taking their powers from them.

* * *

"What do you mean you know how to get through the barrier? Nothing can get through the barrier when it's been fortified like this."

"I think I can do it."

The lightening persisted to shimmer along the curvature of the dome showing minute imperfections in the magic used to protect Rowan. I'm sure he was to blame for energizing the field so that we would not be able to get back inside. There was really no doubt in my mind, he had to be working with Arabella and god only knows what they had planned for Addy, myself, and everyone else attending the

Ascendance.

"What are you thinking you can do to create a tear in the shield?" Tesicqueo asked.

"We have the power of healing and regeneration, right?" I said.

"Yeah, why?"

"I'm going to harness the lightening's energy rippling along the dome and discharge it directly back at it. Surely, that'll create an opening long enough for us to get through to the other side."

"Are you crazy! That's suicide. There's no way you can survive that even with your regenerative powers. What makes you think you can do this and survive?" he asked.

"I'm not so worried about the surviving part, more than the can I do this part," I quipped.

"Ethan, I can't let you do this. You'll die," he pleaded.

"I'm sorry, but you can't stop me."

He moved forward to grab me, a blur of golden orange light streaking through the night air, when I reached out and tapped him with two fingers on his forehead. He fell where he stood, taken by a deep slumber. Ever since receiving the secrets held within the grimoire, I had slowly been sorting and assimilating all of the spells and castings revealed to us. I only hoped Addy had been doing the same because I knew we would need everyone we could muster to stop Arabella and Victor. I'd die trying if it were necessary.

An earth-shaking clap of thunder caused me to look upwards in time to see a vein of lighting collide with the dome, sending uncontrollable energy rocketing downwards along the liquid barrier towards me. I dug my heels into the muddy earth and braced myself before placing both of my palms on the electrified shielding. This time, I held my ground and did not allow the energy to repel me. My hands tingled as the current raced closer. There was an explosion of white and pinkish purple light and plasma as my body absorbed the energy produced by the storm. Everything my new enhanced eyesight took in turned a scorching white. I pulled my hands away from the wall and balled the energy between my palms before hurling it away from me and towards the invisible barrier.

The once liquid wall shattered like glass, sending particles of intense energy flying through the air in all directions. I ducked and turned to cover T from any errant flying energy. His eyes fluttered open as I protected his body from the magically imbued explosion. The energy dissipated and a sliver-like opening appeared in the barrier.

"Now."

I grabbed T and we lunged at the decreasing hole, but, as we passed through a piece of the wall it made contact with T's leg and seared a long gash across his calf and his shin. We landed with a rumbling thud on the protected area on the other side of the barrier just as the hole closed in on itself. T winced in pain, and I reached down to see what damage the wall had inflicted on him. The razor-edged side of the opening had sliced open his leg, but there was barely any blood to be seen because the intense heat had almost instantly cauterized the gash. Thankfully he was already beginning to heal, the tattoo of the serpent on his wrist glowing a vibrant and flaming red aura.

My vision had not yet returned to normal, and in the distance I saw tell-tell wisps of energy in the air moving towards our position.

"We got to get out of here and hide, someone's coming."

"Sounds good to me. Do you think there's anyone we can trust?"

"I'm not so sure about that. You saw who's been lying and planning something horrific, and we have no idea of who else might be working with him and Arabella."

"Welcome back, boys." A voice said from behind my back.

* * *

The words being chanted by the funeral participants floated along the breeze with a lightness and molten calming effect. As they came into view, their robes glided with a rhythmic cadence, which hypnotized me. I watched as they approached the altar and witnessed the deliberate and macabre, yet beautiful movements of their hands, all in unison, as they put the body of Étienne atop the wooden structure without making even the softest sound. They disturbed nothing of the organic and bewitching ornaments adorning the altar and the surrounding ritual area. One of the ethereal robed figures took a torch beside the altar and set the base of it aflame. The dry wood crackled and breathed in oxygen as the fire grew and consumed the entire altar and then the linen-draped body of Étienne.

An unexpected tear dropped from the corner of my eye and listlessly rolled down my cheek. For the first time since leaving Salem, my guard dropped, and I realized how much I missed my father, and how much I had been impacted by his death. It was only compounded by the unknown whereabouts of my mother. I longingly hoped I would see her again and that the same heinous thing that happened to my father had not befallen her. Another droplet inched its way out of my other eye and within moments my cheeks were glistening in the flickering light of the torches encircling me. I felt dizzy and weak. I struggled to keep myself from sobbing and ruining the sanctity of what I was observing, but I couldn't, I didn't want to stop myself. My chest buckled and I relented to the sadness I had been so skillfully hiding for longer than I should have done. My knees resigned to my grief, and I dropped to the ground, bending over and giving my heartache to the earth below me. I grasped the wet sandy despairing dirt in one hand and pounded it with the other. My lungs burned with emotion, and I leaned back onto my legs to try to breathe, yearning for solace. I wanted my mom here with me. I deserved to have she and my dad standing beside me. It wasn't fair dammit. I was innocent, my mom was innocent, neither of us had done anything to garner such pain and sorrow.

The salty globules of torment puddled between my now dirty hands and a tiny pool reflected my face in the light of the firelight. My red and swollen eyes stared back at me full of pain, anger and determination, and then it was no longer my own face I saw. The soft and caring features of my mother smiled back at me. I touched the small pool of tears and the face of my mother remained unwavering in the tiny ripples caused by my fingertips.

"Mom?"

"Ma petite loup, there is nothing is this world or the next that could keep me from you. All you ever have to do is look within yourself, and I will be there behind you with my hand on your shoulder."

"I'm scared, and I don't know what to do or how to move forward."

"You are stronger, more powerful, and more special than you could ever know. I'm sorry I wasn't able to be there to guide you through this, but you will know what you need to do. Trust in yourself no matter what happens. You will be tested by something you will not see coming."

Before I could respond to my mother's encouragement and warning, bright flying flashes of orange light polluted the image of her face in the small puddle of my tears. When I looked up, my gaze was greeted with varying sizes of fireballs spraying into the air, all of which originated from the altar. Looking into sky, as I watched the fire show, I realized the storm above was now gone, and only a clear, starry sky remained above Rowan. I assumed, at first, this was part of the ritual, but quickly realized I was horribly wrong. Many of the attendees began covering their mouths in shock and terror as the night sky sparked and spurted fire. Their faces mortified at the sight before them. Several members of the coven and tribe walked away from the others and purposefully entered the flames of enveloping the altar. We all watched as their flesh charred, bubbled and boiled before cracking open in response to the intense heat and rampant fire in which they stood.

None of those who moved into the fire spoke a word or called for help, they simply stood there and let the flames devour their bodies. The other members watching the grotesque show remained unmoving for a moment before scattering and bringing water from a nearby well to try and extinguish the now raging fire. The smell of burnt flesh was nauseating, and I scanned the entire crowd for any face that might seem familiar: Ethan, T, Quinn, or McIntyre. None appeared. I rushed over to help the members bring buckets of water to the flames. However, when I reached the once beautiful and serene alter, another grim scene faced us. The shooting balls of fire hovered sinisterly in the sky above us. Then, without warning, they shot to the ground towards the members and me. I watched as almost twenty members of the coven and tribe stood waiting, mouths open ready to take the fire into them.

As soon as they had each swallowed the flaming orbs, they turned to the nearest unaffected member and began killing them. It was like they were different people. Children killed their parents as parents killed their children and others took lives from their friends, their families without hesitation. Blood flowed freely from people's throats, heads, and every part of their bodies, as former trusted members massacred them. Bodies dropped freely around the ritual area, creating a grisly wall of bodies.

"Stop it! What are you doing?"

"Addy!"

I swung around to see Ethan, T, and McIntyre running towards me in full stride. I had never been so glad to see their faces. There was no time for greetings or hugs as death and destruction dominated the scene around us.

"What happened? What the hell is going on?" Ethan asked.

"I have no clue. Fire just started shooting into the sky from the altar and then people walked into the fire while others became…possessed by it and started killing others."

"Do you know where Quinn or his father are?" McIntyre questioned.

I shook my head and told them I hadn't seen either of them since Quinn ran after his father to see why he was acting so strangely. Without warning, a flash and explosion behind me cut our conversation short. We all turned to see something, a figure, immerging from out of the flames. Arabella. It wasn't her physical form, more like a fiery outline of her features. She poised herself above the ravenous flames of the altar and looked down at the mayhem before her. She spoke directly to her murderous followers, still concentrated on taking the lives of anyone not privy to their diabolical plans or group.

"We have to do something!" T exclaimed before running towards those doing the killing.

Ethan tried to stop him, but it was no use. T encountered a former friend that marched in our direction and they fought vigorously and violently. Fist flew through the air as they took turns pounding the other.

"What can we do? We have to stop this," Ethan asked.

Ethan grabbed my hand and together we ran towards the fighting that blasphemed the once pure ceremonial altar.

"What are we going to do? We're not even sure how to use or activate our magic."

"We've got to try something. Our magic tends to work when we need it most."

Blood ran freely along the once consecrated earth as we approached nearer the ritual altar, the shapes of our feet leaving gooey imprints in the brown-red dirt. We had to jump over several bodies, their eyes searching in the nothingness for someone to stop the needless violence. We finally reached the boundary of the once sacred circle around the altar where Étienne's body had transformed into the immortal through the flames.

Arabella loomed domineering over the burning circle with a snide and animalistic expression on her face of flames. All of the innocent members who had been present at the ceremony lie lifeless throughout the center meeting place where they had come to say goodbye to their friend and Elder. Arabella's demented followers stood guard around her, their eyes flickering ferociously with the fire they had consumed, the fire that lead them to unleash their vile treachery.

"My dear children, how good it is to see you!"

Her words honestly sounded sincere and motherly, which made my skin crawl. I didn't understand how she could be so evil and care about our well-being at the same time. I both hated and was intrigued by her.

"Why are you doing this?"

"Why? For my precious twins of course, why else."

"How can you be so sick and twisted? What would make you think we'd want all of this? These people have done nothing but be nice to us since we arrived here, trying to escape from you."

"You are destined for great power, and I am here to guide through the process of controlling such enormous magic."

"We don't need you for anything. We already have people with us who actually care about and want to protect us."

"That's right." McIntyre and T said as they came and stood beside us.

Arabella looked unaffected by our stand against her.

"There is nothing or no one that can keep you from me and my plans for you."

As soon as the words left her mouth, something strange occurred within the center of the burning altar. A small opening appeared and Julie walked towards us. She looked just as belligerent and vexed as when I had first met her outside Rowan when I was with Quinn. She came forth from the lashing flames and stood, completely untouched, with one leg out to the side, her arms crossed in defiance of our attempt to go against anything Arabella wanted.

"Julie, what do you think you're doing?" T shouted, unreservedly astonished by what he was seeing.

She simply stared at us without saying a word and gave us no warning as to what was about to happen. People we had trusted with our safety were revealing themselves to just the opposite. Who could we trust? Suddenly, a cracking sound and guttural, raspy gasp drew our attention from Arabella and Julie to where McIntyre stood. A horrific, bone-chilling sight filled our eyes as we turned to look at our Guardian. McIntyre stood unmoving, surprise and distress marring his face, as he looked down at an arm and hand protruding from the middle of his chest. The person's hand clinched McIntyre's heart, which still beat and squirted blood through arteries no longer connected to the rest of his body. When the killer retracted his arm and hand from McIntyre's bloody body, McIntyre dropped to the ground, his face vacant, and his body limp.

Victor stood triumphant-looking at what he had done to a lifelong friend. He showed not a single inkling of regret or sadness at the murder he had just committed. Both Ethan and I, still hand in hand, ran to our fallen principal, friend, and Guardian, but there was absolutely nothing we could do. His heart had been ripped from his chest and a thick red torrent flowed unabated from his chest cavity. A spring of anger and rage erupted in my belly, and I reached out my hand and blasted energy at Victor. The force catapulted from my hand sent him flying through the air and into the yearning and groaning flames. His body landed with a cracking thud as his back snapped during impact with the burning wood. His screams immediately began to fill the night sky, an arrogant killer taken down by an unsuspected foe. He begged Arabella and anyone in the vicinity but his cries for help remained unanswered. Even Julie, his own daughter, stood unsympathetically by and watched her father evaporate into the mouths of flames that fed on his sizzling and smoking body.

Assuming Julie stood distracted by her father's demise, T lunged towards her, knife in hand, yet she reacted quickly to his assault. She cast a large orb of magic from the fire and threw it at him, knocking him to the ground. She then knelt down, looked at the ground and dug her fingers deep into the blood-drenched soil. Then she threw her head back, and stared at us with eyes of coal. The fire highlighted her changing appearance into that of an angry, wild beast. The ground grumbled and shook beneath our feet as the earth below T's feet undulated and began to cave in on itself. The quivering light of the fire created a strobe light effect on T as he fell into the earth, everything occurring within ghastly, slow-motion.

Ethan released my hand and lunged to try and save T before he was completely ingested by the earth. T futilely clawed at the air, reaching for anything to stop his descent. Thankfully, Ethan reached him before he vanished underground. The two of them rolled across the ground and came to a stop safely away from the newly formed crevice.

"Perfect! I love the selflessness you possess for those you love. Thank you for breaking the bond with your dear sister."

The heart dropping realization dawned on me as Arabella spoke. Ethan and I were no longer connected. We were not one in our magic. She hoped this would happen all along. She had played us like fools and we had followed unwaveringly. I heard Ethan shout my name as he scrambled to his feet and raced towards me. I turned and looked at Arabella bathed the incensed fire still burning and saw as she placed her wrists together and opened her palms at me. A stream of blackness, darker than the night itself flew out of her hands and rushed towards me. In defense, I created the same motion I had used against Julie, but Arabella's dark energy shattered my protection spell and violated and invaded every cell of my body. She had known we would not be strong enough individually to destroy her, so she would take whoever of us was easiest to trap.

* * *

She can't do this. This can't be happening. My feet struggled to grip into the blood-soaked earth, as I tried to reach Addy. We had come too far, we had been through too much for it to all end like this now. Too many had died and it had to stop. Arabella's magic, darker than the pits of Hell sought out Addy and devoured her entire body before I could reach her. I jumped to put myself between Addy and Arabella, but Julie waved her hand and tossed me away like a ragdoll. Why couldn't I use my magic? Of all the times, why did it not respond to my anger and emotions? I collided with the ground and bounced, as I helplessly watching Addy be overtaken by the black energy.

The stream of dark energy ceased, and Addy's body slowly ascended into the sky, like an astronaut in space. She floated there for several seconds until finally her eyes opened. I felt relieved she wasn't dead, but as her eyes opened, they gleamed a lifeless black in the subsiding light of the fire. Why? Why could I not save the ones I loved?

"Addy, say something!" I screamed as I pounded my fist into the earth.

"She rests with me now, and you will do the same very soon," Arabella declared.

Arabella turned and faced me, created the same shape with her hands as she had done when she polluted Addy's body and soul. She unleashed her darkness a second time, but before it could reach me, a dazzling blue light appeared between us, causing the stream of polluting blackness to disintegrate. I shielded my eyes from the brightness of the luminous figure protecting me from Arabella unsure of whether I should be happy or more worried than I already was.

"How can you attack your own children, Arabella? Do you truly care nothing for anyone or anything except your unholy desire for power?"

"Véronique, what a nice surprise! I thought I had banished your spirit to the other side for forever after I ripped you from your car."

So that was what had happened to Addy's mom and why there had been no trace of her or anything other evidence at the crash site.

"Sorry to disappoint dear sister, but I'm quick a study, just like you. Now release my daughter from your evil."

"Unlikely. You may have been able to defend Ethan from one of my attacks, but I doubt you can continue to do so for very long," Arabella challenged.

"Are you sure you want to test me?" Addy's mom asked as the glow around her intensified threefold.

"Maybe another time. For now, I will take my leave. Goodbye, dear sister. I'm certain we will all meet again."

A whirlwind of flames enveloped Arabella, Julie and Addy and shot up into the sky before vanishing into nothing but embers and ash. I had lost her, my friend, my sister, my only true family. I had failed.

"Ethan, you have to save Addy. Don't let Arabella destroy her soul."

"V, is that really you?"

"Save her." The light said as its luminescence faded and the only light remaining were the glow cinders from the smoldering altar. My head hurt and, all of a sudden, I felt alone again. I had no Guardian, no family. What was I supposed to do now?

My body wrecked and spent physically and emotionally, my eyes transfixed on where Addy had been only moments earlier. Now, there was nothing but mutilation and death contaminating the once peaceful mountain vistas. As I lay there defeated and despondent, my heart slowed and began to beat in a steady, languid rhythm as my mind struggled to make sense of what had just happened.

T remained crumpled and unconscious beside the gaping crack in the ground. McIntyre, my Guardian and friend, had been brutally slain right before my eyes, and my sister had been taken over by our mother's dark magic, and then snatched away from me. I didn't want to give up. I wasn't a quitter, but, in that moment, I was plagued by thoughts of doing just that. My soul hurt, my life had spiraled out of control. Who could I turn to for help now? Who would be my guide though all of this, to help me master my magic? Would T be okay? How would I save Addy from Arabella's plan? There were so many unanswered questions.

Then, a voice I couldn't at first decipher filled the smoldering void around me.

"Ethan, are you all right?"

Again the voice came to me.

"Ethan, can you hear me?"

McIntyre? My mind and heart were at their limit for supernatural bull crap and I couldn't deal with anything else otherworldly.

"Stop! I can't take any more of this. You're dead. Just shut up and leave me the hell alone!"

It wasn't McIntyre, but T who had regained consciousness and come over to me. He put his hand in mine and helped me to stand up. I dared to look into his eyes, to bare the loss and fear I felt. Tears filled my eyes and began to trickle down my reddened and muddy cheeks. He hugged me and held me tight, not daring let go. In that moment, I realized we had both lost so much to the same evil, conniving person. I wasn't alone. Together we would find some way of getting Addy back and putting an end to Arabella's plans.

"Ethan, I swear we will get her back. We will not let Arabella get away with what she has done here."

"I want to see her tainted blood dripping from my clinched fists."

A fire, unlike anything else I had ever felt in my life, ignited within me. I focused all of my remaining strength on the desire for retribution for everything she had stolen from me, from us. If she wanted me, let her come and get me. I would be ready to face her no matter what the cost. It was my turn to give her a family reunion she'd never forget.

Epilogue

THE FIRST WINTER STORM billowed and surged high above the peaks of the White Mountains. A blistering wind raced down into the valleys and across the frigid waters of the lake just outside Rowan creating white-capped waves that crashed onto the shore and splashed water unto my jeans. It had been two months since Arabella attacked Rowan and took Addy. At least I hope that was what had happened. Part of me feared she was dead, but I couldn't allow myself to give into the possibility. Maybe I was just being selfish. Considering the vengeful desire of Arabella, death may be the better option between the two.

I could feel my nose running as the arctic wind chapped my exposed skin, but I didn't care. I wasn't the same boy I was when all of this started. I had grown up more quickly than I had wanted when life was easy in Salem. Now, I had been hardened and defined by events no person should ever have to witness. I was a man. I was a witch-Native American hybrid. I was consumed by a desire to make things right to those who had sacrificed themselves for us, even if that required me to kill.

During the past two months, I had filled my days with learning all I could from the people here. I physically and magically practiced and trained as much as possible, only sleeping three or four hours a night. I had no other option than doing no matter what it took to set things right. Images of that night flashed across my mind and I closed my eyes, letting the coming storm invigorate me with its polar fury.

A trickling warm sensation touched the palm of my hand. I opened my eyes. The few tears I allowed to escape froze on my reddened cheek as I looked down. Without knowing, I had clasped a rock, with a sharp edge, in my hand as I had thought of that night. Blood dripped down unto the grey bed of pebbles where I sat. The rivulets of life slowly covered the cold, tiny rocks as I squeezed the keen rock harder in my exposed hand. I felt no pain. I was not allowed to feel pain. Everything I had done these past couple of months was a test. A test of how strong I really was. How much I really wanted to get her back if she were alive.

I raised my clinched fist shoulder height as I sat there and admired the rippling flow of blood. Then, I opened my hand and let the rock fall to the ground. It clacked as it hit the other rocks, stained with my life. Within moments, the wound scarring my palm healed. I couldn't be killed, right? I took my index finger of my other hand and swirled it around in the remaining blood pooled in my palm. With my finger, I traced over the serpent symbol on my wrist. It glowed with the same fury I felt in the pit of my stomach.

Someone placed a hand on my shoulder. Tesicqueo. He was the only good thing about this entire situation.

"McIntyre is waiting for us," he said.

"It's time?"

"It's time."

That bitch wouldn't see what was coming and I longed to choke the life from her insidious body. The plan had to work. We had no other option and I would not back down.